EDITED BY SHEILA HARTNEY

Hadrosaur Productions, Mesilla Park, NM

Exchange Students
Hadrosaur Productions
First Edition, first printing, continuous printing on demand

First date of publication: February 2020
Collection Copyright © 2020 Hadrosaur Productions
Cover Art Copyright © 2020 Laura Givens

ISBN-10: 1-885093-89-6
ISBN-13: 978-1-885093-89-9

TABLE OF CONTENTS

Table of Contents

EXCHANGE STUDENTS

Introduction

Sheila Hartney

When I was in high school I was in awe of the foreign exchange students. They came from far away places like Switzerland, Sweden, Turkey, and Norway. I envied them and longed to be one. Alas, that never happened. Those exchange students were sponsored by established programs like American Field Service or International Student Exchange or another such. The exchange students in this volume mostly got here (or there) in other ways. But they got there. Or here.

Several years ago a nephew made a casual remark about exchange students from another time. So I wrote the story "Claudius" about a young man from ancient Rome who becomes an exchange student in a small town in Minnesota.

About a year ago at a con, Mile Hi, I think, I told David Lee Summers that I had several ideas for themed anthologies. He asked me to run some of them by him, and the one he chose was the exchange student idea. It was my favorite.

So we put out the word and submissions poured in. I am delighted with this collection of stories. The range of ideas, and the various ways those ideas have been dealt with is wonderful and awe-inspiring. From a typical slacker teen on another planet, to a devil on an exchange visit to heaven, from exchange students struggling to keep up with a truly foreign – in some cases alien – curriculum, to exchange students up to no good, we have it all. There are dark tales of evil beings, humans who care deeply for aliens, teachers and administrators overwhelmed by the needs of diverse students. There's even a tale of law enforcement personnel crossing dimensional boundaries. Many of the stories underscore the essential and underlying connection between intelligent species, regardless of how alien they seem to each other. There are funny stories, sad stories, even a story about superheroes with an exchange student twist.

Have fun!

Switching Worlds

J Louis Messina

"They chose us!"

I raced into our sanctum chamber, waving the automated acceptance words that appeared on my hand. Sitting on our floating sofa, Mom, Dad, and my brother Kai jumped to their feet.

"Is this about the Conservation Tracking Curriculum?" Mom asked hopefully.

"No. I won the Interplanetary Student Exchange Program essay on why our family was best to represent our planet."

"This is amazing, Lorc," Dad said. He pressed his palm to mine and transferred the neuron letter to his hand, then read the official document. "But you're only twelve. They're exchanging a student that's sixteen. That means Kai has to go."

Kai's mouth dropped; I grinned. I had written it to get rid of my annoying brother. He was always bossing me around, telling me how to do everything. When he turned sixteen, his brain chip upgraded to scholar, another word for know-it-all.

"I'm traveling to another world?" Kai said. "We don't know anything about these Earth aliens. They just contacted us last year."

"Now you can tell us all about them," I said, pushing him toward our bedroom. "I'll help you pack."

We met the aliens in an enormous field with a grand ceremony of our delegates' most prestigious citizens. I held my breath as the cylindrical, silver spacecraft landed, kicking up dust.

Kai paced and wiped away sweat on his forehead. I was

nervous, too. We had to represent all the families on planet Koontz. Talk about pressure.

When the Earth officials walked down the ramp, the crowd cheered, and everyone saluted, shook hands, and made speeches that lasted longer than the space trip.

Because our planet had transmitted the Earthlings' language to our brain's speech centers, I understood every word they said and could communicate on their level.

I examined the adult Earth aliens to see if they had eight arms, or a bug head, but their anatomy appeared like us. Whew! What a relief. I had to bunk with him, and I didn't want a creepy bug alien living with me.

Kai said his goodbyes. We all hugged and cried. Secretly, I couldn't wait to have someone take his place. I'd be the envy of every kid. I bet this Earth alien could teach me all kinds of fantastic things, like how to levitate, or become invisible. Who knows?

As Kai clomped up the ramp and disappeared into the spaceship, the new boy strolled down. They'd told us that the alien boy would be a typical teenager on their planet. When he stepped out of the shadows and into the light, I couldn't believe my eyes.

One row of stiff, green hair stood straight up down the middle, with bald spots on the sides. His face was pleasant, but a big, gold ring hung from his nose. He wore a black sleeveless shirt that clung to his scrawny physique; engraved on his arm was a picture of a skull on fire. He'd definitely stand out like an eight-armed, bug-headed alien.

I held out my hand to shake. The alien slapped it. Assuming that was his greeting, and not wanting to be rude, I slapped it back.

"Name's Switch," the alien said.

"I'm Lorc."

"Cool."

"It is a bit breezy."

When we stepped off the conveyor belt and arrived home, Switch unpacked.

"What was your winning essay like?" I asked, wondering if his intellect exceeded mine in writing.

"We didn't do one, little dude." He tossed some clothes onto the floor. "They picked us at random. Our government thought it'd be fairer that way."

"Oh." I was a little disappointed they hadn't sent their best. Perhaps, however, I was being hasty or too judgmental. "What's your favorite subject in your learning institute?"

"School's for hanging out. Learning's a drag."

I wasn't familiar with these expressions. I began to ask him what they meant, but he put some mechanical device over his ears and started moving his head. I thought it might be massaging his neck.

"Can't hear you," Switch yelled. "Got any snacks?"

I ran into the kitchen and brought back some healthy bean treats. He looked at them and glowered.

"You guys health nuts down here? Where're the chips?"

Chips? Did he mean fragments of food? Maybe they can only eat tiny bits at a time.

"Man, this is going to be a long six months!" Switch flung the treats into the refuse container; then he grabbed a magazine with violent, bloody, and gruesome cartoon drawings on it out of his suitcase and plopped down on the bed. "Don't bother me until dinner."

Dinner didn't go well. Switch sat playing something called an electronic game machine and never looked up. My Mom and Dad tried desperately to make conversation, but he just grunted.

When dinner was finished, he didn't offer to help clean up. I reasoned that on their planet they have a robotic appliance that does everything for them. Planet Koontz abolished A.I. centuries ago because they had become too dangerous to our society. I scrubbed the dishes and sulked. I felt envious.

"So, what's on the tube?" Switch asked.

"The tube?" Dad said. He leaned forward and scratched his chin, trying to decode the word. "We're not familiar with your language choices, yet." He perked up in his seat. "Is that some sort of riding apparatus?"

"You know, TV. Anything good streaming, like action or horror flicks? What have you got to sit and watch?"

"Wait," Mom said, brightening. "I remember researching that. Your planet watches images through glass all day. We don't have one of those. We work constructively together to reinforce bonding and intelligence until bedtime."

"Work?" Switch looked as if his nose ring might fall off. "I'm heading for bed."

"Good idea!" Dad said, rising to his feet. "Then we can get up bright and early for a rewarding day of learning."

Switch glared at Dad, seized his electronic game, and marched to the bedroom. These alien kids weren't as sociable as I thought they might be.

Switch didn't get up until noon. He made a mess of my bedroom and bathroom. At least Kai was neat, and he talked to me even if it was to tell me what to do.

Truthfully, I was a bit embarrassed with him at Group Instruction. It wasn't hard to tell he was a student from another world. He disrupted his teachers a lot, too, saying foreign terminologies like *lame* and *no-way baby*. Then he started a food fight in the refectory. I tried to stop it, but received a plate full of food in the face instead, and the advisor sent us to the retraining center.

"Hey, Dork," Switch whispered to me to keep the training instructor from hearing.

"That's Lorc."

"Whatever. Let's skip the rest of school and go to the mall or the arcade."

"I don't know what those are," I said. "But we'd miss the rest of our assignments."

"I didn't come down here to do alien homework. And I've done enough detention at my school."

"We could go to the Institute's archive to learn more about our culture."

"Hey, dude, I came to party!"

I learned later that party meant to do nothing.

I could see our societies didn't have much in common. I was positive that he didn't have any special powers to teach me, either. However, I was determined to help him become a better Koontz citizen.

* * *

Over the next six months, we did everything to involve him in our daily activities. It wasn't easy. At first, he resisted. But we had to teach him our ways so he could report to his planet. After the first few months, Switch realized we didn't have any of the things he requested from home, and he began getting up early, talking, participating.

He no longer listened to the music device or played his game machine. The biggest moment came when he agreed to get a new haircut, take out his nose ring, and remove what he called a tattoo.

Time went by quickly. We were once again waiting for the arrival of the Earth spaceship. Switch (he later told us his real name was Bob) had become a model citizen of our world.

That's when I became worried. What if my brother Kai had changed? What if the alien world had affected him? Would he come back acclimated to their culture, with bizarre green hair, weird menacing tattoos, and anti-social behaviors? I missed him terribly and wanted him back the way he'd been.

The ship landed. The ramp sprang forth. Switch gave us hugs and said he'd never forget us. In a way, I was sorry to see him go, even missed his peculiar ways. Up he went; down came Kai.

I raced to him.

"Kai!" I said. "You haven't changed."

"No," Kai said. "Brainy as ever. In fact, they didn't want me to leave. But I said I missed my little brother."

"What was it like on Earth?"

"Baffling. You hang out at malls and arcades, eat fast food, and don't bathe for a week. But I brought you back something." He held out a bag. "A product called chips."

I grabbed a handful and stuffed them in my mouth. They tasted good, and I ate until I finished the salty, addictive snack. Now I understood why Switch missed them so much.

"Cool, dude," I said and slapped Kai's hand. "What do you want to do today?"

"Let's party! They gave me a game machine as a present. We can play it all night."

"Good to know we've exchanged some meaningful values," I said, toggling the joystick to destroy the invading alien spaceships on the screen.

We Are Allan

Tim Kane

Today, it's my turn.

Kaden had a Drasel as his exchange student. And its name was Drasel, too. All part of the same creature, or something like that. A little weird, if you ask me. But then everything's weird these days. What with Earth joining the Galactic Union of Species.

The Drasel (we just called him Dray) was pretty cool. He could change shape into anybody he touched. Kaden had him turn into Mr. Harrison during nutrition break so when we got back to class there were two teachers. We watched them argue about who was really real. Totally hilarious.

Charlene went next with xr3 from some place called the Great Globular Cluster. It didn't even have a body. Just some sort of computer virus that uploaded onto all our tablets. In the end, xr3 crashed the whole network because it saw homework as a threat and Mr. Harrison couldn't assign us anything for a whole week. It was the best.

But Charlene complained. Said it should still be her turn because the xr3 thing went to all of us. But a turn is a turn. And now it's mine.

Mr. Harrison agrees. So today I'm meeting Grok from the Muttick/Kev Collective. No one knows anything about them. They're a super secretive species. The people who visit, never seem to come back. Mr. Harrison says it's because they choose to stay. But that just sounds like another adult trying to give it to us kids easy.

I don't even know what this Grok thing even looks like. At least Kaden found out ahead of time that his Drasel thing was a blob. And Charlene knew that xr3 was a computer program (though she'll deny it up and down).

I step into class and the air feels stuffy, like Mr. Harrison forgot to turn on the AC or something. Everyone's up out of their seats, chattering.

It's the first time people really look at me. Mostly they stare right through me, like I'm just part of the furniture. More the idea of Allan than an actual person.

Philip never ignores me, though I wish he did. When I start toward my seat, he swivels and stares, along with his crew of followers.

"Hey, chunky?" Philip calls. "How do you even fit through the aisle?"

I keep my head down and maneuver toward the back. Mr. Harrison never seems to notice. Or maybe he's just gotten tired of trying, like all the other teachers.

The seat next to mine is empty. None of the other kids ever sit next to me. Charlene once announced she wouldn't even touch me. Said she was afraid she'd catch some disease. Which is stupid. Charlene's the one always sniffling and wiping her nose.

But today, I won't be alone. Grok will sit at the same desk with me. He hasn't grown up at this school or heard all the stories. So maybe he'll be okay. No matter what, I can't mess this up.

Instead of a normal chair, there's this odd looking bench sent over by the Galactic Foreign Exchange people. It's long, almost the length of the desk. Please don't let Grok be a snake. I hate those slithery things.

I unzip my backpack, meaning to grab the tablet computer, but then pause. When did I put my backpack down? Can't remember. But it's there, like always. The whole morning feels like operating on autopilot. I don't even remember walking to school.

Mr. Harrison starts teaching and the class settles down. Everyone except Philip, who keeps shouting out comments and leaning over to talk to his crew. Maybe when they pick his exchange student, it'll be some sort of giant spider. Then it can wrap him in webs and finally shut him up.

I keep glancing at the clock. Nine o'clock is when they

usually bring in the next creature feature. I must be pretty nervous, because there's a film of sweat along my arms and forehead. I wish Mr. Harrison would stop droning on about integers.

Just as the hour hand clicks into the nine position, the door swings open showing our principal, Mrs. Lee. Everyone cranes their heads to see behind her. Whatever Grok is, he's gargantuan, taller than the doorway.

"Good morning class," Mrs. Lee says.

Everyone responds with that super-cheery tone of voice: "Good morning Mrs. Lee."

"I'd like to introduce you to Grok from the Muttick/Kev Collective." Kids are practically leaping out of their seats to see. We've never had an exchange student we knew so little about.

Grok ducks under the door frame and enters. The whole room falls silent. All you can hear is the flup, flup, flup of his flipper feet slapping on the tile floor. He looks like a crocodile and whale had a baby together. Green scales cover every part of him. And then there's his mouth, so jammed with teeth, it's like he swallowed a bag of knives. A Great White would be so jealous.

Grok lumbers over to Mr. Harrison at the front of the class. A universal translator hangs from the creature's neck, looking tiny against his ginormous body. He turns to the class and lets out these deep barks and clicks.

The translator blares out the words in English: "We greet the Earth children." Grok pauses, making sure to fix each one of us with his slitted red eyes. "We bring the children wounds of joy."

There's confusion from the class as kids glance at each other. I'm wondering if the translator doesn't know what to do with his grunt language.

Then Mr. Harrison calls my name and everyone swivels to look my direction. I shuffle down the aisle, which seems impossibly long. Philip says something, but at least it's quiet enough that I can't really hear it.

Finally I stand in front of Grok. It's like staring up at one of those dinosaurs at the museum. If I have to do this all week, my neck is going to get wrecked, for sure. I can't believe this thing is supposed to be a kid my age.

Grok slumps down, lowering his body till he's only as tall as Mr. Harrison. Out comes his hand for the shake. His three fingers narrow into black claws, and I don't mean fingernails. His green scales darken, actually transforming into claws. Or maybe he doesn't have fingers at all and it's just all razor sharp talons.

Whatever the case, I have to shake with that.

Grok's pincer-claws surround my tiny hand. I feel them press into my skin, like grabbing a knife blade first. But he's gentle and doesn't push down. A slimy mucus coats his scales and when I pull my hand away, a long strand of the stuff connects us. I want to wipe it off, but maybe that's rude. As I lower my hand, the strand snaps. A glob of the gooey stuff splats on Charlene's desk. She shrieks and backs up in her seat.

"Look guys," Philip pipes up. "Allan finally has a friend. So sweet."

Mr. Harrison sends us back to our seats so he can switch to a lesson about the Mongols. As if anyone is going to listen to a word he says. Grok follows me to the back, but his too wide alligator-whale body bumps the desks as he passes. At least the other kids are shooting him glares, rather than me.

At my desk, Grok straddles the seat, his flipper feet hanging over the sides. He seems to focus on the lesson about how the Mongols rode around, killing pretty much everybody they met. I can hear his translator delivering grunts and clicks to a pair of headphones connected to what must be his ears.

I only have a sliver of the desk remaining. Plus, when Grok leans in, his arms leave smears of mucus. Every few minutes, or so, there's this wheezing sound from the top of his head, coming from a sort of blowhole where he breathes.

Maybe I was better off being alone. Before, I could sulk in the back, unnoticed. Now, everyone constantly turns to stare at me.

Mr. Harrison dismisses me early to nutrition break so I can show Grok around. Outside, the sun shines extra hard. I didn't know today was supposed to be so hot. I show Grok the bathrooms and hesitate a moment. Usually I would hunker down in one of the stalls and gobble up my snack. But today I have

Grok with me and he's monster big. So I lead him over to the cafeteria tables by the grass field.

"We will acquire sustenance?" Grok raises a hand to his mouth, mimicking eating.

"Yeah, this is where everyone eats their snack."

He points to a trailer at the far end of the field, which wasn't there yesterday. The other exchange aliens didn't have that. But then xr3 was a computer program, so there's probably a lot of things it didn't have to do.

"We return to here and meet Allan?"

I nod and Grok turns to head off to the trailer. I guess that's where they keep his food.

"Wait, why do you keep saying we all the time?" I ask. "It's just you, right?"

There's a pause and I can hear his translator delivering more strange noises.

Finally he grunts and the translator switches the words into English. "We are both Grok." He points a long claw at his chest. "This is Muttick." Then he taps the claw against his head. "This is Kev." He smiles, which doesn't do anything but make me nervous — all those teeth. "Does Allan understand?"

I shake my head.

I don't know if you've ever seen a crocodile frown, but that is what Grok did. I can tell he really wants me to get this.

Grok turns around and points at the back of his neck. "Does Allan see?"

I lean in a little. Just a bunch of scales coated in that slime.

"There," he taps his claw at something in between two scales. "This is the tail."

A little closer and then I spot them — two tiny purple tentacles jutting out, with whisps of hair coating them.

"What is that?"

"The Kev digs into the brain." Grok lowers down like he did in class, so his face is level with mine. "The Kev is..." His teeth click together as he thinks. "The Kev is a parasite. The Kev tells the Muttick what to do."

"So you're saying there's a creature living inside your brain?"

"We work together as the Collective. The Kev thinks it and

the Muttick does it."

"Wait," I hold out a hand. "Could you put one of those Kev parasite things into Philip?" I picture it wriggling into the back of his head. Maybe he'll squeal for help. "That would be the best, ever."

Grok looks at me — his red eyes narrowing. "Only to punish. To protect the Collective." Then he heads off to get his snack.

I still can't get the idea of a puppet Philip out of my thoughts. How amazing would that be? I plop down at one of the cafeteria tables and take out my snack – cookies in a wrinkled plastic bag and some chips.

Nutrition break must have started, because when I glance up, there's Philip. His crew surrounds me.

"How come you got the cool alien as your pick?" Philip thumbs his chest. "My dad's a space marine and that's what I'm going to be. So I have to get used to dealing with creepy alien types."

My fingers twist up the plastic bag with the cookies. Please let Philip leave. I don't want this today.

"Hey Allan, you shouldn't be eating all this junk," Philip says. "You're too fat already."

He pinches my belly, squeezing hard like a vise. I grab his hand and try to wrench it off, but he's too strong. What was I thinking being out here at the tables? I should've ducked into the bathroom, as usual.

Philip finally lets go and I twist away, protecting my stomach. There's nowhere to escape to. His crew is all around, chuckling.

"Just looking out for you." Philip grins and snatches my food off the table. He saunters away with his crew.

Worst of all, I can tell that Grok saw the whole thing. He lumbers over and thunks down a large jug of liquid, making the table shudder.

"Philip taunts Allan in public for everyone to see." Grok slurps from a straw jutting up from his jug. "Philip must be Allan's friend, yes?"

"No. He's a jerk." I flick a glance over at Philip, who munches on my cookies while giggling with Charlene.

"Allan must challenge him!" Grok smacks the table with his clawed hand, making the jug hop.

I shake my head. "It doesn't work that way. His friends will kick my butt."

"Even a loss in physical battle holds merit. The public challenge is important." Grok pokes my shoulder with one claw. "Allan must show honor."

"I just want to get back at him. Maybe leave super glue on his seat. I saw it done on the internet." A grin pops up as I imagine Philip struggling to pull his pants off the chair. In the video the teacher had to cut the kid loose with scissors.

"How will Allan gain public recognition for the victory?"

"I would know. And so would you." I shrug. "That's enough."

"So Allan only desires to see Philip suffer." Grok clicks his teeth together again, thinking. "Let us share a poem with Allan."

"Huh?" I look up at the giant alligator-whale. "A poem?"

"Yes, the Kev write excellent poetry which the Muttick deliver with rapturous ease."

"Sure."

Grok turns his red slitted eyes skyward and begins. It's all grunts and clicks. The translator takes a long time to transform the sounds into English:

"From the scraggly branches drips the grey sky
As the oozy waters drizzle and cry
And my heart shrieks – 'Why?'
Terror runs out of my head,
My soul cut open and bled,
And I am left for dead."

"Okay," I say, because I can't think of anything else. Not sure why a humongous monster like Grok would write poetry. That's for greeting cards and stuff. He seems more like the type to smash first and ask questions later. At least it rhymed.

Back in class, Mr. Harrison has us all write an essay on the Mongols and their conquests. Even though I'm inside, a sheen of sweat still covers my skin. My fingers slip on the digital keyboard, forcing me to retype some of the words.

Then I hear it.

Kids in the class snicker and shoot me glances. A message pops up on my screen – from Philip. I click it open and find a drawing of me kissing Grok with a pink heart scribbled above the two of us.

When I glance up, everyone breaks into laughter. This can't be happening. I just want to get away so no one notices me.

"The illustration is a good representation of the collective," Grok says, leaning over to look.

"It's a joke." I'm tired of explaining everything to him. "They're saying we're boyfriend and girlfriend."

"Preposterous. Allan and Grok cannot mate."

I slink down in my seat and punch at the digital keyboard, typing random letters. The conclusion to my essay looks like alphabet soup. I'll have to fix it or Mr. Harrison will yell at me. He totally goes off on kids who waste time in class.

Then the idea comes to me and a smile crosses my lips. I know how to get back at Philip.

We keep on writing all the way up to the lunch bell. As the other kids scamper out, I linger back, saying I want to show Grok around our classroom. Mr. Harrison is more concerned about ushering the flock of hungry kids out the door. He waves me off and then leaves.

With the place abandoned, I rush over to Philip's tablet. Sure enough, he left it on. Always so sure of himself. I open up his essay on the Mongols.

"What purpose does Allan have?" Grok asks.

"Just be quiet. Mr. Harrison will be back in a minute."

The essay isn't that great, and for an instant I consider leaving it. Philip will probably score pretty low with it as is. But that won't be enough. I select all the text and delete. Then, for good measure, I wipe out the memory cache, so he can't bring back a saved copy. There, done.

I'm smiling all the way to the cafeteria tables.

Grok's lunch is a bowl of stew, which bubbles up random-ly. He skewers chunks of grizzled mystery meat with his claws and gulps them down.

"Does Allan intend to challenge Philip?"

"You'll see." The forty-five minutes can't go by fast enough. After eating, I sit tapping my fingers along the table and shooting glances over at Philip. He's off playing soccer, totally oblivious.

Finally, the bell sends us all back to class and sure enough, Mr. Harrison does a spot check of our writing – displaying our essays on the screen at the front of the class. Philip hasn't even noticed yet. It's only when Mr. Harrison calls his name that Philip sits up.

"What's going on?" Mr. Harrison waves a hand at the blank document. "What have you been doing with all your time?"

"But I wrote it," Philip says, his fingers fidgeting with the tablet. "I swear."

"I'll have to mark you down. And notify your parents."

Philip starts arguing with Mr. Harrison.

Me, I'm smiling. That, plus the other homework he's missed this week should get Philip Saturday school.

Grok tilts toward me and does his best attempt at a whisper, which still comes out at noisy grunts and clicks. At least the translator figures out that it was meant to be quiet. "When will Allan announce his victory over Philip?"

"It's not like that," I say, keeping my voice low. "No one knows it was me."

Grok clicks his teeth. "Allan chooses the quiet hurt?"

"Yeah, cause I don't want to get in trouble." I have to keep my gaze down or Philip will notice me grinning.

Grok lays his clawed hand on my shoulder. "This quiet hurting will be the doom of us all."

As I stare down at my tablet, the screen twists out of shape. It seems to melt into the table. I glance up and the walls of the classroom liquefy, everything blending together. Mr. Harrison, Charlene, Philip – they all begin to glow, the light obliterating the details of their faces. The only object that remains stable is Grok.

The classroom dwindles away, taking with it the desks, the walls, and the people. There's only me and Grok surrounded by a humid darkness.

"What ... what just happened?" I ask.

Instead of my chair, I sit on a stone block covered in thick vines. A few feet away there's another block with a small lump under a scrap of cloth.

"Where is everyone?"

"We test Allan to see if the humans carry honor." Grok lays a hand on my shoulder but this time the claws angle down, tips pressing into my skin. "Rumors of your race spread through the galaxy. The ruthlessness of humanity."

Grok reaches out and pinches one corner of the cloth with his claws. "We wanted to see for ourselves."

"Wait, what happened to my classroom?" A chill settles into my bones. "Where am I?"

The lump under the cloth twitches.

"We did not journey to Allan's planet." Grok turns to me, his toothy maw only inches from my face. "Allan came to ours."

I want to say that this makes no sense but things have been strange all day. Like just appearing inside the classroom. That's why I couldn't remember walking to school this morning.

"Allan will never return home." Grok whisks the cloth away, revealing a tiny creature with hundreds of wiggling feet, like a millipede. But instead of the smooth body of an insect, a fine coat of purple fur covers this thing. Then I recognize the two tails, twirling about on the stone surface. It's the thing that burrowed into Grok's head – the Kev.

Grok holds out a clawed hand and the creature scurries on.

I try to stand, to get away, but the vines from the block have slithered up around my legs. They squeeze so tight, I can feel the blood pumping inside me.

"We will fully understand how Allan thinks." Grok turns toward me. "The process will take much time."

The vines curl up my body, clasping around my arms.

"No! You can't do this."

"The Muttick/Kev Collective must protect itself."

"But my parents. They'll make sure I get back."

The vines now wriggle up my chest and neck.

"Allan will return to the Earth parents." Grok tilts my head forward with one clawed hand. "Only, not the same Allan."

I feel it squirming against my neck. Tiny pincers tearing open my skin. I scream for him to stop. Please stop. My body thrashes against the vines, but they only grip tighter.

Then things start to change. My body calms. I want to keep screaming, but my voice falls silent. It's like cutting a cord. One moment I'm in control. The next, I'm not. I can still see and feel and think. Only my body doesn't respond.

Grok aims his red-slitted gaze at me. "Who is Allan?"

I want to scream in his face, but my brain doesn't call the shots anymore. Instead I feel words forming, my mouth opening to speak. Only it's not me who's talking.

"We are Allan."

Home Is(n't) Where the Heart Is

Chisto Healy

Ted gazed at his horns in the mirror. They were small but they were very visibly there. The more he adapted and became part of this place the more it became a part of him. It wasn't all bad. Suffering even becomes tolerable when it's routine, and there was plenty of time in between the torture to socialize and mingle with the other guests. The daily pain just felt like a chore, a nuisance that needed to be done. You did it and moved on.

When he first got here he was afraid to speak to anyone. He never imagined that he would end up in this place and felt like those who accompanied him had to be the worst kind of people. Then it occurred to him that he was here and there were probably others like him. Not everyone down here was Hitler. It also occurred to him that the only way to differentiate the low level bad people from the really bad people was to talk to them. Since then, he had made a lot of friends and everything felt a lot easier to bear after that. Even hardships were okay when you didn't have to face them alone.

Still, as much as he was adjusting to his new life in Hell, his heart still longed for Heaven. Throughout the difficulties of his mortal life, he always believed that it would end in a place where everything was good and his dreams would come true. The idea of Heaven was what made life bearable. Even discovering that Hell wasn't as bad as you imagined didn't take the ache for Heaven out of your heart. In fact, Bub would be mad if he knew but Ted got through his daily torture by daydreaming about what it would be like to live upstairs. When he was on the rack having his limbs pulled off each morning, his mind was dancing on clouds to beautiful harp music that was being played by gorgeous female angels with snow white wings.

In the time he had been down here he found out that no one had ever switched places. There was no hope of being pardoned and sent to live with the angels. It was crushing to not even have hope, but he had accepted his fate and he was really starting to adjust. Ironically, it was his willingness to become a bigger part of Hell that got him exactly what he dreamed. He pushed his ache for Heaven down and embraced Hell and Bub actually got to where he seemed to like him. That's why when the big He came to Bub with the idea of an exchange student program, he chose Ted to go first.

The idea was that the wild ones in the clouds that didn't really appreciate what they had could spend some time seeing how the others live and what life could have been for them, and the ones downstairs could get a chance to have a break and feel God's love. It struck Ted as odd that Bub wasn't opposed to the idea, but for whatever reason, he went right along with it in an uncharacteristically amiable way. Still, Ted made sure not to display how excited he really was at the opportunity to go live in Heaven, even if it was temporary. He was afraid it would anger Bub and make him change his mind and choose someone else. So, Ted swallowed his excitement and went to pack his things. Now he was looking at his horns in the mirror and really noticing how much of a demon he was becoming. There wasn't going to be any hiding that he was the exchange student.

Ted said goodbye to his friends, again trying not to show his true feelings. He walked to the bench where he was supposed to catch his train but he was dancing on the inside. He wanted it to show up fast so he could get upstairs and let out the happiness swelling inside of him. When it finally arrived, he lowered his head and got on slowly, turning back to wave before the door closed. He could barely contain it then. He was giddy.

He trembled and his foot started to tap to the music in his mind and heart. His soul was finally going to be where he felt it had always belonged. He felt his hope returning. Maybe if he did a good job as an exchange student, maybe if He saw how not-so-bad Ted really was, he could be the first to ever receive that pardon. Maybe if the part-time went well, they would take him on full-time. His heart believed it and his mind really wanted to.

The train was really bumpy and loud. Ted was jostled around and had trouble keeping his footing but it didn't come with seats so he didn't have a choice but to try. He fell a couple of times but got back up and held tighter to the pole at the car's center. Then suddenly, the ride got smoother and the lights in the train car got brighter. He looked up at them and when he looked back down there were suddenly seats lining the walls. He smiled and sat down and sighed at how comfortable and unlike train seats in the mortal world they were. Velvet, he thought. Through the window he saw a train going the opposite direction and he laughed to himself at the thought of what a surprise it was going to be for the person in that train when the seat disappeared from under them and everything got dark and bumpy. Then he reminded himself that laughing at things like that would probably be frowned upon where he was headed and he really wanted to make a good impression.

Ted felt a pang of fear then. What if he didn't know how to behave and be good after applying himself so much to fitting in in Bub's world? He really didn't want to screw this up. Before he could give it much more thought, the train slowed to a stop and the doors slid open. Ted jumped to his feet and danced his way to the open door, assuming it was probably safe to do so now. He stepped out happily and squinted against the insanely bright light. He felt a headache coming on and shielded his eyes with his hand. "It's here," he heard someone say, but he couldn't tell who due to the bright light.

"Hi. My name's Ted," he said excitedly.

"You don't have to shout," a second voice said.

"Sorry," Ted said back. "I can't really tell where you are. It's so bright." There was a sigh of disgust from one of the people there to greet him. Ted frowned. He really wished he could see.

"Of course, it must be dark down there," whoever commented on his volume said. Ted felt someone take his bag from him. "Oh thanks. That's really nice of you," he said.

"What's in it? It's not like gross dead things is it?" the

other voice said.

Ted felt confused. "My bag? Um … no. I mean, it's my clothes and effects." Then he started to wonder if any of his things would be considered gross up there. Worry started to nag at his heart.

"Here. Maybe these will help," the first voice said. Ted felt something being placed in his hand. It felt like a pair of glasses so he put them on and the light dimmed significantly. He sighed with relief. Finally able to see, he looked at the two angels there to greet him. They weren't beautiful women with giant feathered wings. The kind one was a middle-aged gentleman in a tailored white suit and the other was a twenty-something female whose face was so twisted by disgust that Ted had no way to know if she was pretty or not. "So what are your names?" he asked.

"Right," the man said. "Bad manners on my part. My name is Adam." Ted laughed and no one laughed with him. He felt nervous then. Sweat beaded up on the back of his neck and he quickly apologized. He looked towards the girl, but she looked away. She turned her eyes towards Adam and asked, "Do I really have to tell it my name? Why do we have to talk to it at all?"

"Remember where we are and remember your manners," the man said to her.

Ted realized then that she had not been referring to the train when she said *it* was here, earlier. "I'm a man," Ted said. "My pronoun is he. Please don't refer to me as it."

She sighed with disgust again. "Men don't have horns," she said. "You're a thing. Besides, the concept of men and women is for the mortal plane. We are both and we are neither. We are angels, one entity without gender, something greater, and that is just proof that you don't belong here, but I guess He wants us to talk to you though so my name is Mary."

"Really?!" Ted exclaimed. Both people just looked at him strangely. "Oh come on. How is that not funny?"

Adam shrugged. "Maybe humor is different up here." He said it with a hint of distaste. "Let me show you to where you will be staying."

"Fantastic," Ted said. "Oh and thanks for the sunglasses.

They definitely help." When he didn't get a response, he said, "Hey Adam, I'm not staying with Mary am I? I don't think she likes me much." He meant it humorously but now Adam was the one looking at him with disgust. "That would be co-ed," he said. "You're in Heaven now."

"Yeah," Mary chimed in. "Lust is for Hell. Men and women do not lie together up here. Gross."

Ted's eyes went wide. He shook his head. "I didn't even mean it like that," he said. "I meant in the same house. I don't want to be in the same house as you, or cloud or whatever."

"How rude!" she said.

"What do you expect?" Adam said to her. "These creatures have no decency. There are no manners in Hell."

Ted was taken aback. "Are you kidding me right now?" he said. "You've been rude to me since I stepped off the train."

"It is entirely different, I assure you," Mary answered. "You are a foul thing of the underworld and we are good men and women who have ascended to the holy kingdom."

"Oh I see," Ted said. He felt his hope beginning to dwindle. He told himself that it would get better and thought, surely not everyone up here is like these two. He tried to think of something else. In his mind he wondered if he was going to get to meet the big man. That was an exciting thought. He would love the chance to thank Him personally for getting him out of Hell.

"Here we are," Adam said. Ted looked up and stared in amazement. The place looked like a mansion and it was all white and sparkling gold. "Wow," he said.

Downstairs, Ted had a single room hut made of bones and organs. The walls pulsed and spit fluids. It horrified him when he first got down there. He had gotten used to it over time but this was definitely the other end of the spectrum. Mary stopped there and Adam led him up the steps to the door. It felt to Ted like there were a thousand steps. His legs burned with the effort but he made sure not to complain. He didn't want to seem like he was ungrateful or looking a gift horse in the mouth.

When they finally reached the door, Adam set his bag down in the front foyer and then bid him farewell and started back down the stairs. Ted just stood there in the foyer not knowing what to do next. Then an angel in a white tuxedo with a gold lapel approached him. "You must be the exchange student," the angel said as he drew near.

"Yes! My name is Ted. Nice to meet you," he answered, sticking his arm out for a handshake that never came.

"Let's get this out of the way," the newcomer said. "You do not belong here and no one wants you here." Ted looked at him like he had been slapped. This was not at all like his fantasies of Heaven had gone. He didn't respond before the angel spoke again. "My name is Gregor. Your room is down the hall and up the stairs." He pointed the way and then walked off.

Ted bit his lip. He thought the man's name would have been Joseph or Moses or something. *Guess that joke ran its course,* he thought. He walked down the hall that seemed to go on forever. Everything was so white. It was beginning to feel like the world's largest hospital. The lights inside the house were almost as bright as the lights outside and he was forced to keep the sunglasses on. When he finally reached the end of the hall and got to the bottom of the staircase, he stopped to take a break. He looked at the staircase that seemed to climb for eternity and then looked down at his bag and he sighed with defeat. He told himself that it was going to be okay. He just had to prove them wrong, win them over and show them that they were wrong. He could do it. Then with a deep breath, he hoisted his bag up and started to climb the towering stairs.

Ted stopped several times on the way up to catch his breath and rest the sore muscles of his arm. He was beginning to think that this was some form of cruel hazing ritual and there was no end to the climb, that he was just going to climb endlessly until the laughing angels felt he had had enough. Then, at long last, he reached the top.

He entered the room ahead and there were two beds of white linen, on either side of a brightly shining golden lamp. There was an angel on the right bed, lying comfortably in a white t-shirt and jeans, reading a book. "Oh wow. A roommate," Ted said as he entered. The angel on the bed just rolled his eyes and continued to read.

Ted set his bag on the ground and plopped down on the other bed which was so soft he sank into it. He felt like he was sitting on a marshmallow. "Hopefully, you're not like the others and you're going to actually talk to me," he said to the angel.

The angel rolled his eyes again and set his book down on the bed. "It seems I am not going to have a choice, demon."

Ted ignored the implications and went on. "My name is Ted. What's yours? You really make that walk every day just to get out of the house? Don't you think having this room sucks?"

The angel gave another roll of his eyes with the added elegance of a sigh of disgust and then said, "My name is Amir. Nothing sucks demon. This is Heaven. Making that walk is of no consequence. We have eternity. There is no hurry. The rush of mortal life no longer exists."

"Well, I'm exhausted and my muscles are angry. You must be in great shape doing that every day."

"It has no effect. Angels don't tire. That is for mortals, and, I suppose, demons." He said the last word with such a poisonous distaste that Ted almost felt disgusted with himself. "Well if you don't tire, why do you have beds?" he asked.

"For comfort, demon. We have all the comforts."

"Ted. My name is Ted. And you definitely do not have *all* the comforts," Ted laughed. "Do people here really not make love? What about couples that spent their mortal lives together? Don't they still have intimacy?"

Amir stared at him for a moment as if he were something so putrid and vile that the man was actually afraid of catching a disease just being in his presence. Then he sighed and answered, maybe for fear that Ted would add follow up questions with greater detail if he didn't. "Intercourse is for reproduction. Angels cannot reproduce. The act has no purpose in this realm. Therefore partaking in it would be partaking in lust which you may or may not know is one of the seven deadly sins."

"Wow," was all Ted could think of to say.

Amir sighed then. "We are not losing anything Ted. We have transcended. We live a life of intense pleasure already as we have become part of God's light and love. We don't long for anything or feel neglected of anything."

Ted puzzled over this for a moment and then wondered how he was going to win these people over when he still felt tired, and hungry and lustful. He literally was not capable of living the way they did. Suddenly, he felt like he was the one that was being neglected of something. He chose to sleep it off and Amir didn't protest. It was when he attempted to sleep that he noticed the music for the first time. There was a sweet melody playing, soothing strings and organs. It was so entwined with the atmosphere that he hadn't even detected it before then.

The pillow was so soft and fluffy, his head sank into the middle. It felt strange and unnatural. He knew he couldn't sleep on it, so he sat up and opened his bag, removing the pillow Bub had assigned him. It was sewed of flesh and filled with the squishing blood and organs of the one the flesh came from. He laid his head on it and felt comfortable again as it was what he was used to. Then he heard more than saw Amir's disgust. The angel actually ran from the room sounding like he was going to vomit, but from what he had learned so far, Ted was pretty sure that angels didn't throw up. Still, the pillow was probably a mistake. Winning these people over was going to be harder than he thought.

Even with his pillow he found sleep hard to find. It certainly wasn't that he was one with the big guy and didn't feel tired. He was exhausted and wanted nothing more than to sleep. It was just that it was so quiet. The only sound was the soothing subtle music carried on the breeze to his ears. He was used to sleeping through turning machines and screams of agony and lustful moans of orgasm. He tried to pray for sleep, to ask God for assistance. It made sense to do being where he was, but it didn't seem to work, for sleep didn't come. He wondered if the big guy hated him as much as his flock did. If that were the case then why would He even invite him here?

The coming days didn't get any better. Amir moved somewhere else immediately and Ted found himself alone, with no one to talk to. The long walk from the room was extremely tiring to him. He continued to do it and continued to try to assimilate and fit in with the rest of the kingdom. He continued to fail at every turn. The food was pleasure and not for sustenance as they had no need for it, but Ted did and he was hungry. His stomach growled and he asked people where to get a real meal. They all just rolled their eyes and looked at him like he was something foul.

He had imagined that Heaven would be a much kinder place. They were all kind to each other though. No one argued or fought. No one treated anyone like they all unanimously treated him. Apparently they just had a hard time accepting outsiders. Between the exercise and the lack of food he was getting unhealthily thin. He stood out amongst the fit healthy angels and his colored clothing didn't help. Amidst all the white he was like a beacon. There was an angel singing one night. Her voice was gorgeous but her body was even better and she wore nothing more than a see-through dress. It was like a veil for her body, although it hid nothing. Ted knew by then how these people were, so he made sure to say nothing and did his best not to stare. He realized then that it was everyone else staring at him and the very visible rise in his pants. The entire concert broke up and the angels disbanded like they were under attack and Ted was left there by himself, alone with nothing but his erection and his shame.

He was a failure at Heaven.

Ted finally got to meet the man in charge during his second month. It wasn't on the terms he would have hoped for. He had grown tired of the underhanded slights and blatantly rude comments. Fed up, he lost his temper and socked an angel named Juan in the eye. Suddenly he was somewhere else. It was finally dark and he was seated on a stiff couch. He thought that he had been cast out into space. Then he saw a window into the kingdom of Heaven and realized he had been punished, sat away from the others. "Did you just give me a time out?" he said out loud.

"Violence has no place here," a booming voice said back.

"But discrimination does? Bigotry? Bullying? Why don't you put all those jerks in detention with me?" Ted said back angrily.

"You knew as a mortal when I was testing you. Why do you not know it now?" the voice said back.

"I don't know. Maybe because you sent me to Hell? Are you saying that I can pass the test and win a place in Heaven?"

"Are you saying that is something you would want?"

Before his arrival here, maybe even when he first got there, that question had an easy answer, but suddenly he was no longer sure. "I think so," he said. "I mean it wouldn't be bad like this if they accepted me, if I were one of them."

"It is not them that decides what is in you, what your heart desires."

Ted sighed. "Can you please show yourself? This is weird."

"There is nothing to see Ted."

Ted sighed again. He felt disappointed once more since his arrival. "No old guy? No big white beard?"

"No Ted. I am everywhere. I am the light and the music and the love that surrounds you. I am the kingdom and the kingdom is me."

"No offense," Ted said then, "but that sucks. It's so impersonal."

"It is the opposite. It could not be more personal. You are actually inside me, a part of me. What is more personal than that?"

"Can I just go back now?" Ted asked. "I promise to play nice."

"Ted, this was not a punishment. You were brought here because you seemed distressed. You needed some darkness and a break from the others, a place to unwind and relax some. You were in need of peace."

"Oh," Ted said then. He supposed it was true. Then the voice was gone and so was his first interaction with the big He. During that second month, Ted decided to keep to himself. He stayed in his room mostly, eating whatever food he could smuggle in and hoard. He spent a lot of time reading. One thing Heaven did have was a killer library. He had never seen so many books in one place. The giant library lacked horror and science fiction which were his favorite genres, but there was enough interesting stuff to pass the time.

By his third month, the comfort of his self-induced isolation was taken away. An angel named Mariko had come to tell him that his seclusion was frightening people. They didn't know what he was doing and they already felt like he was a stain, a blight on their Heavenly kingdom. They needed him to come out at once and be where the others could see him. "I don't want to be alone," he told her. "I want to be one of you."

Mariko frowned. Her hands tightened on handfuls of her white dress. "I'm afraid that just isn't possible," she said. Then she turned and left. Ted decided he wasn't a criminal and he wasn't going to go hang around these people just so they could keep an eye on him. Granted, he was stealing food, but he felt that was about survival. They didn't actually need it and he did.

Each day after that, an angel was sent to draw him from his room. They were all equally nervous and afraid of him, antsy to deliver the message and get back outside. He gave up trying to fit in and started entertaining himself with their discomfort. He felt like it was all he had. He would reference things in hell he knew they would find gross, make sudden movements at them to watch them jump, and hang out naked hoping it would deter them. They were relentless though. No matter how uncomfortable he made them and how terrified of him they were, they continued to come back, day after day.

By the fourth month he gave in and left his room. Of course, he did it without getting dressed first and the shocked faces of the angels made him giggle. He urinated publicly, something they no longer needed to do, and he smiled as he did it. He felt the horrified staring eyes as he relieved himself. "This is what you wanted isn't it?" he said then, addressing them all. "You wouldn't even give me a chance. You didn't so much as welcome me. You want me to be a heathen and something vile from the depths of Hell, bringing darkness and lewd behavior to taint the holy kingdom right? I tried. I wanted to be liked and accepted, to be one of you. I dreamed about it when I was a mortal and even when I lived downstairs, but you had my fate already sealed didn't you? So now I'm giving you what you want. If you don't like it, blame yourselves."

With those words, he farted and then excused himself to do a number two somewhere more private. He thought that the error of their ways would become clear to them and they would come to him with apologies and wanting to start anew. That wasn't the case. They avoided him more than ever after that. If he chose to stay in his room, they let him, probably afraid of what they would find if they were to enter it. He felt more abandoned and alone than he ever had before, in his mortal or immortal life.

At the start of his fifth month, Ted realized that his six month excursion was nearing its close. He felt bitter. He had his chance to leave Hell and become an angel in Heaven and they ruined it for him. He didn't make even a slightly good impression and once he returned to Hell, he would most likely never be invited to return here. Would he even want to come back if he could? He honestly didn't know and that may have bothered him even more. If they were so closed off to the idea of someone from downstairs coming to live there than what was the point of the whole thing, he wondered. None of it made sense to him. He was lonely, tired, hungry, horny, confused, and depressed.

He decided to spend his last month trying again to do the right thing. Maybe if he tried his best, when he left he would at least leave them with regret and remorse. He got dressed and took the endless staircase and long hallway out of the house day after day. He did his best to respect the rules and he made conversation with as many angels as he could, though they usually ended quickly. It was still bright enough to give him a headache and hard for him to sleep. It was painstaking to go out every day and interact with people who didn't have enough compassion to even pretend they wanted his company, but he did it. He did it, day after day. He didn't actually care about them, the angels. He cared that God saw his heart, saw his intentions and integrity. His was the opinion that mattered when it all came down to it. He was the one that decided Ted was more fit for Hell in the first place and if anyone could make the decision to change his residence, it was Him.

When he at last reached his final days, he went to each person he could find, though they didn't see themselves as people or individuals anymore, and told them each at least one good thing about them that he could think of. He wanted to end things on a positive note and he wanted them to see that despite how badly they treated him for the last six months he was still able to see the good in them. It wasn't entirely true and it was a far more difficult task than he had realized when he decided to do it, but nevertheless it felt important. It felt like winning. He was sure that if God knew that, he would tell him that there was no winning in Heaven. Pride was a sin right? Ted didn't know what the big guy would say, truly. They had only had the one conversation in six months and he didn't get much out of it, but winning felt pretty good to him anyway, and feeling good wasn't something he had done a lot of since his arrival in Heaven. That was a concept that felt very backwards to him, but he knew that he would have plenty of time on the rack to think about it soon enough.

On his last day, Ted bid everyone farewell. They didn't return the gesture but they did all stand there to watch him get on his train. They just needed to see for themselves that Heaven was safe once again, that the monster was gone. You know? Screw it, he thought, and he gave them all the finger as the doors closed. Then he sat down, thinking he should have done things differently. He should have tried harder, put in more effort, cut his horns off, done something. As the train moved to take him back to the Underworld he thought about how his one and only chance for salvation was over, and he allowed himself to feel terrible about how awful it had gone.

Then the seat disappeared from under him and he hit the ground hard. The train started rocking and jumping and he slid across the floor, banging his head into the wall. He remembered the angel going the other way when he was on his way there and how he had laughed and he laughed again. He laughed at himself and the pain of the fall, the surprise of it. He laughed knowing that one of those jerks experienced the same thing. He laughed imagining their face. He laughed and laughed and laughed, and he continued to slide around the floor of the jarring train car as he did so.

Finally, the ride came to an end and Ted got to his feet. His head and mouth were bleeding from collisions during the ride. He gave one more small laugh and then walked to the other end of the car to retrieve his bag that had been sliding around as well. He picked it up and then stepped through the open doors into the darkness of Hell. The only light was the fires burning all around, the smell of the flesh burning in them lingering in the air and tickling his nostrils. He could hear screams of terror and howls of pain coming from everywhere. He looked forward and saw a group of his friends gambling over cards and laughing. Just over to the right were several men and women giving in to their carnal desires, out in the open, uninhibited and unafraid. Ted felt himself start to smile.

Then Bub appeared before him, naked as can be with his leathery burnt skin and horns bigger than anything you had ever seen. "Welcome back," Bub said to him. "We've missed you."

Ted closed his eyes and sighed with relief. "Oh thank God," he said.

A Coral Study

Katherine Quevedo

When I got to Mario Reyes's dorm room, I heard him scuffling around, opening and closing drawers as if he had a girl coming over. I smirked as I knocked. If he'd seen my room, he wouldn't have bothered cleaning.

He opened the door. "Hello, Leland," he said. "Please come in." He never spoke in class, but his English was pretty good for an exchange student. His skin was caramel-colored even in the fluorescent light, and his thick, dark hair hung in waves past his ears.

"You can just call me Lee." I followed him in. "So where are you from, again?"

"Ecuador."

"Oh. Quito?"

He shook his head, looking half amused, half irritated, as if I'd conjured a weary inside joke. Probably everyone around here guessed he was from Quito. "I am from Puerto Ayora, in the Galapagos Islands."

"Oh, yeah. Darwin, right?"

"Yes."

I flung my backpack onto his bed and stepped back as it bobbed on the mattress. A waterbed.

Then I noticed the teal plastic seaweed scattered among his bookshelves like houseplants. He'd forgotten to shut one drawer, which held a small plastic castle designed to look carved out of coral. The color had smudged and worn off the edges, as though handled often. No wonder he was such a loner.

"Um, seaweed?" I said. "I take it you're majoring in marine biology. It's like an aquarium in here."

"No, no, a terrarium," he said quickly. The word sounded

poetic in his accent—short vowels, rolled and flipped R's. "An aquarium would have water. There is no water in here."

"Except in your mattress." I nodded at the waterbed. "Does the school know about that?" Waterbeds weren't exactly standard in the dorms.

"Of course," he said. I raised an eyebrow at him. He nervously brushed his hair back on one side, where I glimpsed a pearl earring nestled in the helix of his ear before a dark wave fell forward again and hid it. "Actually, I am a music major."

"Music?" I plopped myself on the sand-colored rug. "Why are you taking upper level bio?"

"Personal interest."

I laughed.

He didn't. "May I play some music while we work?"

"Be my guest," I said, grabbing my backpack and fishing through it. I glanced up and caught him furrowing his brow in confusion at the phrase. He must've thought I'd extended him some sort of invitation. "I mean, music sounds good," I said. "It'll help us power through this paper so we can start thinking about winter break."

He smiled, started up a playlist, and joined me cross-legged on the rug, carefully avoiding his waterbed as though not to draw any more attention to it.

His taste in music ranged from instrumental pieces that made me feel like I was at a Renaissance faire, to the latest pop hits with hypnotic beats and simple lyrics. All melodic, though. I'd expect nothing less from a music major. Then something else caught my attention, something I didn't expect from his major: his impressive knowledge of amphibians.

He dictated whole sections of our report off the top of his head, while my fingers flew over the keyboard to keep up. The few times he consulted our textbook, it seemed like an afterthought, a courtesy for me. And beyond his raw knowledge, his phrasing sounded poetic, like his accent. Philosophical, even. Maybe he'd call it musicality. Not sure what our professor was going to think, but I didn't care. I liked it, so I included it.

Eventually curiosity got the better of me. I paused the music, and he jerked at the sudden silence.

"Mario, sorry, I just have to ask. What's with all this –

terrarium stuff? How do you know so much about amphibians? You have gills or something?"

I didn't realize I'd meant it seriously until I saw his earnest,
trusting eyes. Perhaps he wasn't a loner by choice. He raised
his hand and swept back his hair. This time, not distracted by
the pearl earring, I glimpsed a shadow just beyond his earlobe.
A trick of the light? Then his hair fell forward again.

We stared at each other for a few seconds, then his eyes
widened and he lurched toward the remaining open drawer
and slammed it shut. He sank back onto the rug.

I cleared my throat. "The Galapagos Islands are pretty far,"
I said. "You must get homesick."

His eyes grew misty. "Yes. But after graduation, when I
return home, I will bring your music with me."

We sat in silence for a moment.

"You know," I said, "if you need somewhere to stay during
the holidays – we have a guest room. And a pool."

With focused eyes and a tight mouth, he studied my voice
as I spoke. Nothing more than the movement of air across vocal
cords, the proper positioning of tongue and jaw, and millennia
of natural selection at work. But so much revealed in it. Mario
searched my face as though expecting I'd referenced an inside
joke he wasn't part of. I hadn't.

Finally, he beamed at my offer. Music to his ears.

Take Him to
Your Leader. Please

Jennifer Moore

Mrs Hopkirk hasn't even finished the sentence, and Jackson Hardy's hand's already up and waving. Typical. Just when I think I can't hate him any more than I already do, he has to go and prove me wrong.

"Yes, Jackson," she says, smiling. Teachers always smile at Jackson. Or at least they do if they want to hold onto their jobs. Given that his dad bankrolls the entire school (it's not called the Archibald Jefferson G. Hardy Academy for nothing), it generally pays to smile at his sneering, stuck-up, ignorant lump of a son. The last teacher who dared to fail one of Jackson's end of term papers was out of here quicker than you could say 'unfair dismissal'.

Poor old Miss Leech. I liked her.

"Did you have a question, Jackson?" asks Mrs Hopkirk.

"When do I go?" he barks at her.

"Well," she says, struggling a little to keep the smile in place. "As I was about to explain, this isn't like most language exchange programmes. We're one of a number of select schools across the country who've been invited to take part, and each school only has one place. It's a *very* big deal, but at this stage we're just after expressions of interest."

Even though I'm sitting two places behind him I can still picture the slow, smug grin spreading across Jackson's pasty face.

"Like I said," he drawls. "When do I go?"

"Your enthusiasm is an example to us all," Mrs Hopkirk tells him, through gritted teeth. She turns to the rest of us with a pleading look in her eyes. "This is a once in a lifetime opportunity to explore the further reaches of the universe. To experience extra-terrestrial hospitality. The selected pupil will be an ambassador not just for their school and country but for the entire planet..." What? Jackson Hardy representing the whole of humankind? No wonder she looks worried. "The future of inter-planetary relations between us and the Laxicams may well depend upon the success of this scheme."

She breaks off to dab her forehead with a tissue. "As I was explaining, before I was so *pleasantly* interrupted, the programme is sponsored by the Laxicamic Supreme Council, so there'd be no costs involved. Perhaps we could have a show of hands?" she says. "The more the merrier at this stage... Anyone?"

Jackson coughs loudly, swivelling round in his seat to check if anyone's stupid enough to cross him. As if we've forgotten what happened to poor Petra when she turned him down for the end of year dance.

"Hands up then," Mrs Hopkirk pleads.

This is it! This is history in the making. This is first contact with another species. Who wouldn't want to be a part of it? I'd *kill* for the opportunity. But what's the point? We all know there's only one person in this class who stands a cat in hell's chance of boarding that spacecraft. As far as anyone at our school's concerned, it might as well be called the Jackson Hardy-Laxicama Exchange Programme. The only consolation is we'll be shot of him for a full lunar month.

"Just you then Jackson," says Mrs Hopkirk with a heavy sigh. "Lucky Laxicams. I'll let the headmaster know."

Once it becomes clear that Jackson Hardy's got the place (the headmaster somehow manages to 'mislay' the permission forms from all three hundred and forty-two other interested pupils), the teachers turn their attention to the Earth-leg of the exchange programme. Just as Jackson will be spending a month on Laxicama, so a lucky Laxicamic child will be spending a month here in Harksville. He or she, or rather 'it' (according to Mrs Hopkirk there are no equivalent genders on their planet), will attend classes with Jackson during their stay. So although we all lose out to him yet again, in many ways we're "all winners". Yeah, right.

Mr Dorada from the Spanish department sets up special Laxicamic classes at lunch for anyone who's interested. I go along to the first one, purely out of curiosity, but end up staying for the whole semester. Their language totally rocks! No tedious verb tables to memorise, no masculine or feminine endings to worry about. And best of all, no written language! Just a series of weird grunts and whistling sounds, at different pitches, depending on what emotion you're expressing. It sounds a bit bonkers the first few times you hear it, but once you get the hang of it it's surprisingly easy. Needless to say Jackson *isn't* attending Mr Dorada's lunch club. He claims it's a waste of time, given that the Laxicams all speak perfectly good English, and of course everyone just smiles and nods like it's the wisest thing anyone's ever said.

Wow. There it is. I'm sure I'm not the only one holding my breath as the first spacecraft enters our orbit. We're all of us crammed into the hall – the entire school – watching on the 3D projecta-screen, surround sound and vibro-scent turned up to full blast. The whole school, that is, apart from Jackson Hardy, who's waiting somewhere just off-screen in the VIP area, together with a select few of his fellow exchange students and their families. Oh, and the President of the United States and her entourage. Not that we need to *see* Jackson to picture his smug smirk.

I can't help wishing the Laxicams *weren't* coming in peace. Not all of them, anyway. Just one peckish rebel with a taste for smug, meaty humans – that's all it would take. One little sneaky snack while no one was looking ... I reckon Jackson would be pretty hard to resist.

The tiniest of tremors runs down the hall through the floor sensors, as the giant beast of a metal sphere touches down in Texas, and then everything grows still. I'm still holding my breath when a large hatch opens at the base; still waiting for my first glimpse of extra-terrestrial life. Up 'til now, all contact with our alien friends has been verbal – no one's actually seen them in the flesh. And my goodness, have they got a lot of flesh! An audible gasp ripples through the room as we clock the first giant green slug creature peering out at the waiting cameras. In fact, it's hard to say what hits us first, the shock of its appearance or the gaggingly foul stench that accompanies it. The headmaster runs, heaving, to the main sensor board, and switches off the vibro-scent feature. But it's too late for the kids at the front, who are already vomiting into each other's hoodies, tears streaming down their scrunched-up faces. Perfect! If the smell filtering through our screen system is as bad as this, just think what it must be like for Jackson! For once I'd *love* to see the expression on his face.

The creatures' nose-melting body odour's all sorted by the time Jackson rolls up at school with his extra-terrestrial guest. He (it) still looks like a revolting green slime creature, but at least he doesn't smell. Apparently in Laxicamic circles that particular scent's the equivalent of a polite handshake and a "pleased to meet you". There's no equivalent when it comes to names, though, so the creature suggests we call him Rocky. Bit of a strange choice – maybe they showed old Sylvester Stallone films on the flight over.

Funny, isn't it, how a planet with the same basic chemical make-up as Earth could have produced such wildly different creatures? I mean they breathe oxygen just like us. They need H_2O to survive. They've mastered language and technology. And yet they've ended up with a shapeless blob of lime jello for a body, six eyes on stalks, and a hole for a mouth. And do you know what's even funnier? Rocky may look like a freaky giant garden pest – a radioactive one at that – but he's *still* more of a catch than his human exchange partner!

To give him his due, Jackson *was* right about Laxicamic language skills. Rocky's English is absolutely impeccable. Not that Jackson bothers talking to him of course. Instead he shoves him down next to me and heads for a desk at the other end of the classroom, like he can't get far enough away. Not exactly what you'd call hospitable. Mrs Hopkirk shakes her head in disgust at his rude behaviour but she doesn't say anything. She never does.

Me? I don't really mind. Rocky seems nice enough, once

you get used to his appearance, and it's not every day you get to meet someone from the outer reaches of space. In fact, thanks to Rocky, I'm enjoying registration more than usual this morning. From where we're sitting we've got a perfect view of the green slime trail down the back of Jackson's designer top. He's going to spew when he finds that. Result!

Not only is his English perfect, it turns out Rocky's a bit of an all-round genius. He's finished all the math problems on the board in the time it takes me to get my work-tablet out my bag in first period. He masters Spanish in a single lesson and composes an entire symphony in Music, complete with harmonies so beautiful they have Miss Kringer weeping on the floor. The only subject he struggles with all day is Physical Education, on account of his not having any legs. A minor detail. He still manages to speed round the running track in the blink of an eye, but fails miserably when it comes to the hurdles and high jump. Of course Jackson finds it hilarious and spends the rest of the lesson taunting him with inane insults like, *"not so hot now eh, slug boy? What's wrong – evolution forgot to give you any legs? I'd have thought you could jet propel yourself over on your disgusting stink cloud."*

Rocky closes four of his eyes, in a gesture of polite demurral, and says nothing.

"Take no notice," I tell him afterwards, in my best Laxicamic. I've been practising. "The guy's a total loser. We only put up with him because his Dad pays for the school and pretty much owns the entire town."

"You speak Laxicamic?" Rocky says, answering in his native tongue.

"I try my best," I tell him, wishing my accent wasn't so poor. There's a beautiful lilting quality to Rocky's grunts and whistles that's quite mesmerising. "We've been having lessons at lunchtime."

"But Jackson can't speak a word in our language," he says, all six of his eyes blinking in confusion.

"Yeah, well, that's because he thinks he's too important to have to learn. Plus, he's a mean, lazy imbecile with a donut for a brain." I don't actually know what the Laxicamic for 'imbecile'

Jennifer Moore

or 'donut' is, so I resort to a bit of international sign language along the way. I think Rocky gets the gist.

"It's true," he agrees, switching back to English. "I know I haven't met many Earthlings yet, but he and his parents strike me as particularly unpleasant specimens of your race. At least here in school I can get away from them for a while."

"Two *minutes* with Jackson Hardy is enough for most people," I say. "Let alone a whole month. Do you have to share a bedroom?"

Rocky's black mouth opens a little wider and a sound like machine-gun fire comes tearing out of it. A few of the nearby kids dive for cover, but I've attended enough of Mr Dorada's lunchtime classes to recognise the Laxicamic equivalent of laughter.

"I don't even have to share a *house* with him," he says. "They're so worried about slime on their furniture they make me stay out in the garden. Jackson shouts insults to me out of the window."

Ooh, that's harsh. I reach forward and give him a tentative pat on what I'm hoping is his shoulder. As alien flesh goes it's surprisingly warm and pleasant to the touch.

"Don't worry," I assure him, "we're not all like that."

"Just as well," he says, "otherwise we might be forced to declare war on your planet."

I'm still waiting for the machine gun laughter. Only it doesn't come.

"You *are* joking, right?" I certainly *hope* he's joking, although I wouldn't put it past Jackson to lead the planet to complete annihilation, merely by the unpleasant force of his personality. I mean, if anyone can, it's him.

"Don't worry," says Rocky. "All-out war is not part of our plan. And I've seen enough of your planet to know that Jackson Hardy is not representative of humankind as a whole. No need to breach our inter-planetary peace agreement just yet!"

Phew. If Rocky's amazing intellect is anything to go by, Laxicamic weapons technology must be light years ahead of ours. I wouldn't fancy our chances much.

"I'm afraid you got the short straw when they were handing out exchange partners," I tell him. "We all wanted you to come and stay with us but you know how it is … what Jackson wants, Jackson gets. You'll have to get your own back on him when he comes to Laxicama. Make *him* sleep in the garden, so he doesn't pollute the atmosphere with his obnoxiousness."

"Ah yes. I've been giving his return trip some thought already," Rocky says, "and I have to admit I'm delighted he was chosen instead of you."

Oh. Well, that's a bit of a slap in the face. Talk about a sudden turn around. And I thought we were getting on so well.

"Right," I say, trying not to sound too hurt. "Looks like it all worked out for the best then."

"I think so. He will be perfect."

I've never heard him called that before. Apart from his glowing end of year reports: *Jackson is quite the model pupil. It has been an absolute pleasure and daily thrill to teach such a talented, intelligent, self-assured individual, who quite clearly takes after his father…* It's all very vomitsome and the rest of the class has to sit and listen while Jackson reads it out loud, gloating over his superior grades. I don't think he's been to a single drama lesson all year and he's still going to wipe the floor clean with the rest of us when it comes to his report card: *such rare dramatic genius. Jackson will need a very big mantelpiece for all his Oscars. A radiant example to actors the world over…* You get the idea.

I guess Rocky's clocked on to how things work round here. That's the only explanation I can think of for choosing a spoilt creep with the IQ of a woodlouse, over yours truly.

"But I thought you said he was an unpleasant specimen of humankind?"

"Yes," agrees Rocky. "Exactly what we're looking for in our new research programme."

"What do you mean?"

One of his eyes closes briefly, as if he's trying to wink. "Can you keep a secret?"

"Of course." It's true. I'm fabulous at keeping secrets. I never tell more than three or four people at most.

He makes the funny machine-gun noise again. "I don't believe you for one second," he says. "But never mind. I'm sure you'll keep this one – after all, peace between our races, and the future safety of mankind may well depend on it."

"Oh. Right." I'm not sure I like the sound of that too much. Seems like a big responsibility.

"More to the point, if you tell anyone, they'll try and stop us. And then we won't be able to take Jackson away to experiment on. He'll have to stay here on Earth. With you."

Wow! I did *not* see that one coming.

"You mean this whole exchange programme is just a cover?" Is that what he's saying? "A way of collecting humans to experiment on, without the hassle of stealing them away in the middle of the night, like they do in films?"

"Exactly," says Rocky. "But we're not barbarians. We intend to keep only the dregs of your society – the others will be returned safe and sound. It's in no one's interest to provoke war between our planets, and we only need a select few for our experiments. Like Jackson."

"And you'd keep him there on Laxicama? Forever?"

Rocky's body shakes up and down, sending ripple-like reverberations through his jello frame. I think he's trying to nod.

"That's the idea," he says. "But it's all a bit hush-hush right now, for obvious reasons."

I throw my arms around him, launching myself face first into his warm, squidgy exterior. Mum's going to have a fit when she sees all the slime over my clothes and hair, but I don't care. I love this guy.

"Rocky," I assure him, in my very best Laxicamic. "My lips are sealed."

The Blog of Thomasona Brown

Paula Hammond

Monday

The head of Philip K. Dick just liked my tweet. Seriously, that's never something I thought I'd ever write. But the Literature Department here is, like, so cool and always looking for new ways to engage with the students. If you read their prospectus they even say that the Heads of Hemingway and Faulkner give classes in the Fall. How fun is that?

The Uni are super supportive too. It was their idea to start this blog. Professor Migo says, "If you want to be a writer, then you've got to write." So here I am, Thomasona Brown, exchange student at Miskatonic U and this is my first ever blog. Hello world! Or at least hello MU. Today the intranet, tomorrow the world, right?

I'm sort of nervous because before they moved out to the Valley both my folks went to MU. Mom was from Salem. Dad was Arkham born-and-bred. So it was really important to them that I spent some time at their old alma mater. Can you believe that they actually met in the stacks? Right between *Prinn's De Vermis Mysteriis* and *Picasso's Dream Lands Print Series*. So you could almost say that I'm a child of MU. Later in the year I'm planning a pilgrimage to the exact spot. Maybe take some selfies with me and my honey, Keziah.

Oh, didn't I mention her? Joke – if you know me, you'll know she's pretty much all I talk about these days. Keziah Mason. Funny, whip smart, and a total Betty. Yeah, I know it's sort of un-PC to say that, but it's true. Whenever I look at her, the world just takes a sideways jump. It's all a bit unreal.

We met through the campus paper. They were having an Orientation 'get to know us' thing. And, yes, I actually am making little quotation marks with my fingers as I type that. Confession time tho? While I really do want to write – like professionally – I only went along because someone said wine and cheese. Who doesn't like free bubbles, right? Plus, any excuse to get out of my roommate's hair for a few hours.

Honestly, she's been the only downside to the whole exchange experience so far. It's not that she's unfriendly – just mega uptight, for which I totes blame the parents. I think they're from one of those crazy churches where everyone calls each other brother and sister. Which is, like, so creepy. Anyway, I figure she'll come around eventually but I wish she'd quit with the chanting. Don't get me wrong, it's a free country. If you want to spend your nights mumbling made-up words in candle-light then knock yourself out. But, really, who does cults these days? It's just so '90s. Plus, a girl's got to get her beauty sleep, right?

Tuesday

O.M.G. So. Big news on campus. Jennet Fleishman just aced her midterms. We all know Jennet, right? Super super nice, but not what you might call deep. Someone – who shall remain nameless (how's that for journalistic integrity) – said that she really wasn't herself "if you know what I mean." That would definitely explain some of the trippendicular things she's been doing recently. We Californians, like, practically invented drugs but Jennet has been seriously out of it. I tried to chat to her just a few days ago and she was all "After man will come the mighty beetle whose bodies will host the cream of the Great Race seeking to escape the monstrous doom that will overtake the Elder World." Seriously: wow. She didn't even take a breath. Trust me, whatever she's on, it's not your usual Truckers' Stay Awake pills. I've totally chugged a few of those in my time and all I ever got was a fearsome caffeine headache.

What's odd, though, is that Kez has been pissed about it all day. Like being a stoner was something to envy. And that's what led to our first ever fight. We made up later, natch, but it did shake me up a bit. I really couldn't be with anyone who did drugs. Yeah, I know, so who's the uptight one now? Mind you, sometimes when I look at Kez, I get that Vaseline-on-the lens effect – say it loud, say it proud: I'm drunk on love, girl. Drunk on love. Or should that be drunk on Girl Love? Capitals totally intended, I should add.

Wednesday

Today I discovered that my Professor Shrewsbury – the one from Anthropology who I wave to every morning as he crosses the quad – is Mom and Dad's Professor Shrewsbury. How awesome is that? At first I thought it was his son because I remember seeing pictures of him in Mom's old yearbook. All I can say is that he must have some magical moisturizing routine because he looks super amazing for his age.

Kez says I'm obsessed with the man but, seriously girl-friend, the guy's like a zillion years old and he's still a total dude. Not that I think about him that way. At. All. But you don't expect your Mom's Professor to look like the captain of the football team. Anyway, there's more to it than that.

You wouldn't know it, but MU is really a university of two halves. There's tons of overseas students and, like, loads from other states. But there's also lot of students, like Kez and I, who are sort-of local. Our parents and their parents' parents studied here. We're almost family. So it's only natural that I'd feel some sort of connection to the Prof. who taught my folks. Not that I'm about to start poking around in any dusty, old librar-ies. Seriously! The big downside to this writing business is that everyone expects me to spend all my time with my nose bur-ied in ancient tomes. That's so not my style. Plus books: mega dangerous. Dad has been telling me that, like, forever. I mean knowledge is power. We all know that, right?

Anyway, I prefer to write from real life and MU is so in-teresting. Just this morning the Archeology Department left for their annual field trip. It took me right back to my childhood. Mom and Dad have always been super focused on their work. Even in the holidays, we kids would be dragged off to look at piles of decaying stones while the folks went crazy over some squiggly writing.

Now that I'm officially an author – well blogger – it's exactly the sort of thing I should take an interest in. It's so exotic and people love exotic. Fascinating as I am, I can't spend the whole year writing about just me, right? Plus, the men and women who volunteer every year are so brave. I do hope some of them come back this time.

Thursday

Well, Thursday already, and I'm so impressed with myself. Four days, four blogs. This writing business is a total breeze. And here I was, thinking it would be all angst and torment. Pouring out my soul to a cold, uncaring world. Sobbing myself to sleep every night with sheer, creative exhaustion. But, seriously, all you have to do is keep pressing the keys in the right order. Isn't that how all those monkeys wrote Shakespeare?

OK, OK. Creative Writing seniors, please don't kill me. Hand on heart, I really am enjoying putting fingers to keyboard. Even if, like, right now, that means that all the keys are covered in Essie's Barely There polish. I've totally ruined a kicking manicure, so don't tell me that I have to suffer for my art. Been there, done that.

Being serious for a minute though, Kez is being totes supportive about it all. Well as supportive as the little wise-cracker gets. If I remember rightly what she actually said was "You're bound to be good at anything that involves talking about yourself." And, you know, it is kinda true. I am super self-absorbed, but aren't we all? We're the generation that spent our childhood staring at our own reflection in tablet screens while our parents documented every belch and booboo. We're all children of the selfie-stick, right?

In fact, if you're anything like me – and if you are, welcome to the Awesome Club – you probably have your whole life stored on the Cloud. And how weird is that? I mean, my folks probably have a couple of dozen photos of themselves, max. So I can laugh at the dog-eared pix of Dad's Magnum P.I. mustache and that total Flash Dance thing Mom had going on, but that's pretty much it. If Kez and I ever have kids, the embarrassment's never going to stop. There's some serious blackmail material lurking out there on the Cloud, let me tell you.

Kids. Wow. Did I really write that? Perhaps there's more to

this writing business than I thought. I mean, I'm never totally serious about anything but here I am, opening up and sharing. I know it's not exactly Confessional Stuff but perhaps little Thomasona is maturing?

At my morning tutorial Professor Migo even said that I was "doing really well", although she thought that I needed to expand my horizons. "Get out into the universe and soak it all up." That's how all the big names did it, apparently.

Have I told you about my Prof? She's a lovely lady. Ever so quietly spoken and a bit standoffish, but lovely. Anyway, it's not every day that a Professor praises my work and – you know me – any excuse for a hug. So I gave her a great big bear squeezer. Sadly, that did not go down well. At. All. Message to self. Keep your natural exuberance for wine and Kez.

Friday
Downer alert! Just spent lunch with a couple of fellow exchange students from Caltech. Both Valley types so, natch, I made a bee-line as soon as I heard them in the dinner line. At first they were, like, so pleased to talk to me that I could barely squeeze a word in sideways. Imagine that if you can! But, wow, talk about judgmental. They *did no*t have a single good word to say about lovely old MU and you'll never guess what they called the locals? "Freaks." I mean, hello? California has, like, special vats where they breed all the hippies, goths, punks, and eco-nuts. The place is Weird Central – and I speak as a South Cal gal. Hell, there's a guy that lives next-door to my folks who walks his dog in nothing but ass-less, see-through pants. Like see-through pants weren't enough on their own. And he's, like, the Chief of Police. So, trust me, I know weird.

But the big shocker was when I called Kez over to say hi. You could literally see them back off. Well back off doesn't really describe it. More like run for the hills.

Now perhaps I've just been lucky because, my whole life, I never saw the like. Mom and Dad always taught us to be respectful of others, no matter how strange they or their customs seem. Just because someone doesn't share your world view doesn't make them a bad person. I don't know if there's some homophobia thing going on but they were Class A Ass-holes.

Yes, I'm doing the Putting Important Stuff in Capital Letters thing again because the steaming pile of dog poop emoji doesn't seem very literary. But I am thinking it.

Seriously, the way they bolted you'd have thought there had been a full-scale zombie invasion. Notice I said "full scale" there, because there were already a couple of pre-med zombies waiting in-line. Those guys work so hard that they always look ready to drop. But these were the full-on shambling, pallid, drooling pre-med zombz that we've all come to know, love, and be a bit creeped out by.

Afterwards, Jason McCoy could see how upset Kez and I were and said we could borrow his hound to teach them "a bit of down-home MU hospitality." He's always saying things like 'down-home' which sounds super funny coming from a ginger white boy. Anyway it was nice of him to offer, but I've seen it. That hound is never going to scare anyone. It's just a big, bony Great Dane that sits in the corner of his room looking hungry. He really should feed it more because whenever I visit all I can hear is its damned chewing.

Still, I don't expect they'll stay long. According to Jason, our little corner of the cosmos has a world-beating rep. when it comes to the fields of anti-matter, dark matter, and string theory. I haven't a clue what he's talking about, but he says it takes a special mind to study Physics at MU and they just don't have what it takes.

Saturday

Well, the weekend is here already and you know what that means for little Thomasona and her gal? Party Time!

First up, though, I have to FaceTime Mom and Dad. They're over in Egypt so I don't expect I'll even get a connection. I mean, pyramids aren't famous for their wi-fi, right? Natch I'll be putting on my very best Interested Expression. There I go with those capital letters again. Don't get me wrong, it's not that Mom and Dad's work bores me. I get the appeal of all those terrible spires, and monoliths, and lands that men never knew were lands. But dirt and bones. Gross. Don't go there.

Then there's more of the usual college girl routine stuff: laundry and an hour at the gym.

Healthy body, healthy mind is one of MU's big mantras. Basically you won't get a passing grade unless you do your time in the gym, pool, or on the field. If I'm honest that seems a bit unfair to me. Not all of the students are able-bodied and some are seriously freaked by water. There's an Innsmouth girl in my writing class that has a real phobia about it.

Still, I don't really mind. Anything to keep me young and beautiful, right? Talking of which, I really need to pick out an outfit for tonight. Kez has persuaded me to try out for her sorority and they're super picky so I want to make a good impression.

It would be awesome if we could be sorority sisters. I just hope the pledge isn't too embarrassing. I've already seen some of the frat boys creeping round campus in totally grody costumes. O.M.G. If you ever spot me dressed in dowdy brown robes waving a rubber knife around, just kill me. Better that than finding myself on YouTube being trolled by the fashion police.

Sunday

They say that the best parties are the ones you don't remember. Which means that last night's was probably the best of my whole life. Seriously – the whole thing's a total blank. I got nada. One minute we were knocking on the sorority house door, the next I was waking up in the serious post meridian.

All I get are flashes of this, like, weird old woman. All bent back and croaky voice and, I swear, she had this white-faced, bearded rat perched on her shoulder. Brown and sort of bloated looking with tiny baby hands. The rat, natch, not the woman.

I must have danced my ass-off, though, because I ache all over. Plus I slept, like, the whole morning. OK, so that's not unusual. If MU ever starts a competitive sleeping team, I'm so joining it.

Still, Kez says that I made a great impression which is a relief because, trust me, a drunk Thomasona can be a serious handful.

You know, I've just read that last line back and it occurs to me that I really should stop talking about myself in the third person. It makes me sound like some goofy super-villain planning to take over the world. Seriously, can you imagine? Me, the Miskatonic Sisterhood, and witchy rat lady, creeping round the sorority house plotting world domination? Let me tell you: the only thing I'm planning to dominate right now is this duvet.

If I ever manage to FaceTime Mom and Dad they will be totes pleased with how it all went. As soon as I got my place on the exchange programme, they were crazy keen on me joining a sorority. And they'll be thrilled that it's Kez's. Before you ask, yes, they know all about her. Mom and Kez's family have old Salem connections so when I told her we were dating, she said that she couldn't be more excited and that "all their plans for me would soon come to fruition." She has this odd way of talking sometimes, but that's mothers for you. A little strange but you love them anyway. Just like my Kez.

Interplanetary Relations

Margret A. Treiber

"No way," I replied. "It's seedy and dangerous there. I have to stay clean if I want to get a decent internship next year."

"Of course it's seedy," Ralph whined. "It's the vice district. That's where all the fun is."

"I've already had three applications rejected. If I get into any trouble, I'll blow any chance of an academic future."

Ralph shook his head. "You need to pull that stick out of your ass and stop worrying all the time."

I looked at Petra. "It's your call. You're the deciding vote."

Petra tilted her head to one side, feigning deep thought. "Vice District. Hmm." She closed her eyes and then smirked. "We've been on this world an entire month and seen nothing but museums and libraries. Ralph is right. We need to have some fun. Besides, you are the future diplomat. You need to study some of the local nightlife."

"Yeah, Tom," Ralph said. "I'm right."

"Don't let it go to your head. I don't see how an alien tourist trap is going to educate me on local customs." I tucked my passport, wallet, and valuables in places I would notice if someone tried to pickpocket me. Petra rolled her eyes at me.

"Hey," I said. "Better safe than undocumented on a strange planet. Remember what happened to Hans. It took an entire semester to process him back."

Ralph and Petra followed suit and stashed their valuables safely away.

We strolled into the vice district. It was just as dirty and sleazy as I expected. Sordid looking people with unwholesome expressions eyed us as we walked by. My pulse raced as I felt the sensation of being targeted.

"Are you okay?" Petra asked.

I nodded. "Yeah, just uncomfortable."

"This is what we signed up for." She winked at me.

Signs flashed around us in several different languages, including several human dialects. They advertised and enticed. My curiosity started getting the better of me. This was obviously a tourist trap, heavy emphasis on the trap part, but it was exhilarating.

The stores and stands sold food, drinks, drugs, sex, and vices I had never heard of. One cart sold various helmets that when donned, threw the wearer into moaning ecstasy. Ralph started veering toward it. I grabbed him by the arm and stopped him.

"What?" he demanded.

"That's a Vehor device," I explained. "The sign isn't in Human. Put one of those things on and you will probably fry your melon."

"You are such a drag." Ralph shook his head.

"Dude, I'm only looking out for you."

"There." Petra pointed to what looked like a club. The sign had four human dialects on it, and each read 'Party!' Drunken students and tourists were flowing in and out of the place with feverish exuberance.

"Yeah, that doesn't scream kidnapper paradise," I scoffed.

"Come on, Tom," Petra said. "Stop being a dick."

"Fine, let's go."

The three of us entered the club. It tried to look like a typical Earth club but it was off. The lights were just the wrong shade of tacky and the decor was still alien enough to leave the human senses uneasy. The matted, red carpets showed surprisingly little wear, even though they were faded in a way that only excessive traffic and years of service would produce. However, the patrons appeared to be similar to the guests of a college hangout, except there were more people of stellar descent around.

Lights flashed and the music boomed. A Tumna woman screeched as she fell to the ground in a drunken stupor. Several men of different species helped her to her feet, each competing to be the most chivalrous.

We approached the bar. The bartender scanned and tagged each of us with drink ID bracelets to prevent poisoning. Ralph didn't lose any time in ordering. A round of Graviton Bombs was served in mere moments.

Petra hit the dance floor and Ralph began his assault on the female coeds. However, it seemed like the human women were in the mood for something more exotic than Ralph from Irvington, New Jersey.

Leaning against the bar, I people watched. The sheer number of represented races blew my mind. There were species I never even read about. Maybe Ralph and Petra were correct, there was value to this outing.

I sipped my drink slowly, wanting to remain relatively sober so the other two could party freely. I spotted Petra dancing with a Foroncian dude. The two seemed to be having a great time. Ralph was still striking out but didn't seem at all discouraged.

The music got louder and the lights pulsed faster. The beat was contagious. I even caught myself being sucked into it, as I bobbed my head to the rhythm and drank.

"Hi." A girl sidled up next to me and activated her translator. "I Myel."

"Hi," I replied. "I'm Tom."

"Nice meet you," she replied with a heavy Lhongan accent. I wondered how my human accent sounded through the translator.

The Lhongan were physically similar enough to humans to undergo the same medical procedures, and their appearance was close enough to be mistaken as human without too much scrutiny. Their faces tended to be rounder, and they were about a foot taller than the average human. Culturally, humans knew little about the Lhongans. The diplomats were still engaged in initial negotiations. Since humans and Lhongans were both suspicious of other cultures, progress was slow moving.

"Buy drink?" she asked. She was attractive, but she looked undernourished. Her cheeks were sunk in and she looked pale. Her clothes were tattered in a way that suggested poverty.

"Yeah, yeah," I nodded. "What would you like?"

She turned to the bartender. "Mobon turundi."

I switched on my translator. She saw and smiled.

"Translate Lhongan?" she asked in broken Human.

"Not so well," I replied. "A few words. You're the first Lhongan I've met."

"Me Human few words. You first." The bartender handed her a drink. She guzzled it.

"Whoa, slow down," I said.

She laughed. "No time. Have to fun fast. Another mobon! You drink, yes?"

I swigged the rest of my drink and nodded. "Yes!"

The bartender heard and complied. A second later, I was trying my first mobon turundi and she was chugging her second drink. Before I knew it, she was ordering two more.

"I can't drink like this," I said as the next round arrived. "I have to stay sober for my friends."

"Sober no fun." Myel gulped her drink and motioned me to drink mine. I obeyed.

She ordered another round. The effects of the liquor started to hit me. I wasn't sure what was in the mobon turundi, but it was sweet, heavy and very strong.

"We go quiet place?" she asked.

"You are fast, I..."

"Myel!" A large, gruff Lhongan man appeared. "Y smon fo sop ker–" My translator kicked in. "–come here." He grabbed her by the arm and yanked her. She resisted, swallowing the rest of her drink.

"Girn you, Master," she screamed and struggled to break free. She dropped her glass and reached for mine. I let her take it. She managed to inhale it before the man pulled on her arm again.

"Leave her alone!" I yelled. "Stop hurting her."

The man studied me and laughed. He tugged her arm again. She whimpered.

He motioned to me. "Is this what you want?" He released his grip, dropping her to the ground. She jumped back up defiantly, then fell back down unconscious.

Ralph came running up. "Dude, what are you doing?"

The Lhongan man grabbed Myel by the arm again, this time as if to drag her away.

"Look at her," I replied. "This guy is about to grab her. She can't even defend herself."

"Dude!" Ralph repeated. "Remember the S&M party and the girl you tried to liberate."

"I was drunk," I replied. "Drunker. And this is different. Look at his size and she's practically skin and bones."

"You need to think this over," Ralph stated.

"I have." I turned and addressed the Lhongan. "Let her go."

"You want her?" he asked. "You pay out her contract."

"Sure," I replied. "How much?"

"Ugh," Myel moaned and rolled over onto her back.

"It's okay," I assured her. "He won't hurt you again. How much?"

"Twenty-three hundred," he answered.

It was almost all my savings, but I had it. "Done." I held up my wallet and initiated the transfer.

He checked his wallet and nodded. "Good. She is yours." He glanced scornfully at her and then left.

Myel clutched her head and sat up. "Wold me," she muttered.

"No, wold him." I replied making an assumption of what 'wold' meant. The translator didn't pick up most colorful colloquialisms.

By now, Petra had seen that some kind of drama had taken place and approached me at the bar.

"Everything okay?" Petra asked.

"Yeah," I replied. "This is Myel. She's going to be staying with us for a while." I looked at Ralph. "Hands off."

Ralph snarled at me. "Don't worry, I won't touch your girlfriend."

"She's not my girlfriend. We just met."

"And she's staying with us?" Petra asked.

"She's cool," I replied.

"Well this night's a bust," Ralph scoffed. "Let's go home."

"Petra was—"

"Yeah, he's a jerk," Petra interrupted. "He kept asking how much I charge."

"Nice," Ralph laughed. "Petra the ho."

"Shut up." Petra smacked him.

"Let's go." I offered my hand to Myel. She took it and I helped her to her feet. She stumbled as I led her out of the club. We walked back to the apartment in relative silence.

When we arrived, Myel was still barely coherent but she managed to speak. "Human room big." She smiled and stumbled forward. I caught her before she fell.

"I'll sleep on the sofa, you can take my bed." I led Myel to my room and sat her on the edge of my bed. "Go ahead."

Myel pulled off her clothes and fell back onto the mattress. My heart pounded and my palms began to sweat. She was breathtakingly beautiful. Every part of her, perfect. It took all my will to avoid staring at her.

"Get some sleep. I'll see you in the morning."

"You no stay?" Myel patted the bed.

"No, you've been through enough tonight."

Myel jumped up and grabbed me by my arm. "Stay you. Make sad go."

"I really want to," I replied.

Myel pulled my face down and kissed me. I didn't resist. Her lips were soft and warm. It sent a chill down my spine.

"Stay," she whispered. "Make good feelings." She began to reach her hand down my pants.

"No." I pulled back. "I can't take advantage of you. Besides, you're completely hammered."

"What is hammered?" she asked.

"Intoxicated," I replied.

"I want be hammered," Myel whined. "I want be hammered and wolded." She made a motion that indicated one body part entering another.

"I'm sorry," I replied. "You are so beautiful, and I really like you. But I can't."

Myel pouted and flung herself back into the bed. She immediately fell unconscious and snored loudly. I left and got comfortable on the sofa.

"We're talking about this in the morning," Petra yelled from her room.

I moaned and went to sleep.

I awoke to the sound of activity. Petra and Myel were

sitting at the kitchen table eating. Myel was no longer in her rags but in one of Petra's outfits. It was too short and hung off of her loosely. However, it was a vast improvement over her previous garb.

"Good morning," I greeted.

"Morning," Petra replied. "Sleep well?"

"Like a rock," I answered.

"I woke up to find Myel cleaning," Petra stated. "I had to stop her to sit for breakfast."

"Myel, you don't have to clean up after us," I said.

"I already told her," Petra explained. "She thinks we're slobs."

"Was filth," Myel said.

"She won't tell me what happened, though."

"Contract gone. Need new life." Myel clutched her head and finished downing her bowl of cereal. "I pee now." She stood up and dashed to the bathroom.

Petra cast a sideways glance at me.

"What? This dude was hurting her. I told him to stop. He said if I didn't like it, I could pay him for her. So I did."

"Crap." Petra looked over to make sure Myel wasn't back yet. "How much?"

"Most of what I had." I shrugged. "I still have enough to eat. I came to study anyway. I don't need money for that."

"We'll cover you, but what are we going to do to help her?"

"I don't know. They told us not to get involved with the government here. The embassy won't help unless it's one of us. I don't know anything about her embassy. We can't call student services because she's not a student."

"Maybe we can make her a student," Petra suggested. "We CLEP her in, then she enrolls and transfers back with us next semester."

"I guess we can try," I replied. "The computers have translation programs. We can let her take our classes online with us."

"Okay, you get her set up and I'll get her clothes and stuff."

"Okay," I agreed.

That day Petra found an air mattress and set it up in her room. She also picked up some clothing that would fit Myel. We decided to hammer out the rest of the details once she settled in. Myel skulked around the apartment, obviously upset. However, she was not unpleasant company.

After a week of cramming for midterms, I was decompressing with some mindless entertainment.

"What do?" Myel asked.

"VR infotainment." I deactivated the sensors and her face materialized before me.

"Why no study?"

"Eh," I replied. "I needed a break. My brain was getting tired."

"Brain should sleep earlier, study all awake time."

"Yeah." I laughed. "You're right. It's just been a strange week."

"Strange, yes." She shook her head and grinned.

"Are you okay?" I asked.

"Okay," she answered. "Sad."

"Sad? We will make you happy. Now you're free you can do anything you–"

"Yo!" Ralph burst in. "Huge party tonight in the Earth Club. You in?"

"Nah," I replied. "It's the middle of the week. Got too much work to do."

"You're so lame," Ralph replied.

Myel started poking at her translator. "He walk. How lame?"

"It's an expression," I explained. "It means I'm no fun."

"Because you no party and yes study?"

"Exactly," Ralph replied. "He's pathetic. He only thinks of school and his future. He never does anything crazy or fun, besides bringing you home."

Myel blushed and looked away. "I not crazy fun too. I work hard."

I took Myel's hand. "You don't have to anymore. You're free now."

Myel pulled her hand away and ran out of the room. I could hear her sobbing as she slammed her door.

"What did I say?" I asked.

Ralph shrugged. "Women. Who knows? Maybe in her culture, it's an insult to be nice to them."

"I hope not. I like her."

Ralph grinned. "Hook up with her yet?"

"No," I answered. "She doesn't need some jerk hitting on her right after she was freed from another guy. She needs time to get herself together."

"So, she's not into you?"

"What? Yeah, no. I don't know. Not the time for this crap."

"Ah, she's giving you mixed signals," Ralph stated.

"Doesn't matter either way," I stated. "I'm not taking advantage."

"Boy Scout," Ralph scoffed.

"Pervert," I replied.

"And proud of it." Ralph smacked me on the shoulder. "Off to Earth Club. Have fun being boring."

I powered off the VR and went back to my room. I sat on my bed and studied until I passed out.

The following day I had classes starting from early morning. Ralph agreed to keep Myel company while I was out since he was too hungover to go anywhere anyway. After my afternoon classes, I walked into the apartment to find her and Ralph studying at the kitchen table.

"No," she shouted. "You not trying."

"I am so," Ralph objected.

"Tom, Raf no study. How student no study." Myel turned back to Ralph and pointed at him. "Student, study!"

"I don't get it!" Ralph threw his arms in the air. "She studies my classes for one day and is suddenly an expert. I study the lessons six times and I don't get it."

"What class?" I asked.

"Stellar navigation," Ralph replied.

"That's a tough one," I said.

"Not hard," Myel shook her fist. "Study. No, go party drunk night."

"Hey!" Ralph complained. "I only went out one night this week."

"One night should study. No." She shook her head. "Speak like Dron."

"Dron?"

Myel dropped the pad she had been studying and ran out

of the apartment. I followed. "Wait," I called after her.

"No," she replied. Increasing her pace. "No."

I launch into a full sprint. She stopped and let me catch up. I was running so fast, I overshot her and had to step back. She shook her head at me.

"Where are you going?" I asked.

"Back," she stated. "Beg for contract."

"What? You want to be a slave."

She looked at me like I had grown another head. "No slave. What think?" She started laughing. "You think," she continued to laugh. "You think save slave girl from bad master."

"Okay, I got something wrong."

"You save drunk student from angry teacher. No allow vice. Snuck out, caught."

"But he grabbed you."

"Dron is … is…" She pulled out her translator and made an advanced query. "Old School. Not suppose to physical, he do. But he best, so let him."

This time I laughed. "He's your teacher? What was with the contract?"

She checked in the translator again. "Advanced graduate studies with Lhongan. Pay contract if fail or drop out." She pointed at me. "You flunk out me."

"I flunk out you." It hit me like a planetary freighter. I destroyed her academic career. "Oh no. How can I help?"

"Can't. I beg now."

"Please let me come. I'll tell him it was my mistake."

"Okay," she replied. "Your trup."

I nodded, assuming 'trup' meant ass.

We walked to a part of the city I had not been to. I was struck by the diversity. Apparently, our dormitories were in an extremely homogenized area. An odd mix of architectures collided, Lhongan, Tumni, Veheen, Koow, Splatg, and some I couldn't identify, all melding into an incongruous, but unique skyline. The colors and textures were like nothing I had viewed anywhere. It was art, living art that people lived in. And the people, they were part of the creation, moving bits of mastery, the city expressing itself. I stopped to drink it in.

"You no ever see city?" Myel asked.

"No, except that one time I met you. I never left the human sector before," I replied. "It's breathtaking."

"Human new here. No merge yet. Will same human soon."

I knew what she meant. Soon the human sector would integrate with the rest of the city, losing the distinction between us and them. One day we'd be another color in the collage, the way our planet was just beginning to blend into the galactic community.

Myel allowed me another moment to ponder my existence before she grew impatient and nudged me forward.

We arrived at a large academic building. It was utilitarian in design, gray and square. The windows were each covered in uniform beige blinds. There was no sign of self-expression on any of the externally facing structure.

Students sat on stone benches studying. There were no other activities. No socializing, no music, just textpads, and hushed discussions.

"You take school very seriously here."

"Advanced program. Hard work." Myel grabbed my arm and led me into the building. We walked down a long bleak corridor to an office. The door was slightly ajar. In contrast to the inert exterior, this room was alive.

The walls were covered with primitive star charts and maps. Shelves were lined with ancient navigation instruments. The man from the bar, Dron, was seated behind an antique-looking desk. Myel knocked tentatively. Dron snarled and motioned her inside.

"Speak," he said.

"I here to beg," Myel stated.

"Why? Your male paid to free you from your bondage." Dron spoke in perfect Martian Human, obviously for my benefit.

I stepped forward. "I'm sorry. I made a terrible mistake. Please take Myel back. I accept all consequences."

"Accept consequences?" He pounded his fist on the desk. I felt the room shake and jumped backward. "Are you a student?" he growled.

I nodded. "Y-y-yes. I … I attend university in the Human sector."

Dron stepped out from behind his desk. He advanced and loomed over me. Even for a Lhongan, he was huge.

"You think you can take our females, have your way with them and return them when you're finished?"

"No ... no..." I whimpered. "I didn't, I didn't touch her."

"So, she wasn't to your liking?" Dron bent his head to meet mine. It felt like he could destroy me with a single word, his eyes glaring, projecting terror and impending pain.

"No, she's beautiful, I ... I didn't want to take advantage. I really like her. I just didn't understand." My stomach churned.

"You didn't understand?" Dron growled. "Of course not. You're not her equal in any way."

"I'm sorry," I squeaked. For a second, I thought I had peed on myself.

"What exactly are you studying?" Dron straightened up, still scowling at me.

I looked down at the ground and sighed. "Interplanetary relations."

"Interplanetary relations!" Dron bellowed.

"Maybe I should change majors."

Dron laughed. "Maybe you should study harder. Maybe you should meet people without making false judgments."

"I..." I had no words.

"You're a junior student?"

"I'm a senior undergraduate. Next term is my last semester before my graduate internship."

"Where will you be interning?"

"I don't know yet. Competition is tough for my program."

Dron tapped on a pad and then handed me a record-chip it dispensed. "You will intern with one of our diplomats. He's my friend. He'll whip you into shape."

"Thank you, but why?"

"You need discipline. Grel will exact my vengeance on you with daily beatings and hard labor."

I almost fainted.

Dron laughed again and shook his head. "I hope your wits are stronger than your physical prowess."

I saw Myel holding back her laughter. I tried not to smile.

Dron continued. "I looked into you after we met. I had

your information from the financial transaction. Do you think I would allow some random stranger to simply take my teaching assistant? You just learned the most valuable lesson about cultural relations, and Grel was just complaining that he needed a vetted exchange student. You'll do."

"Thank you," I said.

"You're welcome, and most of your payment will be returned to your account. I took the liberty of buying myself a good dinner with your funds."

"Thank you."

"You already said that. Now go." He waved his hand, dismissing me. "Myel–"

I walked out as quickly as possible without running. I could still hear Dron shouting at Myel halfway down the hallway. As I questioned my life choices, I wondered what fresh hell I just signed up for.

Advanced Precognition

Emily Martha Sorensen

"All right, class, get out your assignments. Yes, Miss Baker?"

Startled, Sarah raised her hand.

"*Yes*, Miss Baker?" the professor repeated, sounding impatient.

"Um," Sarah said nervously, "I thought this was our first day. What–?"

The professor let out a long, dramatic sigh. His eyes rolled heavenwards. "Every class I get a slacker. Of course I haven't announced the assignment yet; the *point* of this class is to remember things I haven't asked yet. As per our course aims?"

Sarah gulped, sliding down in her seat. "I – I don't think you've–"

"I hand them out on the last day of class." The professor gave her an irked glare. "Honestly, how–"

The whole class tittered.

"–did you even *pass* Beginning Precognition?" he finished.

Face burning, Sarah slid further down in her seat. She hadn't passed Beginning Precognition; she hadn't even taken it. She was here on a dare from her roommate, who had claimed that students on the Reason track couldn't possibly handle classes in the Mysticism building. Now she was beginning to wonder if her roommate had been right, and she'd been an idiot.

"No," the student next to her said.

Sarah stared at him, befuddled. What was he talking about?

"Miss Baker!" the professor barked. "Why aren't you taking notes?"

Sarah fumbled in her satchel for a notebook and pencil, and found her pencil had snapped in half. She turned to her neighbor. "Could I borrow–?"

"I already said no."

"Here." Someone held a pencil over her shoulder. "I brought this for you."

Sarah took it, relieved.

The professor put his feet up on the desk, pulled out a thick tome, and started to read. Sarah stared at him, stared at the blank paper in front of her, and looked around at everyone else. What were they all writing? How could they be taking notes when the teacher said nothing?

With less than five minutes of class-time left to go, the professor leapt up from his seat and talked at such a break-neck pace that Sarah barely managed to record five sentences. At last, humiliated, Sarah dropped the notebook into her satchel and buried her head in her hands.

I'm never, never, never going to pass this class.

"Don't worry about it!" the student behind her said cheerfully. "You've saved me enough times when I've forgotten things!"

Sarah turned around, startled. "Oh – uh – thank you for letting me borrow your ... uh ... pencil."

"Nice to meet you, Sarah! I'm Tanja. We're friends next week."

Sarah blinked. "Huh?"

"I have next period free, too!" Tanja looked delighted. "We spend it trying to figure out which paradox you have a mental block against. We figure out it's Salinski."

"*Huh?*" Sarah stared at her.

"Uh..." Tanja looked worried. "Did I forget to let you introduce yourself again?"

"Do you have trouble remembering the past?" Sarah asked weakly.

"Yeah," Tanja giggled. "I have an awful memory. The last time I tried taking a class in the Reason building ... brrrrr." She shivered. "Can you believe the Logic professor claims looking at the answers on a test ahead of time is *cheating?*"

"You two might want to study together," the professor said from the front of the room, packing up his deck. "It's the only way either of you are going to pass."

"Do you think that's a threat or a future-seeing?" Sarah

whispered, alarmed.

"Both," Tanja grinned. "'Foretelling your own actions and thereby making them happen.' That's Salinski!"

Tanja was a very, very confusing person to study with. If you could decipher her madcap insights and put them into some semblance of order, it was impressive how much knowledge she had. Unfortunately, she rarely remembered even half of what she knew.

"I hate this class," Tanja wailed, throwing her midterm in the trash. Both of them had failed it. Sarah was starting to get very, very worried about the final exam. "All the other classes I can just coast on through. Mind-reading? Easy. Clairvoyance? Please. I passed Supernatural Studies without even studying. But here, it's like the professor is trying to – to – to – *challenge* me!"

Sarah looked at her own test gloomily. She had only answered three questions correctly, and she wasn't even sure if that had been foreseeing or just guesswork. So far, she had only had two future visions she was sure were real, and both had involved Tanja complaining.

"And just *tell* Raine you're sorry," Tanja said, looking peeved. "It's getting ridiculous."

Sarah stopped. "What are you talking about?"

"The feud. It's so utterly stupid."

"Who's Raine?"

"It's not fair!" Tanja wailed. "If I'd lived two hundred years ago, people would have thought me brilliant! But now that we know paradoxes, seers can't sound mad anymore! We're supposed to make *sense!*"

"You could take medication," Sarah suggested. "I've heard time-drift potions can do wonders for–"

"And take a chance of losing all my precognition?" Tanja asked incredulously.

Sarah sighed. "Maybe we're doing this all wrong. You don't need help seeing the future; you need help remembering what you've seen. Have you tried using mnemonics?"

"Men-what?"

"People who can't see the future use them to study." Sarah

looked at her test grimly. "People like me."

"I dunno." Tanja looked unenthusiastic. "If you mean memory tricks, those don't work on me."

"All right." Sarah held up a notebook. "Let's try something else instead. You have trouble keeping memory in your brain. So why not keep it on paper instead?"

Tanja stared at her. "On paper?" she repeated.

"Yes." Sarah tossed the notebook at her. Tanja fumbled to catch it a second early, and it fell to the ground. "Try writing whenever you remember something. Write in blue ink if you think it's the past, red if you think it's the future. I'll space it chronologically after the final exam. Then you can look at it during the final and see the whole class in logical order."

Tanja looked surprised. "That might actually work." She flipped the notebook open, grabbed a blue pen, and stopped. "It's blank!" she cried in horror. "All my hard work–"

"You haven't written anything in it yet."

"Oh. I could have *sworn*..." Tanja shook her head, dropped the blue pen in her pocket, and grabbed a red one instead. She plonked to the ground and started writing.

Sarah sat beside her and pulled out her home-made flash cards. She flipped the first one over and squeezed her fist in frustration. Eight times a day, she had reviewed these. She recognized the writing, the dents, the worn edges. But the terms had disappeared from her mind again. She *hated* those paradoxes.

"You're going about it all wrong, too," Tanja mumbled, not looking up from her notebook.

Startled, Sarah looked over at her.

"Studying. This isn't a class where you can learn things logically. You've got to use your intuition."

"What intuition?" Sarah muttered, glaring at the flash cards in her hands. "I don't *have* any intuition."

"Sure you do." Tanja snatched the flash cards and threw them over her shoulder. "Tell me about Jinkan."

Sarah squeezed her eyes shut, rubbing her fists into them. "Jinkan Paradox. Jinkan. Jinkaaaaaaaaan..."

"Stop trying so hard. Paradoxes only work if you're *not* trying to remember them. What did you eat for breakfast this morning?"

"Huh?" Sarah gaped.

"Or tomorrow. Or yesterday. What did you eat?"

"E-eggs," Sarah stammered. "And toa– *Remembering the future at all when it is not predetermined!*"

"See?" Tanja said smugly. "Now tell me about Harighan."

"I don't–"

"For crying out loud," Tanja said in exasperation. "Just tell Raine to quit it and stop being stupid."

"'Changing what you remember from the future so that it does not occur'?"

"*See?* Now try Dinskan."

Sarah tried to let her mind wander. She stared at the walkway, the trees...

"'Confusing the future with the past'?" she asked slowly.

"No, that's Dinskan."

"You just asked me about Dinskan!"

"Really?" Tanja squinted at her.

"*You're* Dinskan."

Tanja grinned. "Kinagar."

"'Forgetting things you've prevented' – hey, this works!"

"Just try not to overuse it," Tanja cautioned. "Wringalin Paradox says the better you remember paradoxes, the more difficult it can become to think logically."

Sarah stared at her in horror.

"But I'm the living proof that's not true!" Tanja said happily.

In the end, Tanja passed their final exam with flying colors. Even Sarah, with the vaguest, fuzziest beginnings of future memory forming, scraped by. For some reason, that made the boy sitting beside her fly into a rage.

"She can't pass when I didn't!" he screamed. "It's not fair! She sat beside me to distract me! She *knows* I hate her! Of *course* I couldn't concentrate!"

Sarah turned and stared at him. "Who–?"

"You're such a jerk! I hate you!" He threw his test at her and stormed out of the room.

Sarah stared after him, jaw dropping as a fuzzy future memory tickled the back of her mind. "*Who...?*"

Tanja yawned. "Raine."

Sarah clutched her forehead. "There's someone just as crazy as you."

"Crazy, but with a passing grade!" Tanja crowed, waving her final test.

My Book Report on *Starlight*

Joachim Heijndermans

It's strange. The school isn't like I imagined it would be at all. I figured it would look more like in the movies, with long hallways of lockers and posters that say things like: 'reading is fun' or have quotes by famous people I've never heard of. But it's nothing like that. The hallways aren't even hallways, when you get down to it. This place looks more like the dome at a spaceport, but with even whiter walls and a giant glass ceiling that gives you a great view of the outside. And there aren't any posters of any kind. Instead, there are these blue metal spheres that float by, projecting little holo-clips of people talking and playing sports, but it's all in Carillian, so I don't understand any of it. It's a beautiful school. And I don't like it.

"You nervous?" Mom asks. I shake my head, even though I'm lying. To be honest, I'm terrified. Every step I take makes my backpack feel even heavier, like an anchor keeping me away from my new class longer and longer. A part of me wants to grab Mom's hand, but I'm not going to. I'm not a kid. I can do this on my own. But I'm still glad she came with me.

We hear a pinging sound coming from above. A tube of blue light appears in front of us, like if someone were shining a spotlight down at the floor. A man zooms down through the tube. When he reaches the ground, the light vanishes, leaving only a blue circle to indicate where the tube once stood. He's from Caril, but he's dressed in Earth clothes, with a tie and pocket protector and everything. It's too bad, since I actually like the clothes they usually wear on this planet, with all the frills and color patterns that look like cherry blossoms in a garden. These clothes makes him look like every other teacher I've ever had, aside from his bluish skin, four green eyes and a flat nose. He smiles his sharp looking teeth and introduces himself to Mom in Carillian, then turns to me and shakes my hand.

"Hello, Graze. How do you are? I am prinzeepal Solalaron," he says in a thick accent. It's the first time I've heard someone from Caril speak an Earth language. I'm actually glad to meet someone I can understand, even if it is another adult. I doubt I'll actually talk to him all that much. Adults never seem to really talk with you, just at you.

"I'm fine. And it's Grace, like 'place'."

"Ah, of course, yes. Apologizing," he says. He then turns to Mom and goes back to talking to her in Carillian, gesturing with his hands and clicking his teeth rapidly, while Mom does her best to keep up with him. While she can understand him for the most part, I can tell from her face she's wishing he'd slow down just a little. I just wish I understood what he's saying at all. Right now I'm guessing he's bragging about the school and what the students do all day. It'd be nice if he actually told *me* any of this, but I guess he's leaving that for Mom to translate.

"Grace, you liking the sports?" he asks.

I nod. "Gymnastics," I say. I could tell him about the championships I won back home, and how my team managed to make it to nationals, but I don't. I just clam up and look away, peeking at the school grounds outside of the glass dome. The principal just nods and smiles, then says something to Mom in Carillian.

Mom turns to me. "Sweetie, you're going to your class now. But since most teachers and students aren't fluent in English or Spanish, and their English teacher won't be here until next month, you're going to be assigned a helper who is."

"A helper? What does that mean?" I ask.

"It means that a student from a different grade is going to sit in with you every now and then and help you along with assignments and translating whatever you don't understand. He'll be your '*study-buddy*', so to speak."

"OK," I mutter. I don't know what to expect from this 'helper', who I'm not calling my '*study-buddy*', I'll just be glad that I'll be talking to someone I hope is going to be around my age. Though I am curious what kind of student it'll be, since Dad once told me the people of Caril don't know many languages outside of their own. "Does my 'helper' really speak English?"

"Yes, he doing the speaking very well," the Principal says. "Better than me," he laughs. "Top student. Good grade very."

"Well, doesn't that sound great, Grace?" Mom says, trying to be uplifting.

"I guess," I mutter back.

The principal says something to one of the metal spheres, which causes it to zoom away. While we wait, the principal starts showing Mom some artwork that the students made, as I look through the massive window at the Carillian landscape outside.

The purple grass on the school grounds has been cut very short and into weird shapes. I have no idea what they're supposed to be. They look like boneless animals that are falling in on themselves. There's a groundskeeper robot who's pushing its lawnmower around. The sky has an orange tint, while off in the distance, above the azure mountains that mark the border of the valley, I can see Bron Wyverns flying. This planet really is beautiful. I hate how much I like looking at it.

Mom calls out to me. "Grace, your study-buddy is coming."

I groan, loud enough for her to hear me. She is the reigning champion when it comes to making me feel like I'm eight again. I'd regret asking her to come with me on my first day here if I wasn't so terrified of going alone.

She points to the end of the hall, and I nearly jump up three feet in shock when I see him. Here I'm expecting a skinny Carillian kid, one with glasses and a lisp like they always give to geeks on TV. Instead, a nine foot, four-armed, pale-skinned, one-eyed creature comes toward us, his feet never touching the ground as he glides through the air. With his single half-blue, half-green eye, he looks at me. I've never seen anything like him.

The principal introduces him to Mom, who then introduces him to me. "Honey, this is Bowie-san-Gath. He's another immigrant student, like you, but from the Zig system. He speaks over eighteen languages–"

"Nineteen," a voice echoes in my head. Mom heard it too,

as she looks just as frazzled as me. It's his voice, though he doesn't move his mouth when he talks. I don't know if he even has a mouth, or a nose, or ears. It's like his head is just there for that one big eye of his.

"Oh, sorry. Nineteen," Mom corrects herself. "And, as you probably guessed, he speaks English. He'll be helping you with anything that you have trouble with. At least until you feel comfortable enough to study on your own."

He holds out his hand to me, but with his six fingers upward, showing me his palm. "Pleasure to meet you, Grace. I am Bowie-san-Gath, from Zig-Gimma-Tjon."

"Ehm, hi–," I mutter. I place my hand on his, which I'm hoping is what he wanted me to do. He doesn't seem to get angry, so I'm taking that as a yes.

"How are you liking the school?" he asks. It's weird to keep hearing his voice in my head. How does he even do that?

"It's fine, I guess."

"Trust me, it will grow on you in time, as it did for me."

"How long have you been here?"

"Nearly a *qiollicath*. That is roughly a 'year' on your planet."

"Oh," I say, which is the dumbest response I could think of, and yet I said it anyway.

"Would you like me to escort you to your class?" he asks. I find myself looking at Mom, needing assurance that it's okay, feeling even more like an eight-year-old. Why not ask her to hold my hand as we walk to it? Urgh! Stupid!

"Yeah. Cool," I say, trying to sound self-assured. I have no idea who I'm trying to impress here.

"Right this way," says Bowie-san-Gath. "It's on the eighth floor, right above auditorium *Demma*. All you need to do is step on the lift-stream."

"The what?" I ask.

He points to the blue circle thing on the floor. "The blue circle thing, if you wish," he says.

"Huh? That's funny."

"What is?" he asks.

"It's like–," I say, but I stop. "Never mind," I chuckle. For a second there, I thought he read my mind or something.

"I did read your mind," he says. "Low-level telepathy. It is not deliberate, so I must apologize."

"Hey! You stay out of my head, you hear me!" I snap.

"I will try," he says.

I find myself looking back at Mom. She gives me a nod, telling me it's OK and I'll be fine without saying it aloud. That doesn't make it any less scary to follow this giant pale alien guy onto glowy light. When I step on the blue circle, we're suddenly zipped several floors up. It feels like I'm pushed up by an invisible disk, though there's nothing beneath us. When we finally stop, Bowie-san-Gath motions for me to follow him.

We enter another hallway, walking past the classrooms. I catch a few glimpses of what's going on inside (mostly students staring at the teacher in the front), but I don't want to be left behind by my – *ugh* – "study-buddy", who walks very fast for someone whose feet don't touch the ground. He then stops in front of a classroom with a blue door.

"This will be your class. Your teacher is Ms. Gorarawin. I will make introductions between you two."

"Okay. And then what?"

"I will sit in with you for the remainder of the morning, but then I must return to my own classes and studies afterward. I hope that is all right with you."

My first instinct is to say: *no, please don't leave me here all alone with no one to talk to.* But I tell myself I can do this. I'm alright. I'm fourteen, aren't I? I steel my face and strike an *'I'm cool'* pose, and say, "Yeah, that's fine. Whatever."

"There is nothing to be scared of," he says.

"Who's scared?" I say. He looks at me for a bit, which I think might be a comment, then opens the door without actually touching it. We walk in.

The whole class, all Carillian students, turn to look at us. Even though one of us is tall, six-armed, pale-skinned and has only one eye, I know it's me who catches the most attention. Some girls whisper. A few guys give each other looks, the *'what's up with her?'* look. The teacher, an older lady with silver hair braided into three rows, walks toward us. She shakes my hand and greets me in the only three Carillian words I know (which are *hello, how* and *you*) before she goes on and loses me with these long drawn out sentences.

"Ms. Gorarawin welcomes you to her class. You are to sit over there in seat *Hwo-ax*, which means B-12. She is currently covering level-two mathematics. However, since you have not mastered Carillian yet, she will allow you to perform extracurricular activities."

"What does that mean?" I ask.

"You may do other things, as long as she deems them productive and befitting of your school time. You came prepared for this, did you not?"

"Are you reading my mind again?"

"No. I just assumed it's the reason why your backpack is so full."

He's right. Since I didn't get any of my new schoolbooks yet, my backpack if filled with some old school books from back home, a few journals, Mom's old Carillian dictionary, and a copy of a novel I never got around to reading. I look at the teacher, who's giving me this expectant look, so I put my backpack down, open it, pull out the novel and hand it to her. "Is this okay?" I ask.

She looks at it, inspecting the cover and the back. I think it might be the first time she's seen a book printed on paper. Once she sees the picture of K'un Di, the author, on the back, she smiles and hands it back to me, saying something in Carillian to Bowie-san-Gath. He doesn't answer her, but she talks like he has. I wonder if you can only hear him if he wants you to?

"The book is fine. You may read during class, although I would suggest you try and see what the other students are studying. Do not be afraid to ask me to translate anything for you," Bowie-san-Gath says in a tone that I think is supposed to be inviting, but sounds more like a lecture. He doesn't really talk like a student or a teacher. More like a hallway monitor, or someone who really digs school to a weird degree. I nod and take my seat, opening the book to page one, while my alien 'helper' sits beside me.

It takes nearly ten minutes for me to actually read a word, as I use the book to hide my face more than anything. It takes another ten before I start to remember what I just read. I keep peeking around to see whether the students are still staring at me, which they're not. They're just doing their school work, listening to the teacher and passing notes to each other. Perfectly normal schoolkids in a perfectly normal school, on the other side of the universe. I've never wanted to go home so badly. Actual home. Not this planet. I'm doing my best not to cry, and even that I'm blowing, as tears roll down my cheeks.

The first week went by really quick. It's Friday (or sjo'zath as it's called here), and while everyone has been nice to me (for the most part), I still feel like an outsider.

For example: yesterday, right before lunch, these two girls came up to me and asked me something. Bowie-san-gath wasn't here, so I had absolutely no idea what they wanted. I smiled and shrugged, after which they laughed and walked away. Another girl, Urasuwa I think her name is, snapped at them. After that, no one has bothered or laughed at me. I wish I could stand up for myself like that. But I just don't know what to say and I feel super awkward when they all laugh. I know it's probably a joke amongst themselves, but I just can't shake that feeling like they're laughing at me. Whether it's in my head or not, it's awful being on edge like this.

Ms. Gorarawin checks in on me from time to time, always asking the same thing each time. "You ... okay are yes?" followed by "Gud jop," when I nod to her. She mostly lets me read my book, which is fine, I guess. It beats doing homework for now, though I don't know what I'll do once she realizes I finished the book already. Twice, in fact. It's much better than I thought it would be. It's got action, some cute romance parts and plenty of space travel. Good stuff, and it keeps my mind occupied from other things, like how no one understands a word I say.

I know it's been only a week since I started, but the language issue is really kicking me down. Mom is helping me out after school with her old books on Carillian, but she can only do so much considering her busy schedule, and her old study material crashes repeatedly whenever I boot it up on my tablet. Bowie-san-Gath is not much help either, as he retreats into himself most of the time. I know a lot more words than before, but it's the sentence structure and the speed at which native Carillian speakers talk that's really kicking my butt. It's like everyone is running laps around the running track, while I'm on my hands and knees trying to keep up. And now they have students coming up to the front of the class, each doing some kind of speech about something, I'm left staring at them, in the dark to what they are talking about. I just wish I knew what was going on, even for just a little bit.

It's lunch, and I'm sitting by myself again. I'd sit with my class, but not saying anything for thirty minutes straight while I chow down is much worse when you're with others. No one ever told me you could even be lonely in a crowd.

"Hello," says a voice in my head. I flinch, knowing exactly who it is without looking up.

"Hi, Bowie," I say.

"Bowie-san-Gath, if you please," he says, sounding somewhat annoyed. "May I join you?"

"Sure," I sigh. It's been a few days since I've seen him when he sat in with me last Friday. He'd transferred translated copies of homework assignments from his old classes every now and then, but he hasn't shown up in person till now. It's the first time he's met up with me for lunch.

"Enjoying your meal, Grace?" he says, crouching down so he doesn't tower over me.

"Meh."

"Is the food not to your liking? The cafeteria staff can show you visual options if you have trouble reading the menu."

So that's why they kept showing me pictures. To be honest, on my first day I didn't know what to think of it. I've never had a lunch of mostly beans, fruit and beets. Imagine my surprise when I looked up these 'rambutans' they gave out for dessert on the MAYNE-Frame, only to find out they're actually a tropical fruit from Earth.

"It's not the food. It's just..."

"Just what?"

"Nothing," I sigh. He sits down beside me, and while I'm happy he does, I don't show it. I don't know why he annoys me so much. He hasn't done anything to get on my bad side. If it were up to me, he'd be in my class all the time. Maybe it's the fact that he makes me feel like a side-project. I'm just something to deal with when class isn't in session, or if he's got all his homework finished. I might as well be the class pet in a glass cage, an aquarium without water.

"Terrarium," he says.

"What?"

"A waterless glass containment unit for non-marine animals. Terrarium."

I stand up, fighting the urge to slap him across his white domed head. "Stop reading my mind!"

"I don't mean–," he says, backing away as I shake my finger at him.

"Yeah, you told me, you don't control it. But it's still really creepy. Now stop it!"

It's then I notice people are looking at me. I can feel my face turn red when all the other kids start mumbling among themselves, throwing glances my way. I don't know why, but I drop back down, grab my book and hide behind it. I hope that they'll either ignore me or that the ground will swallow me up. Either sounds good enough.

"Are you enjoying '*Protovech Ghan*'?" Bowie-san-Gath suddenly asks, pointing to the book.

"Proto-what?"

"'*Protovech Ghan*'. The novel you're reading. It's the first part of the '*Odakkar*' saga by K'un Di, isn't it?"

I hold it up, pointing at the title. "Yeah, it's by K'un Di, but it's called *Starlight*."

"Ah, yes, I see. I've only read it in its original Zon. *Starlight*, was it?"

"Yeah."

"Amusing. That is not a correct translation of the title at all."

"Why? What does 'Protovech Ghan' mean in English?"

"The Sun Queen's Laser Spear."

I chuckle. "No offense, but I like *Starlight* better as a title."

"None taken," he says. "You've been reading it non-stop since you started school. I take it you enjoy it?"

"It beats doing nothing or getting homework I can't read," I say, trying to sound cool and aloof. I don't think he buys it, because I get the feeling he can tell from my voice that I'm about to re-read my favorite chapter.

"Are you at the part where Solea meets the Harbinger yet?" he asks.

"Just about. I–," I say, stopping when I know I just gave myself away.

"Second read through?" he asks.

"Third by now," I mutter. To my surprise, I hear him laughing. It's a pleasant laugh, one that is understanding. I laugh too, which I realize might be the first time I've done that in front of him.

"I'm sorry I snapped at you," I say.

"I'm sorry I read your thoughts."

"Start again?" I ask.

"What do you mean?"

"I think we got off on the wrong foot," I say. "Tell me more about yourself. Why'd you come to Caril for schooling?"

He locks his hands together. "After some ... issues on my home world, my previous diplomas and degrees have been rendered invalid. I had to retake my classes on Caril so I can have the appropriate grades and certifications for this part of the galaxy."

"Oh. But you like it here, right?" I ask.

"It is pleasant enough. But like you, being the only one of my kind here with no one to speak my native tongue with was intimidating."

"Yeah, I bet. But I only know English and Spanish. You know a dozen more languages than I do," I say, chuckling. "Did it take you long to learn Caril?"

"It's not so difficult once you practice it. I mastered it in a tymwull – a month."

"Jeez. All I know you could fit on a single page. It'll take me more than just a month," I sigh. He looks at me, without saying anything. I break the silence. "So what about friends? You seem to be popular here."

"I do not have any friends. Not in the way you define it."

"Why not? You're easygoing, as far as I know."

"I suppose I am not in the habit of making friends. Even for lunch, I sit alone."

"Really?"

"Yes. My studies keep me preoccupied. It seems friendships are simply one of those things that I am unfit for," he says, sounding actually kind of sad. "How about you? Are you fitting in?" he asks. "Made any friends yet?"

I laugh, but it's not a happy laugh. "I haven't. And I'm not fitting in either. Either I avoid people, or they avoid me."

"How come?" he asks.

"Because I have no idea what to say to anyone, and I don't have a clue to what's going on in class. I sometimes feel I might as well be on the moon."

"Which one?" he asks, looking up at the ceiling as two of the large moons pass over us, the blue one being much bigger than the rainbow colored one. The third one should be on the other side of the planet at this point.

"Good one," I chuckle.

"Humor is not as alien to my kind as it may seem. You will find my culture is quite versed in the art of comedic timing."

"Yeah? Know any good Zig knock-knock jokes?"

"No, but our Xenxnex cabaret is similar to the Owarai comedy from your planet. Are you familiar with it?"

"Not really."

"It's a Japanese style of comedy. It is very popular on some of the outer colonies, like the Brbrrrb satellite near Tensemt and Colo, where the Technarcy have embraced it."

Wow, those are a lot of names I'm probably not going to remember. "You've been all over the galaxy, haven't you?"

"I have moved around quite a lot."

"Do you miss your home planet?"

"Not really. But you do, don't you?" he says.

"It's obvious, isn't it?" I groan.

"It is all right to be homesick. But–," he starts.

"Yeah, I've heard that. From my mom, my dad, even people I've e-mailed back home. But that's not what's bothering me."

"Then what?" he asks.

"Can I be honest?"

"Of course," he says, moving closer to me. His one eye changes color to a deep brown. I'm not sure if that means something.

"I'm actually really bored here."

"Bored? Does Ms. Gorarawin not assign enough homework?"

"I think she does, but I get the feeling she doesn't give me all of it. Just mini math assignments. Outside of that, she just lets me sit there and read."

Bowie-san-Gath chuckled. "I know several students who would prefer that to actual homework."

"Yeah, I get that. But how am I supposed to fit in when I get pushed aside all the time? I can't add anything to a conversation. I can't give answers to a question. I'm the Earth girl in the back, who no one can talk to. I just feel like a whole bit of nothing. Like I'm just wasting my time until class ends, and then I have to do the whole thing again the next day. Like today, when one of the kids – Horth, I think his name is – went up to the front of the class and talked about something with all these pictures to back him up. And while everyone else is commenting and asking questions, I'm just sitting there, gawking at them. I feel so stupid, like I should be in the remedial class or something. I mean, what was he even doing? What are any of them doing?"

Bowie-san-Gath presses two of his long fingers against what I think is supposed to be his chin, and sits there, lost in thought. I figured he drifted off somewhere, bored by my story, when he suddenly sits up and pulls out his schedule planner.

"Your grade seems to be in the midst of their Yurngahli-do."

"Oh, okay," I say. "And what's that?"

"Basically, it's an assignment where the students hold a presentation about any literature of their choice."

"A presentation? Like a book report?"

"Yes, exactly like that."

"Any book?"

"Yes, any book, as long as the presentation conveys the content in proper terms."

"What does that mean?"

He rubs his head for a bit, trying to find the words. "You need to be able to retell the story under a set time limit, and it is encouraged to explain what it is about the book that spoke to you the most. Like I said, it's a small assignment."

"Oh, okay. And does everyone in my class have to do this?"

"Yes. Everyone except you, of course."

"Yeah. Right. Of course."

We sit there for a minute or two without saying anything. Me, chomping down on my PB&J, him absorbing water spheres through his chest. I try to think of a new topic, but I just can't seem to get my mind off of book reports. I'm glad I don't have to do one, but at the same time, I'm not. I mean, I have been reading the same book for nearly two weeks straight. I could do a report on it. It'd be better than sitting around and doing nothing. But I couldn't go out there and talk in front of the class. I barely speak a word of Carillian. It's insane. It's impossible. It's–

"Are you thinking of participating in the Yurngahli-do?" Bowie-san-Gath asks.

"Are you reading my mind again?" I ask.

"I didn't have to," he says. "Your face speaks more to me than a mild mind probe ever could."

I feel myself blushing. "Forget it. It's just a stupid idea. It's not like I even have to do it."

"No, that's correct. You are not obligated to."

"Right. I mean, I'm not sure I even can do it."

"True," he says in the most deadpan tone ever. "Your Carillian is poor, so what would even be the point to go up in front of the class and speak about a book you don't even like?"

"Excuse me, but I happen to like *Starlight*. Just because I don't speak Carillian, doesn't mean I can't do a book report on it. I could do just as well as anyone else."

He turns to me. I see my reflection on his face as he quietly stares at me. Then it dawns on me what he's trying to get me to realize. Sneaky alien kid.

"Look, just because I can do it, doesn't mean it will be good. I wouldn't even know where to start."

He quietly hands me a small driver. "Place that in your tablet. It should help."

"What is it?"

"My old Carillian/English dictionary. It also has a phrase generator and can adjust poorly formatted sentences. It should still have all my notes."

"Wow, thanks. Did you get this when you first enrolled

in school?"

"No. It was a gift from a Carillian peacekeeper."

Peacekeeper? I'm afraid to ask, but I've heard Dad talk about the Caril government sending soldiers to wars in the past.

"I don't know about this. I don't–," I begin, but Bowie-san-Gath calls one of those blue spheres over. He mention Ms. Gorarawin's name, after which the ball zooms off. A minute later it returns along with Ms. Gorarawin, smiling broadly. Bowie-san-Gath talks to her, pointing to me, the book, and the blue sphere that shows some clips from today's class. I catch a few words here and there, realizing what he's setting up for me. I am actually getting excited about it.

"Ms. Gorarawin has agreed to allow you to participate. You will have twenty minutes to present your speech on *Starlight* in front of the class in any matter you deem fit."

"Great! So will you help me with the–"

"I'm sorry, but I cannot assist you with a book report. I have not the time to help you on this."

"What? But it was your idea–!"

"No, it was yours. I simply helped you along with making the first step."

"But ... can't you just help–?"

"Are you asking me to put my own schoolwork in jeopardy to help you on an assignment?"

I don't say anything. I feel like such a jerk now. He's right. That's exactly what I'm asking him to do. "But there's no way I can do this on my own," I stutter.

"I beg to differ," says Bowie-san-Gath. "Besides, you were the one who said you were bored, right?"

"Yeah…"

"I believe this book report is what you need to break the barrier. A way to share who you are with your class."

"But why can't–?"

"–I help you? Because I have six exams that hour that I need to complete to pass my classes."

"That hour? Don't you mean that day?" I ask.

"No," he says. From his tone, I can tell he's neither kidding or lying.

"But ... but–," I stammer, wanting to finish with '*I can't*'.

"Yes, you can," he says. "I feel that you doing this on your own is the push you need to overcome your shyness and fears. Call it a baptism of fire, to quote one of your planet's writers."

It's ridiculous. On the one hand, I don't think I can do this. But on the other, I can't just sit around doing nothing forever. I live here on Caril now. This is my home and this is my school. He's right, even though I don't like it. If I can do this alone, I show the class who I am and what I'm like. I have a voice, and I want to be heard. "All right. I'll do it. I'll do my book report on *Starlight*."

"Excellent," Bowie-san-Gath says.

"One thing," I say.

"Yes?"

"What's *Starlight* called in Caril?"

He laughs. "*Tyun-fo*, as in *The Light of the Sun Queen*."

That's actually not half bad, but it still can't beat *Starlight* when it comes to titles. I repeat the title to Ms. Gorarawin, who smiles and nods, then pulls out her tablet and begins writing something down. She slowly talks to me while showing the schedule. She marks the last box with a 'G', which I think stands for 'Grace'. "Toleallir?" she asks me.

"Uhm, yeah. Sure. Fine," I say, turning to Bowie-san-Gath. "What did she say?"

"She said you will be doing your report on toleallir. Thursday."

"Ah, OK," I say. "Which Thursday?"

"This upcoming one," he replies, before hovering off to the lift-stream. "Good luck," he says, waving at me, while I stand there, speechless and frozen with panic. I have five days to prepare. Right now I'm glad that Bowie-san-Gath is the only one who can hear me screaming in my head.

I'm stuck. Trying to read is a chore. Not that I didn't understand the material. I got the book just fine. But trying to retell it in a language I barely grasp is impossible. The English/Carillian dictionary is lying there by my feet, waiting to be used, but I just can't make any sense of the sentence structures.

I'm pacing back and forth, biting my nails, trying to figure out some way I can pull this off. I stop when someone knocks at my door.

"Grace? Honey? You coming down for dinner?" Mom asks.

"In a little bit."

"Dad found a place that makes pizza and brought some home."

"Pepperoni?"

"No, sorry. They don't make sausages out here. Are peppers and tuna all right?"

"That's fine," I sigh. She opens the door and peeks in, instantly seeing my frustration the second our eyes meet. "What's wrong?" she asks.

No point in hiding it. Not from her. "I agreed to do a book report in front of the class this Thursday."

"That's great," she says.

"No. That's not great. I'm going to look stupid, standing there with nothing to say."

"Didn't you read the book?" she asks.

"I read it four times. I know the story front to back. I can dream it. But I can't talk about it because no one will know what I'm saying."

"Oh, I see. Can't ... what's his name? Your 'study buddy'? Ziggy-zen...?"

"Bowie-san-Gath. And no, he can't help. He's doing six exams that hour."

"You mean that day, sweetie," she laughs.

"No, I don't."

"Oh," she says. "Do you need me to help you? I can help you write out what you want to say after dinner."

"That would help. Or you could come to school with me and translate?"

"Sorry, honey. I can't. You know I would if I could, but I have to meet the housing representative and–"

I stop her. "I know. I'm not serious," I say, although part of me is a little bit. "But even if know what to say, how do I know I say it right?"

"Well, how about you eat first? I'm sure you'll think of something once you've got some food in you."

We walk downstairs to the kitchen. Dad and Danny are already chowing down, with Danny holding his pizza in one hand and a red robot toy in the other. "Rrr! Gigator-7 has come to save the pizza planet."

"Don't play with your food, Danny," Dad mutters.

"Gigator-7 needs to eat too, Dad. He's been fighting the Omni-armies all day."

"Oh, and how did that go?" Mom asks, playing along.

I envy Danny. He doesn't have as a hard time fitting in. He already made a few friends and picked up some Carillian, even watching that robot show on TV without any problem. I watch him play for a while as Mom cuts me up some pizza, listening to him recreate today's episode of Gigator-7. He uses his toy to show Mom and Dad all the moves that Gigator used to beat up Tarno-saur. Left kick. Right punch. Barrel roll slam. He makes it sound so real. Like it actually happened.

Then it hits me. An idea. I know how I'm going to do my book report on *Starlight*.

"Danny, can I borrow some of your toys for school this Thursday?"

I watch the clock ticking down. It's almost hour 70, two-thirty in Earth hours. I'm holding onto the box of book report stuff like it's a treasure chest. I hope I'm not making the biggest mistake of my life. For all I know, I'm gonna go down as the girl who played with toys in front of her class. I'll get a zero-minus on my record for the rest of the year. They'll put me in some sort of remedial class, where I have to carry Bowie-san-Gath's books until he graduates.

No. I'm being silly. I'll just go up, do my thing, and get it over with. It's time I stop being the wallflower from Earth in the back of the classroom.

"Graze?" Ms. Gorarawin says, motioning for me to come on up. I feel like I'm on autopilot, as I want to stay seated and curl up into a ball and vanish, but instead, I get on up and walk down the steps, passing by the other students, with the box in my arms.

"You begin, yes?"

"Yes. Thank you – so-fath," I say. I take a quick look around the class. Most of the students throw each other looks. A few of the girls laugh. Ms. Gorarawin gives me two thumbs down, but I think that is meant as encouragement, as she's smiling and nodding. I take out my copy of *Starlight*, and hold it up for everyone to see. I'm really doing this. Here goes nothing.

"This is my book report – mae Yurngahli-do – on *Starlight* – *Tyun-fo*. It's a novel – tiullitan – about Solea, the Queen of the Starlight," I begin, opening the box and pulling out my old Aspen Holiday Amy doll, which I've put in a yellow dress and taped a fork to her hand. Some of the students laugh. My heart skips a beat. For a second I think about bolting out of the classroom while I still can, but I keep going. "She's the creator and the ruler of all the suns – ila zonea. She's a good queen. But she's at war – brokarr - with an awful enemy: the Dark," I say, pulling out Terror-man, the scariest toy from Danny's collection, and I begin my report.

One by one I take the dolls and toys out from the box and place them on the desk, while I roll off the names of the cast. Once I've given every toy their name, I talk about the first part of the book, where the Sun Queen comes out from hiding after the destruction of the green sun of Torra. I pause every now and then to translate a few things with the Carillian dictionary, or I just use props from my box to gesture it (the green sun of Torra is played by an orange). I get stuck a few times, but Ms. Gorarawin jumps in to translate. After a while I talk without any hiccups for so long, I don't even worry about looking at the class anymore. All my nerves are gone, as I move onto the last part, where Solea is attacked in her castle by the Darkling army, loses all her servants and has to fight by herself, which I play out by slapping Danny's old Terror-man toy with my Aspen Amy, although the battle ends with her being thrown from her tower, played by the teacher's desk. She falls into the inky sea of ebony, ending the story on a bleak note. But then, when everything seems lost, her sun spear suddenly comes floating out of the inky blackness. To be continued.

"So I really liked this book. I didn't think I would, at first. I mean, I kept putting it off, never giving it a chance. But it didn't turn out as bad, and I'm glad I finally did give it a go," I say, not sure if I'm still talking about the book or not. I look over the class, seeing everyone intently listening. "Well, that's the end – dexfini - of my book report – mae Yurngahli-do – on *Starlight*

– *Tyun-fo*. Thank you – so fath – for listening."

I stand there, holding Aspen Amy and Terror-man in my hands. The rest of the class is looking at me. My heart stops. Then, one of the boys in the front row, Horth, begins to clap. The students sitting next to him join in. Urasuwa, the girl two seats in front of me, yelps out. Soon, the whole class, Ms. Gorarawin included, are clapping. No one is laughing. Not one of them made fun of me. I feel so ridiculous, for even thinking they would. Then, I hear a voice in my head. "Well done."

I look around, seeing the tall figure of Bowie-san-Gath in the back of the class, throwing me a wave. The lunch chime blares from the blue spheres, causing the classroom to empty out. I walk to my desk with my box of props, where Bowie-san-Gath is waiting for me.

"Hey," I say. "You watched it?"

"Yes. It would have been regrettable had I missed it," he says.

"You skipped your exams for me?"

"Of course not. My instructor still thinks I'm there. Small mind trick I learned long ago. But I wanted to be here and see how you did. And I believe it was a success. You should be pleased."

"I am. Thanks for your help."

"What help?" he says, making a strange sound that I think is a laugh. "You did all this on your own."

"Well. You still helped by being a friend."

He looks at me. His single eye shines a new blueish color, with dashes of orange added in. Is he blushing? "We are friends?" he asks.

"Yeah. I figured we are."

"Hmm," he mutters.

A finger taps me on the shoulder. It's Urasuwa, who has hair braided into six tails and a pencil-thin visor on her nose. "Graze ... goud worke," she says, before saying something, which I think meant either "seeing book" or "watching wood".

"She asked if she can see your book. She has never read it and your presentation has piqued her interest," Bowie-san-Gath says.

"Oh. Of course," I say, handing *Starlight* to her. "So-fath," I say.

She looks at the cover and flashes me a smile. I smile back. When I turn around, I see Bowie-san-Gath heading out of the classroom. He waves at me before the door closes behind him.

I've been in school for a tymwull – a month. Things have gotten a lot easier now, especially since I became part of Urasuwa's group. One of the students in the fyio-gi class lent me a Carillian copy of *Starlight* for my tablet so I can learn some words and phrases, and Urasuwa has been helping me whenever I get stuck. Also with the arrival of Mr. Subra, the English teacher, I now attend his class on Carillian for English speaking students (I'm the first to attend any such class on the entirety of Caril, so I'm top of the class).

I've also joined the school gymnastics team. Mr. Frunadnar, the keileion (that's like a coach) doesn't need to do much talking when barking orders at us. He's all right though, and he let me know through Ms. Gorarawin that if I keep up with my studies and practice, I might be able to make the school team next year.

I don't see Bowie-san-Gath as often. He's still around, throwing me a wave when we pass each other or leaving me a book that helps me practice my Carillian. So I'm surprised he showed up right before class today.

"How are things?" he asks.

"Things are good," I say, before trying it in Carillian. "Ginn to finwa si garr."

"Hinn, not ginn," he says. "But not bad."

"And you? How'd your exams go?"

"They went well. Very well indeed. In fact, I am to be transferred to the more advanced levels in the school's southern campus."

"Really? Where's that?"

"A few days travel from here."

"Oh, but that means–," I mutter.

"Yes. I'm sorry to say, but it does," he says. His eye turns dark, a near black. "That is why I wanted to give you this before I leave." He hands me something wrapped in brown paper. It feels lighter than it looks.

"Thanks. But this isn't goodbye, you know? I've had my fill of goodbyes."

"Then we shall meet again. And when we do, I hope you'll have finished my gift. So until then, see you soon, Grace."

"Later, gator," I say.

"What?"

I turn red. Great. Way to go, Grace. But I think he knows how embarrassed I am, as his eye turns a greenish color. He waves and floats off.

"Grace, quero da hui ki forre?" asks Urasuwa, which means 'what did he give you?' I shrug and begin peeling the paper off the gift. It's a small file driver, which I quickly load onto my tablet. A picture of Solea, queen of the sun, pops up on screen. I read the title.

"'Solarmax: part 2 of the Starlight saga', by K'un-di, with annotations in Carillian and Zon," I read aloud. There's a message encoded with it, popping up as I load the first page.

"Dearest Grace. I hope this next installment will illuminate your life on Caril. Signed; Bowie-san-Gath. Your friend."

Flunk, Juggle & Frog

Jonathan Shipley

Luke Armbrewster sat pale and tight-lipped in the ante-office of the Dean of Students. His grades had not been good – no, his grades had been awful. And he didn't even have the full picture yet. He knew he had two D's and one F. Wunderkind Lucas Armbrewster had *failed* a class. His family would freak ... the whole community would freak. He was supposed to be some sort of Great Human Hope, the best of the upcoming generation, leapfrogging hom culture forward with new tech ideas from prestigious Zjhaccœse University which had the best time-space mechanics program in the ... in the universe, for all he knew. Nothing on Terra compared.

And now he was *flunking out*. It could not be happening, and yet it was. And if anything could be worse than that, it was flunking out because he was clueless. He went to class, worked like a dog, but couldn't get a hold on the concepts. He couldn't even guess on tests anymore. He was leaving whole sections blank because he couldn't make sense of the questions. Why was this happening? He didn't just feel stupid, he felt retarded. His only consolation was it wasn't just him. All the kids from Terrano space were having a tough time. Did that mean they were retarded as a species?

"You – young hom." The thin orange secretary with a huge beak nodded in his direction. "The Dean will see you now."

Luke pulled himself to his feet and trudged through the door. This was going to be bad.

"Mr. Arrumbrooster," the Dean said, stretching out the name the way many of the native Zjhaccœse sauroids did. He was big-bodied and green and looked like a scaled-down T-Rex. "Please sit. We have a problem." He clicked his claws together in an unnerving fashion.

Luke sat, clasping his hands together to keep them from shaking, and waited.

"Your grades from this term are abysmal," the Dean said. "For you to continue your coursework here, you will be required to do accredited remediation as well as retake the failed classes."

Luke tensed. He flunked more than one class? "Can I continue my coursework here?" he asked hesitantly. Or was he being thrown out? He couldn't flunk out – he just couldn't.

"You *may* continue your coursework," the Dean said. "Whether you *can* is another issue."

At first Luke thought that was a slam on his intelligence, then realized they were talking about something else.

"The scholarship is the immediate problem," the Dean continued. "With these grades, there is no way the University can justify exempting your tuition. You may enroll under the terms stated, but you must pay your own way."

Luke was hearing this as snippets of good news, bad news. He wasn't being thrown out – he was losing the scholarship – he could re-enroll and try again – he had to pay for it himself. "Uh, thank you," he said awkwardly and stood to leave.

At the door, he paused as whole picture started to sink in. "Are there uh, any student jobs available?" he asked.

The Dean shook his head. "There are ample jobs in the City, but the University itself has no work-study program. Good day, Mr. Arrumbrooster." He clicked his claws together again.

Luke walked slowly back to the dorm, turning over possible jobs he could do. He didn't even know what jobs were out there in a predominantly saurian culture. Wait tables, maybe?

Dillon Halliper, another Terra student, caught up with him in the Quad and fell into step beside him. "Brew," he nodded.

"Dill," Luke nodded back. The two of them weren't exactly friends, but all the hom students knew each other. There weren't that many of them. He and Dill had an Intro to Rift-Wave Mechanics together and were always jockeying for position. Even when the only positions in question were bottom of the class and second from the bottom, they kept playing the game because they were both competitive in nature. And who wanted to be absolute worst in class?

After an awkward silence, Dill said, "I heard you had a meeting with the Dean. Me, too. I can stay, but no more scholarship. You?"

"Same." There was a lot not being said here, but they were clearly in the same boat. "Any ideas for jobs? I would scrub toilets before going to my family for more money." *And having to tell them I'm flunking out.*

Dill nodded, apparently understanding the unspoken as well the spoken from his own situation. "Here's the problem. Scrubbing toilets won't come close to making tuition. None of the menial part-time jobs will." He turned and inspected Luke in an oddly explicit way. "You're not a bad-looking specimen, Brew. Good face, good body, good posture – the whole package presents well."

Luke tensed, not knowing where this was headed. "So?"

"So I'm thinking you'd do better than OK as an entertainer."

Was this some variation of "with your looks, you ought to be in flix"? Luke knew he had looks – he'd been told that all his life. He'd even been told he was wasting his time in spatial engineering when he could be modeling instead – as if getting by on his face was somehow superior to studying hard. But this from Dill was just strange. "What kind of an entertainer?" Luke asked suspiciously.

"Here's the thing." Dill sidled closer. "We're in a non-hom culture where homs – monkeys to them – aren't so well respected. You've heard all the monkey jokes, right?"

"Oh, yeah." Luke was constantly bombarded with "dumb monkey" jokes from his dorm mates. They were all lame, but non-homs seemed to find them really funny. "So what does that have to do with entertainment?"

"The point is, lizards like laughing at monkeys. I think we can make that work for us, make some money off it."

"You mean a comedy routine?"

"Yeah, but heavily slapstick with pratfalls and juggling and silly costumes."

Luke frowned as the image crystallized. "A clown act, Dill?

A *clown* act? I did not come to the oldest university in the sector to get a pie on the face."

"So go scrub toilets for pennies," Dill shrugged. "I'm not exactly thrilled with the idea either, but I can't go to my family for money. They'd have me on the next ship back to Terra and that would be the end of college for me. But maybe you've got better options." He turned and walked off.

Luke took a deep breath, balancing options that were all pretty shitty. Go home a failure ... call for more money and admit he was flunking out ... become a clown. Put like that, the clown thing didn't sound so bad. And he was already a laughingstock around campus, he and the other "dumb monkeys." "Hey, wait," he called, jogging after Dill. "Let's talk about this ... even though a clown act is just pandering to the dumb monkey stereotype."

"Yeah, I know," Dill said. "It sucks. But not as bad as going home. And I really think we can make good money on the party circuit."

They continued walking in silence for a while. "OK," Luke finally said. "I'm in. How do we get this going?"

Dill grinned. "I've already got leads on some party planners in the City. We'll put together a couple of short routines and go audition for them. Oh, and I guarantee you'll be offended by the routines I have in mind, so be prepared, Brew. It's all very dumb monkey."

"That I figured," Luke shrugged. "Do I do anything in particular, or just stand there and look pretty as a pie target."

"Juggling," Dill said. "If you can keep juggling some items, it would really help the look of the routine."

"I'm no juggler."

"You're taking hyperpatial engineering, Brew," Dill shot back. "You can figure out the physics of keeping a couple balls in the air."

"Any time, younglings," the blue-scaled party planner called from the back of the empty hall.

Luke glanced around the hall. It wasn't a huge space – about right for fifty guests, depending on the size of the species. These party halls were popular with lizards, apparently because the size differential among saurians made home entertaining awkward.

"Wake up, Brew," Dill hissed beside him. "We're on."

Luke hefted the metal spheroids a moment, then launched them into the air to commence the act with a little juggling. They figured that a little motion and the stupid costumes were enough to catch the audience's attention. And they did look stupid, Luke freely admitted. He was wearing neon-pink boxers over purple sweat pants with red suspenders and bowtie. Dill was equally garish in shades of green and blue. Considering all they had to work with were dyes and their own clothes, they'd done pretty well at creating a clown look. Of course, it also meant that his only pair of sweats were now purple and half his boxers were pink, but he could live with that.

The act continued with pratfalls, suspender snapping, and whipped cream down his pants, then climaxed with a pie in the face. His face. Through it all, he was supposed to keep on juggling as if nothing was happening. He never imagined it was so hard to do anything with cream pie in his eyes, but he'd practiced juggling with his eyes closed and could pull off the ending. Then it was over. They bowed in unison and while they waited for the verdict, Luke wiped his face with a towel.

"Not a bad little opener," the party planner said, coming forward, "but pretty tame for a monkey routine. Something louder, more bombastic would work better. More hitting and howling, you could say. And dancing. And play up your lack of tails as much as possible. That's always good for a laugh. And cattle prods are always funny. Well, got to run. Think about it and call me." She breezed out the door, as much as a sentient of that size could breeze.

"More hitting and howling," Dill mulled. "I guess that's possible."

Luke glared at him. "If you're imagining you'll hit and I'll howl, forget it. I didn't sign on as a punching bag. And don't even think about a cattle prod."

"And then there's that tuition that's not going to pay itself."

Luke shut up. But he wasn't liking this direction at all. Then he couldn't hold it in anymore. "I can't go there, Dill. Maybe I'm an idiot, but I won't be a fool, too. I'll work some menial job, if that's what it takes, but not this."

"And you'll be out a whole semester with that menial job,"
Dill shot back. "Think about it – rift-wave mechanics after a lay-
ing out a semester. That's like volunteering for an F ... another
F."

"I'll manage, thanks," Luke said tightly, though he had no
idea how.

And that's how they left it.

The joys of menial labor. As always, Luke got to the party address early, changed into his tux, and was ready and waiting
when the first guest arrived. So serving drinks didn't pay half
as well as the clown act. At least it was a normal job, not making a fool – a dumb monkey – of himself in public. He kept
suspecting that Dill was right and staying in school was worth
a certain amount of humiliation, but Luke just couldn't do it.
He just hoped to hell he remembered anything about anything
when he tried to go back to class next semester.

But the joys of menial labor called. The tux was a huge
improvement on neon pink and purple, but schlepping drinks
was a lot of running around. Now that he thought about it,
he was still playing to stereotype. He'd been hired because
monkeys were fast on their feet and good at weaving through
crowds of bigger, slower saurians. But "fast monkey" was better
than "dumb monkey" any day.

As this particular party picked up, he was surprised to find
a five-foot frog in a corner by himself. Oh, he knew there were
amphibs on Zjhaccœse, but had the impression that lizards and
frogs didn't mix much socially, maybe because he'd never seen
it. So seeing a frog at a lizard party was fairly unusual, and this
particular frog didn't seem to be enjoying himself all that much.

Luke swung by on his next circuit through the living room.
"Refresh your drink, sir?"

The frog looked up and for a moment they studied each
other, two singleton species in a house full of lizards. Luke had
heard that the local amphibs were really bright, but to the eye,
it still looked like a five-foot green frog in fancy dress.

It blinked big saucer eyes at him and said, "Kinda far from
home, kid."

"University," Luke shrugged.

"Kinda far from campus."

"Well, I'm on break at the moment. Just me, not the whole University," Luke clarified when he saw another question coming. "I'm taking a semester off, working odd jobs to put together the tuition for next year."

"So, flunked out, eh? So why don't you pack up and–"

Luke grimaced as that hit a nerve. "I better make my rounds," he said abruptly and darted off. How did a total stranger know he was flunking out of school? Was it tattooed on his forehead or something?

He started his rounds again but found he couldn't concentrate on what he was doing. He felt a strange need to justify himself to this stranger. Or maybe to justify himself to himself. He headed back to the frog.

"I'm not stupid," he began. "Back home I was really good at both differential and solid state physics."

"And home would be … ?"

"That would be Terra in the Sol system," he said. "And no, I'm not packing up and leaving."

"So what were you studying that didn't agree with you?" the frog asked curiously.

Luke braced himself. "I'm almost afraid to say. I get a reaction whenever I say I'm studying to be a rift-wave engineer."

The frog exploded with laughter but sobered immediately.

"Yep, that's the reaction," Luke said woodenly. "Everyone automatically assumes I don't have the brains for it. And understandably, it turns out. Right now I'm so clueless that I don't even understand what it is I don't understand. Yet back home I was winning awards right and left."

"Well, that's hardly something to brag about when 'back home' is such a small pond."

Luke felt a sudden surge of anger. It was bad enough that he felt stupid now. He didn't need some smartass frog suggesting he'd always been stupid and the awards meant nothing. "You think I'm a 'dumb monkey' – isn't that what sentients here call my kind?"

"You might want to lower your voice," the frog suggested. "I don't believe this is one of those parties where the hired help bellows at guests."

Luke took that slap in the face as a signal to move on – fast. With a stiff bow, he retreated across the room to offer drinks to a group there. From there he headed for the pool, where a group of larger lizards were enjoying a sludge bath, then out to the balcony.

Suddenly there was the frog right in front of him. "A moment of your time," he said. "I need a favor, monkey. A handsomely paid favor you are well equipped to handle."

Luke grimaced. First insults and now some sort of sexual proposition? Did he come across as that pathetic? "I may be just the hired help," he muttered savagely, "but *that* I don't do. And I don't believe this is one of those parties where guests should openly solicit the help."

"No, it isn't," he said quickly. "I was referring to some discreet eavesdropping."

"Oh." Luke felt his cheeks grow warm at a fairly major error in interpretation. He really wanted to just walk away, but there was that mention of money. And money drove his life right now. "Maybe I could do that ... for the right price."

The frog murmured a figure, then nodded toward the lizards in the sludge pool. "Those are the ones. Hover close to them and report to me after the party at the service entrance behind the building."

All this suddenly fell into place. The frog had to be a private investigator on the trail of the lizards in the sludgepool. And the frog had come to him as an extra pair of eyes and ears. That in itself was interesting – maybe even more interesting than the money. The way these Zjhaccœses looked down their noses at homs, a monkey waiter would be completely beyond suspicion, just a dumb animal delivering the drinks. Maybe, just maybe, there was some mileage in that with a PI.

So he was especially attentive to the needs of the sludge-pool for the rest of the evening, refreshing drinks almost instantly and storing up snatches of conversation in progress. He even stayed late on the pretext of cleaning up when the pool lizards lingered late. By the time he came down to the service entrance, the rest of the catering crew – not a monkey among them – was almost ready to leave. He dawdled a few minutes more until they were all gone.

As he was changing back out of his tux into street clothes, the frog appeared like a ghost out of the shadows, giving Luke a start. The frog was so good, it was creepy, really living up to the reputation of his species for being quick and cunning. This PI would be a good connection to have.

Luke forced a grin over his initial surprise. "Pretty slick. I was looking for you and never saw a thing."

"So what did the monkey hear?" the frog asked.

Then there was the monkey business. The guy just didn't get it. "This may be news to you," Luke began with an edge to his words, "but 'monkey' is not what my kind likes to hear. It's a racial slur – like calling your kind 'frogs'."

"That I hear all the time without a second thought," the frog shrugged. "I had no idea your kind was so sensitive about labels. But I can just as easily call you simian, mammalian, or whatever –"

"My name is Armbrewster. Lucas Armbrewster."

"Is there a monosyllabic option in there somewhere?"

"Luke."

"Then, Luke, what did you find out?"

Moment of truth. "I heard a lot of contented gurgling in the mud, but I assume that's of no interest. Then the blue-scaled one mentioned overdue bounty and the gray one gave an excuse about the climate being wrong and that an exchange in-kind might be the better option. The third lizard, the biggest one, never said anything while I was there. Is any of that meaningful?"

"I don't know about meaningful, but it's interesting."

Luke stepped closer. "Then I have a proposition for you. We use this case as a trial run of my usefulness – an audition, so to speak. If I'm not that useful to you, you pay my fee as agreed and we're through. But if I am useful, then we forget the fee and you give me a job."

"Doing what?"

"Oh, being in the right place at the right time. Eaves-dropping at parties is one example, but I'm also quicker on my feet that most of the species around here. I could shadow suspects pretty easily. And stereotypes being what they are, who's going to suspect the monkey? Working for a PI firm is a better opportunity than filling drink orders, so I'll make sure you like the results. That blue-scaled lizard, for instance – I've seen him around on the party circuit. I know who he runs with."

The frog seemed to be actually considering the offer. "Okay," he said. "You can have your audition. But no promises. Your kind isn't exactly easy to work with."

Luke rolled his eyes. "Watch those stereotypes ... boss. The obvious may not always be true."

"But since I'm the boss now, let me tell you one obvious thing that *is* true."

From the tone of voice, Luke knew something negative was coming. He should have known. This job interaction had gone too smoothly when nothing on Zjhaccœse ever went smoothly for him.

"When it comes to rift-wave mechanics, you consider the fourteen wave-forms, find which one is the best match to your sample, and interpolate from there."

Luke looked up, startled. "Wait – *you've* studied rift-wave theory?"

"For a couple years when I was at the University ... like most youngsters, I had my phase of wanting to go out into the unknown and discover new worlds."

"You could tutor me," he said slowly.

"Perhaps. But only if you prove to be a very good legman for me. Thinking through your tentative duties, I can already tell you're going to be very busy for a while."

Luke digested that with a suspicious stare. "You sly frog. Not to mention manipulative and self-serving."

"Ah," the frog said. "Now who's resorting to stereotypes?"

"Brew," someone called across the Quad.

Luke turned to find Dill heading his way. Considering how they left things, this ought to be awkward, but he discovered he really didn't care so much anymore. He was out of school for a semester, but he had a plan for coming back.

"I heard you've been waiting tables," Dill said. "You know you can do better than that if ever you want to come back into the act. The money's good, Brew."

Luke shook his head. "No thanks. I'll stick with what I'm doing. Slow and steady will get me there. Besides, a semester off gives me time to work on concepts. I actually understand rift-wave mechanics now."

Dill's eyes narrowed. "Really. I'm taking that class again and it's still pretty dense. How come you understand it?"

Luke gave an elaborate shrug. "Some of us monkey around. Some of us leapfrog ahead."

A Visit From Lady Lydia

Ken Goldman

"In a world of diminishing mystery, the unknown persists."
— Jhumpa Lahiri, *The Lowland*

"Known is boring; unknown is tempting!"
— Mehmet Murat ildan

"There is no such thing as the supernatural. There is only the natural that we don't understand."
— Lady Lydia Zephyr, online vampirette

The scene played like a bad horror movie, the two characters standard Hollywood issue. The vampire, her victim. Check and check.

But the scene was real ...

From the shadows she appeared like an apparition, a full bodied beautiful woman whose appearance did not suggest the strength of which she was capable. The young man hardly resisted as she pulled him backwards into the darkness of a nearby alleyway. Maybe he expected an anonymous blow job from this dark female seemingly emboldened by alcohol. He'd had enough beers himself to let that happen, even under this bizarre circumstance.

"Do you know what I am?" she asked.

"I have no idea who you are..."

*She tugged him closer. "Not **who** I am, you fool. I asked you **what** I am!"*

The man managed to stare at her, but said nothing. In the pale wash of moonlight she appeared heavily made up yet still alluring, although her skin was white as porcelain. She loosened her grip, allowing him to speak freely.

*"**What** you are? I'd say you're a bit presumptuous, if this is a mugging. I'm carrying little cash, and you don't seem to have a weapon. I could break you in half, you know, so you're fucked all around." He struggled, but again she held him fast. "Look, if this is some drunken attempt at a seduction, or if you have some irrational hatred of men—"*

The woman crooked her arm around the man's throat. "You are a fool. I need no weapon, and this is no seduction. This is my survival. And yours!"

"And you, lady, are a bad cliché. So get your fucking hands off me."

The man laughed, unaware he had proven the woman's statement accurate.

*He **was** a fool…*

One of Len Haskin's dutiful students turned on the lights as the young teacher slipped the DVD back into its case. Facing his class, he grinned and slipped into hip mode. "Okay, gang. Movie Review time. Questions? Comments? Thumbs up or down for this morning's creatures of the night?"

Adele Somers, always bucking for an 'A', took the shot. "A good movie, Mr. Haskin. But vampires aren't real, are they?" Her pearly toothed smile followed. "I mean, no one lives forever, right?"

Ronny Corbin, his testosterone bubbling at full boil, whispered, "Not as real as those tits, Adele! They'll always live forever right here." The kid pointed towards his crotch. Haskin ignored him, although he agreed the kid was right about Adele's attributes. If he were ten years younger and not her teacher – Christ, the girl could pass for a full grown woman *now*.

The girl's question wasn't unexpected. High school kids were always curious when it came to the darker realms. Haskin's senior class responded on cue, having just viewed that teenage angst '80s classic, *The Lost Boys*. (*"Worms , Michael! You're eating worms!"*) The vampire flick was part of his film class's horror unit, so of course some student had to ask if the movie depicted real vampirism.

"No, Adele. I highly doubt it. Not if you're talking about someone transforming into a bat and flapping around the room. However..." Len paused for dramatic effect. "I imagine there are those who practice vampire-like customs. Cults exist for all kinds of aberrant behavior, including the urge to administer some serious hickies. But I'd guess those folks are mostly wack jobs, outcasts whose lives would otherwise be empty, or, more likely, who are just pissed off at the world."

Craig Rabin, a heavy-set tattooed and body pierced Goth wannabe, looked up from his smart phone. "You mean guys like me, don't you, Mr. Haskin?" Len had never seen the boy attempt to smile or to pay attention, which of course came with the ever-present black attire. But in the age following Columbine, ticking time bombs like Rabin had to be taken seriously.

"For some that lifestyle is a sort of religion, Craig, like those who pay endless homage to their smart phones. And finding like minded peers often serves as a bonding experience for other ersatz vampires. It may not be the Scouts, but cults do serve a purpose, a kind of emotional meth for those needy enough." Haskin felt like adding ... *And you would know something about that, wouldn't you, you unemployable prick?* Preferring to keep his job, Len kept that judgment to himself. Even the best teacher had to remain safely open-minded and essentially spineless, not an easy thing when asked about premarital fucking or the existence of vampires.

Rabin's attention returned to his phone. Another student offered commentary.

"But vampire bats are real, isn't that right?" The question came from Bart Guffman, a good looking and likable enough student, whose I.Q. probably was similar to his shoe size. "I mean, they suck blood just like those kids in the movie, right?"

Seeing his opportunity for some cleverness, Haskin went into full Bela Lugosi mode. "Geeve me a bite of yourrr neck, yesss?" The joke fell flat. What would millennial kids know of a movie made more than fifty years before their parents were born? "Okay, yes, vampire bats are real. There are several species of the little suckers, and they all drink blood, Bart. It's their primary food source and readily available. Mammals, birds, but rarely humans. They do hunt at night, though. And they're ugly as hell, little fanged flying rats. But they're mostly harmless."

Craig Rabin spoke again, an event about as common as Haley's Comet. "I found something on my phone that may interest you, Mr. Haskin." The kid got to his feet, held up his phone. "There's this site online – It's filled with people who say they're vampires. *Real* vampires! They have chat rooms, web pages, all kinds of shit. There's this woman online now. She's no kid, either, if you look at her photo, which means she's not jerking around. She's local, too. Interested?"

"Bring up your phone, Craig. I'll put it on the screen, make some use of this high technology the school has graciously supplied." He hooked the phone into the large HD TV unit. The image onscreen caused some girls to gasp.

Rabin was right. These weren't kids' photos online; these were adults, and their photos showed bleeding fanged creatures whose faces probably were enhanced by Photoshop to look like the real deal. Many of them had active text addresses; that meant they were willing to talk, and remaining anonymous seemed of no concern. The young woman Craig had selected could have come from central casting. Erotic and raven haired but with milky white skin, she seemed some gothic Cleopatra. Her name flashed beneath her photo.

"Lydia Zephyr?" Haskin asked. "That can't possibly be her real name."

"I think she prefers Lady Lydia. Women vampires like that sort of royalty shit."

The bell rang, signaling Haskin's Film Class period was over, but Craig and his classmates didn't budge. They seemed to expect their Goth pal Craig to make his point.

"Text her, Mr. Haskin. See for yourself. Maybe this Lydia lady will want to visit our class. That'd be cool, rustling up a real vampire, don't you think? None of those sparkling *Twilight* Hollywood pansies, but the real deal? And a female yet!" Haskin's students nodded in agreement.

"Text her, Mr. Haskin! Will you. Please?" from Adele.

Len shrugged. "Yeah, Craig, That'd be cool. It might cost me my job, but what the hell. Now scram, all of you…"

* * *

Well, what the hell…

His class gone, Len hit the computer's FaceTime button and waited. Incredibly, within seconds Lydia Zephyr appeared onscreen, live, or seemingly so. Her dark eyes appeared almost cat-like. Or maybe bat-like.

"Your chubby Goth student told me you'd make contact. Am I his homework assignment?" The woman's voice was breathy, sexy enough to seem well rehearsed.

"Lady Lydia, huh? Your real name?"

The woman managed a shit eating grin. "Well, Lady Lydia sounds a bit affected, but 'Linda Smith' – that's an unimaginative moniker for a creature of the night, don't you think, Mister…?"

"…Haskin. Leonard. Film Studies teacher over at Washington High on the South Side. And it's my real Judeo-Christian name. Well, Jewish, actually. So you won't have to worry about crucifixes from me." The woman's expression seemed a blank slate, so he dropped the clever repartee. "Okay, so, Lydia, you're on the level, then? See, my senior class seems to think there may be such things as…"

"…as vampires? Real bloodsuckers? I know you're skeptical, but we all harbor our own nasty little secrets, don't you think? I'm not ashamed of mine."

Len grinned. The woman's flirtation was obvious but effective. "Fine. You want to put your money where your fangs are?"

"This isn't Tinder, Mr. Haskin. I don't show my goods so easily."

"So, you've got nothing?"

"Well, I won't do the bat-transformation right now – that's so amateurish. But here's something for you…" Lydia's onscreen image sank out of sight for a moment, then reappeared. Smiling now, she displayed elongated fangs. "Convinced, Leonard?"

Haskin had to laugh. "Very clever, but nuh huh. You slipped some false teeth into your mouth while you weren't onscreen. Big whoop, but no cigar, Lady Lydia."

"Well, I would morph into a bat, but I don't think you're ready for that." The woman managed a Playmate-of-the-month pout. "Don't tell me the teeth aren't a turn-on, Leonard. You want a little bite, maybe? I'd be happy to oblige."

Her flirtation came full throttle now, but this was no hormonal teenaged girl. Lydia Zephyr *(no, Linda Smith!)* was a woman in full bloom, but also maybe a bit warped.

Len knew it was game-on now. "No bites, Lydia, not unless we get to know each other better. However, you *can* do something for me."

Lydia leaned forward. Her lips puckered as if she were about to leave a lipstick smear on the screen. Seething with innuendo, she whispered, "And what would that be, Mr. Haskin?"

"Len, okay?"

"Fine."

Their verbal sparring felt tacky, but the woman's breathy utterance coupled with her image on the monitor had the desired effect on Haskin's libido.

"You know where Washington High is?"

"I can find it."

"My Film Class students asked about vampires. You know kids. The supernatural fascinates them. And a vampiress such as yourself must be a wealth of infor–"

"–Vampirette, okay? That's the correct term. And there is no such thing as the supernatural. There is only the natural that we don't understand. Capeesh?"

"Got it. So, care to stop in around 10:30 for a little Q and A? I'm in Room 215. Tomorrow's a double period. Plenty of time to strut your stuff."

Lydia laughed loud. "Why, Leonard, you know what they say about vampires appearing during daylight. You wouldn't want me to dissolve in a pool of goo on your floor, would you?"

"So it's thanks, but no thanks?"

She spoke low, as if sharing a secret. "Well, you also know what they say about having to invite a vampire in, right? You've invited me. So I'll be there, Leonard. Tomorrow. Although I have some plans tonight. Midnight plans."

"A rendezvous with another creature of the night, I'm thinking."

Lydia giggled, but the response fell short of girlish. "Not

quite. A feeding. Probably from some young stud like yourself. Don't misunderstand, Mr. Haskin – *Len*. It's harmless stuff, really. A pricked finger, at best. Most guys are usually grateful for the experience that follows." She licked her lips and smiled, faux fangs still in place, and the screen went dark.

Len Haskin grinned at the young woman's moxie, the same dopey grin he'd worn as a horny adolescent on the prowl. He had good reason. He was nursing one enormous erection. Well, then...

He had a few minutes before his next class to take care of business.

At the bar the young woman sat, her legs on full display from the high stool. She waited for the inevitable. Near midnight, it wouldn't take long.

"Mind if I sit here?" The well dressed collegiate-type didn't wait for her answer. "What're you drinking, hey? Wine?"

"It's red, isn't it?" Smiling, the woman applied a brief Blush touch-up, then gave the guy the once-over. The man appeared younger than her usual selections. Probably a pre-law or pre-med student. Looking him over, she laughed to herself. "Isn't it a little late for you to be out?"

The guy didn't appreciate the joke coming from a woman clearly older than himself, but nonetheless she was beautiful. He ignored the comment. "A cabernet, then?"

The woman finished the last of her drink. She nodded.

He called the bartender over, pointed to her glass. Extending his hand, he leaned towards his new companion. "I'm Cliff."

Squeezing the young man's hand lightly, the woman spoke close to his ear. "I'm whoever you want me to be."

Within the half hour the two walked together beneath the boulevard's dim street lamps. Being late and a weeknight, traffic was light. The woman waited for the right moment. She stopped cold, kissing her escort near the entrance of an alleyway. He seemed surprised but quickly responded. She slipped her tongue into his mouth, crushing her body against his. The young man followed her into the alcove's darkness. She knew he would. Easy.

"I don't even know your–"

"Shhh..."

Moments later the woman exited the alleyway alone.
In thick rivulets, blood dripped down her chin.

"It's sunny out, Mr. Haskin. Not promising weather for a vampire's visit." Adele Somers had a point. Ten minutes into 3rd period already had passed.

Len shrugged. "When we spoke yesterday, our Lady Lydia didn't seem concerned about daylight. I'd say that sunlight thing is probably a myth anyway. Miss Zephyr is probably a bored woman playing 'Let's Pretend.'"

"A bored woman with huge ta-ta's," Craig Rabin mumbled.

As if on cue the door opened and there she stood, displaying a toothy grin – but showing no fangs. The woman wore a black skirt that stopped at her knee with a plain white shirt, a surprisingly conservative ensemble. "Okay, then, kids. Let's pretend, shall we?" She winked at Haskin, an action noticed by his students. Two girls giggled when the woman, crossing long legs, parked her ass on Haskin's desk. Someone wolf whistled.

Len extended his hand. "Thanks for coming. I'm glad you didn't enter through the window, Miss Zephyr. Our principal would frown on that."

"No one sees me except those I choose to see me."

Haskin's brow raised, but he kept his thoughts to himself. "Class, our guest speaker is your basic practicing vampire, Miss–"

"They know what I am, Mr. Haskin." She turned to the class, pointed to the window. "It's a bit bright out today. Would someone mind pulling the shades?"

Several students looked at each other. Quick on her feet, Adele Somers darkened the room. Lydia mouthed a quick "Thank you." She straightened her posture, still perched on Len's desk.

"Okay, then. Your teacher mentioned you had some questions for me. I'm all ears, kids. Except for the part that's teeth." Practically every hand went up. "Not necessary to follow school rules today, guys. Just ask. Okay?"

Suzette Davis took her shot. "Are vampires really dead? Or undead? Are you–?" Suzette never spoke up in class before. As far as Haskin knew, she never spoke at all.

"I'll let your teacher decide that. He pressed my hand, my flesh, a moment ago. So, Mr. Haskin, tell your students – What did you feel when we ... touched?"

Len went flush before he realized where Lydia's question was going. "It felt cold, Suzette. Miss Lydia's touch felt very cold."

"Want to feel, Suzette?" Lydia asked.

Falling silent again, the girl shook her head. She clearly didn't want to know.

From the back of the room came a male voice. "Do vampires live forever?"

"I live in the moment. Forever consists only of moments. So, yes, in that sense vampires live forever. As do I."

Behind her, Haskin leaned close to the woman so that only she heard. "Nice save. I'm writing that one down."

Another student, a girl, spoke up. "Will you show us your fangs?"

"No."

An uncomfortable silence followed before the next question came.

"Do you drink blood?" asked Bernie Huffman, a boy who never failed to spit whenever he talked.

Lydia didn't miss a beat. "Tell me – If you cut your finger, do *you* drink blood? Or, perhaps when you were younger, your mother kissed the boo-boo?" She turned to Len, saw him smile at her answer. She smiled too. "A question most ask of me, knowing so little of what I really am, Mr. Haskin. Next question?"

"Do you kill?" from the Indian kid, whose name Len never could pronounce.

"We all kill."

"No, I mean do you kill people? Bite them?"

"Only if they appear tasty."

Craig Rabin shouted, *"Answer the damn question!"*

"Very well. In nature, it's the female who kills. Almost always. As for myself – well, I *am* female, as you can see." A laugh from Lydia, and that was all.

Haskin leaned forward and spoke low. "And the Oscar goes to..."

Rabin interrupted. "About sunlight…"

"A lie based on superstition," Lydia answered.

"But you wanted the shades pulled!"

"The sun was in my eyes."

"Crucifixes? Stakes in the heart? Morphing into a bat?"

"Those beliefs make for good fiction."

Rabin sneered, mumbling something to himself.

Honor Roll Student Adele spoke up with one hell of a question. "Who made you?"

"The same who made you. Your maker. My maker."

"Do you mean God?

"No. Do you?"

Adele's attempted smile didn't work. The woman's answer would have to do.

Craig Rabin wasn't buying any of it. "Tacky, Lady Z. Very tacky." Stepping forward, he raised his phone and snapped the woman's photo. Holding the screen for all to see, he added. "See? *She's visible!* Lady Z., that raises serious questions about your authenticity, don't you think? For a vampire, you're more like Donald Trump!"

Without losing her grin, the woman motioned for Craig to come forward. She cupped her hand and whispered to him.

"Don't fuck with me."

At the bell, Lydia got to her feet. Heading to the door Len's students thanked her, while a few kept their distance. Adele Somers bravely shook the woman's hand, then whispered to her, "Yeah, your skin, it's cold. Like death." Craig Rabin smirked and moved on. With the classroom emptied, Len closed the door, turned to his dark guest.

"That was heavy stuff. Not entirely informative, though. You fudged a bit."

"Much better to keep them guessing, Leonard. Adolescents, they're such curious souls. Like that Goth kid with all the ink and piercings, the headbanger that found me online."

"Craig Rabin is a curious kid, all right. But I think he's in training to be a full-out ass hole. The nose ring is a dead giveaway. You want to bite someone, he'd be a good start."

"Taking a chunk of Mr. Rabin's favorite arteries can be

arranged."

"For all that, you really didn't admit to much, you know. Rabin had a point. Your answers were mostly cryptic bullshit, textbook vampire lore – *Lady Lydia*."

The woman managed a warm smile unlike those she previously offered. Her eyes locked with Len's.

"You can call me Linda."

Haskin smiled too. "So much for the vampire act, then?"

"We're mysterious beings, we creatures of the night, Leonard. But I'll share one secret." She extended her hand. "Your cell phone, please."

Haskin appeared puzzled. "A selfie to show you really don't appear onscreen after all?"

The woman tossed her thick black hair provocatively and took the phone. "No, Leonard, that's vampire Hollywood hype. What I want is – I want to give you my number. Okay, there, I said it. No bullshit." She punched the keys and handed the cell back. "However, if you'd like, I *can* let you in on something else." Reaching into her small purse, she added, "Have a look?"

She inserted the false fanged teeth. Haskin leaned close, took the woman's face into his hands pretending to examine it.

"I knew it! The lovely Lydia emerges from the dark to reveal herself as mortal!"

She tapped her palm across her chest. "Very mortal. Be still, my heart."

"No stake required?"

Her smile appeared again, now faux fanged.

"None at all."

Craig Rabin put away enough beers to drown a moose. He topped those off with one potent bomber of a joint. Leaving his pals at the school ball field, he found himself on Main Street near midnight, passing the local watering hole called Moxie's. Soon he would be old enough to enter, not that he hadn't tried. But his twenty-first year wasn't far off, and before long he'd be bumping uglies with the local sluts he'd seen entering the place. The crowd inside was shouting whatever lyrics they could figure out from *"Louie Louie."*

Taking in the bump-and-grind music that drifted to the

sidewalk, he noticed the woman in the black mini emerge. She was alone, and stopped to stare at him. He stared back.

"Craig! It's you! Out this late, and on a school night!"

It took a moment for the voice to register, a longer moment for him to recognize the woman's face.

"Adele? Jesus, I never would have recognized you in a million years. You look so – so *old!*"

"Older, you mean, right? I wouldn't want to look *old*, Craig."

Rabin burped a taste of his beer. "Jesus, Adele, I didn't mean–" He paused, trying not to slur his words. "I mean, look at you! You're so made up, you could pass for thirty!"

"It's a rare talent, Craig. Gets me into these local bars every time. You think they'd let in a high schooler?"

Craig laughed. "I guess girls can pull off that kind of shit. Me, not so much, not even with a phony I.D. But I'd never figure someone like you would want to be in this place. I mean – you, *here?*"

"A girl can get thirsty."

"Yeah, but, I mean – *You're Adele Somers! You're on the fucking Honor Roll!*"

"Only during school hours. That 'A' student is off duty now. And my parents – well, since the divorce, my dad doesn't give two shits where I go."

"I guess we have that in common."

"And maybe more," she added.

The two started along the boulevard, although it was more like Adele walked and Rabin followed.

"You sure don't talk like a Washington High senior, 'Del. I mean, tonight you don't look like one, either. Not even close!"

"I'm actually a little older than most kids think. And much smarter. The Honor Roll, that's kid stuff."

Front Street appeared vacant, a side artery that saw no traffic at this hour. The girl made the turn, and the two walked in silence. Adele Somers could be damned intimidating, but she was also one major piece of ass. That ass looked fine in the pale light.

"Do you think of me as a kid, Adele? I'm not, you know. I've been around."

"I'm sure you have, Craig. I've watched you in class. You really put that phony Lady Lydia in her place today. I detest phonies too."

"Especially wannabe phony vampires," Rabin added. He paused, looked at Adele. "Are you really older than everyone thinks?"

"Oh, yes, Craig, much older. Want proof?" She smiled beneath a dim street lamp. Pushing him against a beat up Chevy, she wrapped her arms around him and pulled him close. The boy's wide grin spread. This was more than Craig Rabin could have ever asked for. His erection nearly shot through his pants.

"Right here?" he asked. "I mean you want to do it right–?"

"I'm old enough, Craig. Are you?"

"Fuck yes!"

Smiling, the girl showed teeth. "That's good. Me, I'm pushing three hundred!"

Grabbing Rabin by the throat, Adele Somers sank her fangs deep into his neck.

Claudius

Sheila Hartney

Marilyn blamed it on the internet.

She had taken a break from the Gordon account to research some vacation possibilities. So there she was, idly cruising on-line, clicking from one site to another and it just popped up. *Host A Temporary Foreign Exchange Student.* The graphics were appealing, Egyptian pyramids, the Coliseum, Stonehenge, some cathedrals and she thought, why not? She'd never had kids of her own, just the three rambunctious stepsons during her brief second marriage, and she figured one kid would be a breeze after that experience.

There wasn't much to the application form, a few questions about why she wanted to host a student, did she have a separate bedroom, who the responsible adult would be. She worked from home, and figured that would be in her favor. No doubt there would be some kind of a home inspection before any student would be placed, so she just answered those few questions and hit the send button. Her phone rang six weeks later.

"This is zzzt Constantine. You are Marilyn Hegstrom? You want zzzt host tempozzzt exchange student?" The connection was very poor, as if the call were coming from somewhere deep inside a mountain. She had trouble making out everything the man was saying.

"Yes, this is Marilyn Hegstrom, and yes, I would like to host a foreign exchange student."

"Tempzzzt exchange student" he corrected.

"Well, yes, aren't they all temporary?"

She heard Constantine chuckle. "No, not all of them. Just some. Listen, we have zzzt and I need a home quickly for my

117

Claudius."

"How quickly?"

"Zzzt, away. Now. My Claudius is from Rome." There was more static on the line, and Marilyn didn't quite catch the next thing he said, it sounded almost like 'third century' but it was probably some kind of address or zip code. Not that she'd have any clue what the zip codes were in Rome, if they even used them there. Constantine went on, "He's a good kid, zzzt no trouble at all."

Marilyn thought, Whatever happened to the home inspection? She said, "I'd be more than happy to take this student. When will he be arriving?"

"Oh, zzzt arriving right now, zzzt this time. I'll get him to you immediately." Constantine hung up and Marilyn went into panic mode. She quickly changed the sheets in the guest bedroom, made sure there was some empty drawer space in the bureau and hangers in the closet and headed downstairs to see how the refrigerator was stocked. She'd probably have to make an immediate grocery run, considering how much teenage boys could eat.

The doorbell rang. There stood a short, skinny kid who looked a bit ragged and unkempt. His hair had apparently been cut with dull shears and clearly needed to be shampooed. His large brown eyes had a distinct look of confusion. Marilyn looked past the kid and saw a black sedan of indeterminate make and model pulling quickly out of her driveway. How rude, she thought.

The kid handed her a large envelope. Inside was a sheaf of papers clipped together. On top was a note. "This is Claudius, your exchange student. He is from Rome, and may take a little time adjusting to his new culture and temporary milieu." Underneath were what looked like official documents. A brand new passport, what looked like school and vaccination records. The very last paper had a credit card, no it was an ATM card according to the printed information. The PIN number was 7645. That would be easy to remember. The year of her birth and her age. Nice coincidence.

There was a hand printed note at the bottom: *This ATM card is to be used for expenses connected to your student. If you need more than a thousand dollars in any month, please call the number on the back of the card.*

Marilyn looked at Claudius more closely. Those eyes. Oh, my. He was going to be a heartbreaker in a couple more years. Especially once he got cleaned up. Right now he didn't make a good impression. Good grief. Was that a *toga* he was wearing? And where was his luggage? Surely a kid coming to spend a year as an exchange student needed, well, a year's worth of clothes and stuff. All he had was a burlap sack, not even the backpack that kids all carried these days.

"Well, Claudius," Marilyn said, "let me show you to your room, not that I've had much time to set it up, and we'll just go shopping right away." She leaned in to him and sniffed. "You definitely need a shower before we go anywhere." Claudius just stared at her and said something she couldn't understand. "I'm afraid I don't speak any Italian, Claudius. Don't you speak English?"

"Omnis latina lingua discere debet."

"Well, whatever. Come along inside and we'll get started."

Claudius seemed very curious about everything in the house. His eyes got huge when she turned on the hall light. It was as if he'd never seen electric lights before. Maybe he was from some unusually isolated part of Italy that somehow still didn't have electricity? She couldn't imagine. It was two decades into the 21st century, after all. When he saw the bathroom he exclaimed, "Mirabile! Habes latrinam suam!" He poked at the hot and cold knobs, as if he wasn't quite sure what they were for.

"Yes, a bath would be a very good idea, unless you'd prefer a shower."

Claudius just stared at her. She turned on the water, adjusted the temperature, then turned to grab bubble bath. All she had was lavender scent. It would have to do. When she turned around he already had most of his toga, yes, it definitely was a toga, unwrapped.

"Wait a minute, young man. At least let me get you a towel. Wait! Here," Marilyn quickly poured the bubble bath into the water. Claudius's eyes widened at the sight of the foaming bubbles.

"In paradisio sum," he said, and took his toga off completely.

Marilyn fled the bathroom. What on earth was she thinking? A teenage boy living with a single woman? So many people would think the worst. So many things could go wrong. She leaned against the bathroom door. What if he didn't turn off the water? Would she be able to go back inside and prevent the inevitable flood? After a couple of minutes she heard the familiar squeak of the faucets being turned, and thought she could hear Claudius sighing with pleasure.

At first the principal of the town's high school was a little reluctant to enroll him. "I just can't understand why we weren't notified by the exchange program ahead of time. Back when we used to get exchange students we always knew about them a month or two before they got here." Alan McCurdy ran a hand through his thinning hair. "To be honest, Mrs. Hegstrom—"

"Oh, please, call me Marilyn."

"Marilyn. I just don't know what to say. You say he's from Rome?"

"Actually, I think he might really be from some very small town somewhere in Italy. I'm not sure he'd ever seen electricity or hot and cold running water before he got here."

"You don't say." McCurdy looked sharply at Claudius.

She didn't mention that the first time she made spaghetti he didn't seem to have any idea how to roll up the noodles and sauce with a fork and spoon. Or that pizza seemed equally unfamiliar to him. Marilyn felt justifiably proud of how far he'd come in the two weeks he'd been with her. He was dressed like a typical American teen, his hair was neatly combed, and he smelled faintly of soap. And now he could eat spaghetti properly.

"Well then, don't you think it's time to have another foreign exchange student? I'm sure both Claudius and your students will benefit. Plus, his English will improve far more rapidly if he's with kids his own age."

The principal sighed. "No one wants to come to a small town in Minnesota these days. At least that's what the program we used to use told me a few years ago. But honestly, I really don't understand why we didn't get advance notification that he was arriving." McCurdy gave Claudius another long look.

"What did you say the name of the program was?"

Marilyn told him, and when she got to the part about the call from Constantine, McCurdy looked startled, and took another long look at Claudius. When she finished with another plea to accept Claudius in his school, he sighed.

"I really ought to have some documentation for him."

"Oh, I'm sorry. I should have given you this right away." Marilyn pulled out the envelope Claudius had given her the first day. "I believe this has everything you need." Now the envelope only contained the official looking papers. The ATM card was safely in her wallet, the passport and note in the top drawer of her desk.

"Thank you." There was a pause while McCurdy looked through them, muttering a bit. "This does appear to be in order, although the school records are sketchy at best. This Constantine fellow seems to have thought of everything." He looked up at Marilyn, a bland expression on his face. "I'll enroll him in some basic classes, and let the teachers know not to worry much about his academics. Let's see, first year algebra, let the teacher figure out how much math he knows, P.E. of course, American history, Freshman English, I think Steve will cut him some slack until his language skills catch up..." McCurdy mumbled a bit more, and fifteen minutes later Marilyn walked out, feeling triumphant. There were some advantages to living in a small town. Given McCurdy's reluctance to enroll Claudius, even with the paperwork she gave him, it probably would have been impossible in a more bureaucratic big city public school.

The first few weeks the principal emailed Marilyn almost daily.

> Marilyn, can you get Claudius to understand he absolutely must use a fork to eat his food?

> Marilyn, I'm putting Claudius back to basic math, as he doesn't seem quite ready for algebra.

A week after that:

> Marilyn, the math teacher tells me that
> Claudius likes to use Roman numerals to do
> his math.

Another week went by, then something a bit more ominous showed up in her in box:

> Marilyn, I'm afraid Claudius is a little too
> competitive in P.E. Can you explain to him a
> little more about the concept of sportsman-
> ship?

Marilyn thought that was something the PE teachers should be doing, but she spent the weekend watching football with him and trying to explain it. As much as his English had improved, she wasn't certain she succeeded. At least the Vikings won their game, which made up for it.

As Claudius learned more of the language, Marilyn tried to find out a little more about her student, maybe something about his family.

"No family."

"Oh dear, you're an orphan then?" That might well explain his unkempt state when he first arrived, his total lack of luggage, let alone shampoo or deodorant, or why he hadn't gotten any mail or phone calls since he'd arrived. Impulsively she said, "You should think of me as your mother. You can call me Mother Marilyn."

He looked at her with those wonderful brown eyes and repeated, "Mother Marilyn."

"So tell me more about your life in Rome."

Claudius dropped his eyes. "My time no good. Your time better." She thought that was an odd way to express it, but after that brief statement she couldn't draw him out any more. Still, as the weeks went by, he seemed to be fitting in better at school so far as she could tell, and the emails from Alan McCurdy had dropped off considerably. That was progress. The only thing that continued to bother her was that he didn't seem to have made any friends yet.

* * *

"Claudius! Time to get up!"

Marilyn waited at the foot of the stairs until she heard him moving around before she went back into the kitchen to start breakfast. It was some six weeks into the semester, a bright early October morning. Looking out the window she could see that the trees were past their prime, their shed leaves in deep drifts on the lawn. Soon enough there would be snow, and it occurred to her that having a teen around to do the shoveling would be convenient.

Twenty minutes later Claudius entered the kitchen, smelling sweetly of his favorite lavender soap. She wondered what the kids at the high school thought of the lavender. Maybe … maybe that was why he didn't have any friends yet. They might be making assumptions about him that might not be true.

"Ave," he said.

"English, remember?" Sometimes he still reverted to his native language, which honestly didn't quite sound like any Italian Marilyn had ever heard.

Claudius stopped, then said, "Good morning, Mother Marilyn." She liked it when he called her that.

She wasn't much of a breakfast person herself, and drank a cup of black coffee while Claudius ate heartily, three boiled eggs, four pieces of thick cut toast – she'd made a loaf overnight in the bread machine – with butter and jam, and a large bowl of oatmeal. He'd grown some since arriving, and it looked like she might need to buy him new clothes soon. Still, he was small for his age, although come to think of it, Marilyn didn't know exactly how old he was. She needed to take another look at his passport.

"Vale," he said rushing out the door to catch the bus. That still didn't sound like Italian, but what did she know? A couple of semesters of college Spanish were long forgotten, and probably wouldn't help anyway.

A couple of hours later the phone rang. Caller ID showed it was the school.

"Mrs. Hegstrom, I thought I should call and speak to you directly, rather than handle this by email."

Marilyn felt a rise of nervous anticipation. He hadn't called her Mrs. Hegstrom since her first visit to the school. "Please, it's always Marilyn. Is something wrong?"

"I'm afraid there is. There was a problem in P.E. class today. I'm sure it was an accident, or at least unintentional, but a kid's arm got broken and unfortunately the eyewitnesses all say that Claudius did it. I've already talked to the other kid's parents, and since the school will be covering all the medical bills, they're willing to take our word that it was an accident. But Coach really wants Claudius out of the class."

"Oh, I'm so sorry!" Marilyn found it hard to picture Claudius doing anything like that, but she also knew young males could be very physical and not always know their own strength.

"I want you to know I'll put him in another class for the rest of the semester. Maybe woodworking." McCurdy paused. "On second thought, sharp tools and Claudius might not be a good combination. I don't know. Some kind of art class, or I could assign him to help out in the cafeteria. I'll think of something."

Marilyn hung up and sighed. Claudius remained a puzzle. He still didn't quite fit in, but she could tell he was trying. He'd been there less than three months. She thought of how far he'd come, and decided he was doing quite well, everything considered.

When Claudius arrived home that afternoon he wasn't alone.

"Mother Marilyn," he said. "This is Antonius. He's also from my Rome. He's a temporary student, same as me."

"Is he also at your school?" Marilyn couldn't understand why McCurdy hadn't mentioned another exchange student, even if Antonius had arrived after Claudius."

"No, he is at the religious school here."

"Oh, you must mean St. Bridget's." Marilyn had always thought it odd that the Catholic school in a town settled by Swedes was named after an Irish saint.

"Ave," Antonius said.

"English, Antonius, we speak English here."

"I am very pleased to meet you," said Antonius, bowing slightly. Marilyn was charmed. What a nice young man. It looked like Claudius was finally beginning to make friends after all. The boys helped themselves to apples and walked into the living room, chattering to each other in that funny-sounding Italian.

Why hadn't she thought of it before? Maybe he just needed to connect with more foreign exchange students like him. Probably that website for his program would have some information she could use. She went into her office and fired up the computer.

How strange. At first she couldn't find it again. She searched all the terms: Host families, foreign exchange students. All she could find were the usual ones, AFS, International Exchange. There'd been something different about the one that got her Claudius. That's right, temporary families. There it was. Marilyn looked more closely at the site. Well, that's strange. She could have sworn it had said Temporary Foreign Exchange Students, but now she could see that it clearly read Temporal Exchange Students. This was definitely the same website. Those were the same graphics of pyramids, the Colosseum and all those other old places. Temporal, not temporary. To be certain, she went to an on line dictionary. Oh, yes: *Of, relating to, or limited by time: a temporal dimension; temporal and spatial boundaries.*

She pulled out the note that had arrived with Claudius. How had she misread it? "New culture and temporal – not temporary – milieu" it said. Had she mis-heard everything Constantine said? She looked back at the website.

"Host a temporal exchange student and learn about the ancient world." Ancient world. Rome. The toga. Taking baths. Not knowing spaghetti or pizza. Being surprised at electric lights. Suddenly everything added up. And now Antonius.

She heard them chattering away in Italian. No, not Italian. Latin. She turned from the computer and looked at the two young men. Temporal exchange students. Where, no, when had they come from? And why, exactly?

She looked back at the computer screen. How many others, how many Temporal Exchange Students were there? She looked back at Claudius and Antonius. A smile stole across her face. This was going to be an interesting year.

Easy Peasy

Holly Schofield

Get there early: that's the number one lesson for an interpreter's kid. Thanks to Mom's work in the Canadian embassy, I had a complicated life. This was my fourth high school in three years and, crap, it had a lot of hallways.

Eventually, I found Room #128 near a sunny courtyard complete with maple trees. It was good to be back on Earth, and especially back in Ottawa, my original home town. But now I had no friends.

Again.

I pushed open the door, slowly.

Empty. Good. I raised my phone to take a picture of the classroom to comm to Mmolmorr, my best friend back at Moon Base One.

"Welcome to our class." The deep voice behind me sounded happy, too happy.

I held in my sigh and turned around. The teacher wore a simple sleeveless coverall like mine – that was good. But he had a wide, welcoming smile and he was holding out his arms for a hug – that was bad.

"Uh, hi," I said and stuck out a hand. "I'm Geri."

"And I'm Frank." The teacher lowered his arms. They were even whiter than mine and had lots of fine red hairs. He solemnly shook my hand, clearly used to adapting to the different cultures he'd have run into at this school. Wonder what he'd make of Ssliberrs' greetings; most Earthers didn't like multiple face licks at first meeting.

"Have a seat anywhere." Frank gestured to the two big tables while he went to a side wallscreen and began to swipe up the day's lessons.

No way was I doing that. Most kids would have their favorite spots.

Frank saw me hesitate. "Take one of those," he said, pointing at two chairs opposite the wallscreen. "Piotr and Pawel won't be in today. I'll bring in another chair for you tomorrow."

I eased into a seat. Maybe this wouldn't be so bad. Maybe I'd fit in and even make some friends. Maybe I could find someone that liked coding and playing with language as much as I did.

The bell rang and a chattering bunch of kids swarmed in.

"Hi, I'm Lulu." A slender Asian girl with purple hair and a trendy slash-hipped coverall threw herself next to me.

"Welcome to our hovel, eh. I'm Abayomi." The dark-skinned girl slid in opposite us and grinned over. Miniature holo'd robots pranced around her active-all and her head wrap was full of glittering holo-jewels. A soft Nigerian accent fluttered her vowels although the phrasing was pure Canadian.

"Love your holos," I said, knowing that if I tried to wear clothes like hers I'd just look foolish. Instead, like always, I wore the plainest coveralls I could print and my mousy brown hair was brush cut in the same style I'd had since I was ten. That's the second lesson interpreters' kids learn: play it safe.

Twelve other kids introduced themselves and then Frank started the lesson. We did math (I rocked), science (I rocked again), and history (not so much). Then, just as I was getting hungry for lunch, he said, "We're going to emphasize sociology this term, in particular, the concept of heritage." He beamed at all of us. "Roots, people, roots!"

Abayomi caught my eye and winked. I shrugged back, unsure what she meant. Probably that, with my bland appearance, I could be anyone from any country, ever. Well, except I couldn't be a Ssliberr. The humanoid aliens were still the only signs of advanced life we'd found, despite all the exo-planet probes and studies in the last twenty years. I shoved aside thoughts of Mmolmorr's smile—best to forget about her. Mom's job took us where it took us, and I'd better learn to suck it up. Mom did her best.

Not that Mom cared about our family's cultural background – to her, our family reinvented ourselves every generation.

"Heritage! What is it? Anyone?" Frank beamed.

There was nowhere to hide. I pretended to study a poster on the wall about Canada's 200th birthday celebrations happening later this year.

"Clothing?" said Abayomi, stroking her active-all, making the robots jump. "Hair styles?"

I stuck up my hand, then quickly shoved it back in my lap, realizing the others had just spoken naturally without the formality of a hand raise. "Religion?" Mom was such a strong atheist that I was a pro at that assignment – I probably still had some notes on it.

"All good!" Frank bounced to the wallscreen and flicked our words onto it. "What else?"

I did a mental shrug. My thing was computational linguistics, not sociology. Any heritage topic was fine with me, just so long as it wasn't food. Mom had no special food traditions or culture and those projects were always tough. Her idea of heritage food was squirting ElectrikOrange cheese on her printed GravyFrys and calling it poutine.

Across from me, a skinny kid in a hockey jersey – Alain? – shifted in his seat and his stomach gave a loud gurgle.

Everyone laughed. Alain looked sheepish. "Sorry, I missed breakfast because of an early ice time and I'm starving. But food is heritage, right?"

"Food!" The others chimed in. "Yeah, let's do food!"

Frank clapped his hands. "Sure! Sounds like a plan! Let's have a potluck and call it homework!"

Everyone cheered.

Except me.

Earth was supposed to be a fresh start. A new chance to shine. Instead, I was to fail at fitting in *and* at the first homework assignment. I was a total loser. Only Mmolmorr thought I was special and she was 384,000 kilometers away.

At least, in this school, my desk was big enough to let me bury my head in my arms.

"It's not the worst day of your life, Geri." Mom rolled her eyes just the slightest.

Yeah, right. What did *she* know about the complexities of

high school life?

She kept talking right through my scowl. "You're caring too much about social acceptance. Just be yourself."

She'd insisted I prop up my slate on the far side of the small hotel-room table and set her image to be actual size. She even made me print the same ChicknBit-and-Biskit dinner from the hotel suite's food printer as she'd printed at her office. That way, it was like we were eating the same meal together at the same table, instead of her being in the translation headquarters thirty floors below.

I explained to her in great detail how I didn't care about hockey or clothes but I did want to connect with these kids somehow. She kept glancing over at her other screen, though, and I knew she was only taking this meal break because of me. Finally, I just sat there silently stabbing at my ChicknBits. I slid my feet up onto the other chair. If I had to eat alone in this anonymous hotel room, I might as well be comfortable.

"The sociology project doesn't have to be so hard. How about Métis food? That's your heritage too. There's bannock, and, er, things like that? You could research what other Métis food there is." She wasn't going to let go of the subject.

Now it was my turn to roll my eyes. "Bannock is just fried dough, every culture has *that*. And you don't really know my dad is Métis." We'd been through this before, when I'd failed yet another heritage project back in elementary school. My father had told Mom during their one-night stand when she'd gotten pregnant with me, that he had some First Nations blood way back on his side along with plenty of Caucasian. Trouble was, Mom couldn't remember much more from what she creepily insisted on calling their "night of passion."

"Well, I know he either has Cree or Ojibwa blood," she said, forehead wrinkling.

"But, Mom, that doesn't necessarily mean he's –"

"Just pick something and go with it. You're overcomplicating things. Your teacher just wants you to learn some history and meet his curriculum requirements." Mom swallowed a piece of Biskit and shrugged.

Great. The only thing I could be *certain* about our family genetics was that we had an abundance of cynicism.

I shrugged right back at her. "I'd rather do British. Or Irish." I was sixth-generation Canadian on Mom's side and I'd never been to the UK. But Frank didn't have to know that.

"Oooh!" Mom set down her coffee mug. "I just remembered a dish my Granny, that's your Great Granny, used to make right up into her nineties. I had it once as a small child. She invented it in the nineteen-forties, after World War Two. You take some toast –"

"Toast!" I cut her off. "Heritage foods don't involve toast!"

"P'raps it's derived from a British dish, or maybe Scottish." Mom kept talking with her mouth unmotherly full. "One of those EU countries, anyway."

"Scotland and Ireland aren't part of the EU anymore, Mom. What marks did *you* get in history?"

Thankfully, she was busy tapping something out on another screen and didn't seem to hear.

"Darling, I really have to finish this speech. Friday's the big day – Ssliberrs from different embassies all over Earth are being flown in for this meeting. Then there's going to be a huge social get-together in this hotel, in the big ballroom on the main floor. Come by right after school, okay? I want to show you off to my Ambassador. It's such a shame you never got to meet her on the Moon."

That was because I'd weaseled out of all the boring adult events up there. "Mommm! I hate having to wear a slit-all and face sparkles."

"It's only for an hour, Geri. I want more time with you before you head off to university or other endeavors. Promise me you'll get presentable and stop by?"

"Fine, okay, whatever. As long as there are snacks."

"I'll be sure to save you some Nanaimo bars. Hey, how about making those for your project? They're Canadian, you're Canadian, Canada is a culture in its own –"

"Mommm! I don't even know what a Nanaimo is!"

"It's a city. On the coast somewhere?" Her eyes drifted leftward again. "I'll say good night now. Make sure you get to bed on time."

"I'm nearly fifteen, I think I can do that. Just make sure *you* don't stay up all night. Old people need their rest." I clicked off and immediately commed Mmolmorr but she didn't answer. I missed her wide face and thick lips, cute as a frog's. She was probably off on a spur-of-the-moment trip with her first mom, second mom, and three sisters, visiting her many aunts, eating Vootll cakes and drinking fizzy Dadaww juice. Her family life had so many holidays and celebrations and customs, I hadn't learned them all yet.

I couldn't finish my Biskits. Things made with Earth flour tasted dirty somehow – must be all that actual soil the wheat grew in. My six months away sure had changed me. I dumped the rest in the recycle chute, grabbed a bowl of Mega-Crunch cereal, and picked up my slate.

Time to focus on my secret coding project. Mom's type of work involved memorizing a whole bunch of words and sounds. Oral stuff wasn't for me. I preferred text. The human and SSsliberrian scientists had cobbled together a prototype of a translation program – that was what Mmolmorr and I commed with – but I was going to ramp it up with extra coding until we could exchange even our deepest thoughts.

I checked my slate every ten minutes all evening. Still nothing back from Mmolmorr.

Doggedly, I started coding. The prototype dbase the scientists had made already had a bunch of phrases, but I wanted to add things that were more relevant to me and Mmolmorr – we didn't want to talk about the weather, we wanted to talk about teenage life, feelings and everything. I added a whole bunch of segments – sentences and clauses – until my eyes got too tired to focus.

I checked for new messages from Mmolmorr again. Still nothing.

I put on my pajamas only two hours later than I'd told Mom I would, then I hunted through my suitcase for the one item I always packed first: my scruffy old teddy bear who had travelled with me through every move.

I clutched her tightly as I crawled into my too-soft hotel bed.

By Friday, I still hadn't started the heritage project. I spoke up before Frank could start the class. "Um, my family history is complicated so I don't have anything that stands out. Can I pick a culture that's not mine?" I did make a mean taco.

"Well, adopted kids can," said Frank and a freckled white kid whose name I couldn't remember nodded. "However, everyone here has a mixed background," Frank continued, "and they're making it work." He looked at Lulu. "Take a banh mi sandwich for instance, it's a combination of Vietnamese and French cuisine from colonial days, yet Lulu's not complaining about the complexities of that." He immediately looked abashed. "Sorry. That was unkind of me, but, Gerun–er, Geri, the project's due Monday. You have to pick something soon."

"Yes, Frank," I muttered. Crap, he'd almost used my full name. I'd never live *that* down!

But he wasn't done yet. He fixed his blue eyes on me. "Everyone has culture. I mean, my own family makes a mean Yorkshire pudding, even without having access to any authentic cow meat. I'll be bringing some of the ol' pudd on Monday." He turned to face all of us. "And just a reminder, folks, no programming a food printer. Or having your parents make your dish." He swung into the next lesson, coding, and I got every question wrong.

At lunch, Lulu sat next to me. "Tell us about the Moon!" she said, black eyes shining like her hair.

Piotr, one of the twins who'd been away on my first day, overheard and slid in next to her. He stared intently at me. "Yeah, tell us!"

I got lost in his kind eyes for a moment but then Pawel shoved him along the bench so he could squeeze in and clatter down his tray.

I launched into a story about the time Mmolmorr and I had taken a rover and spent the night "camping" in a collapsed lava tube just outside the dome. "No one around us for a hundred klicks!"

"Woah, that's cool!" Piotr flashed a grin through his thin red lips. "You're actually friends with a Ssliberr!"

"They're just dumb Froggies," said Pawel around a mouthful of grilled cheese.

I started to stand up.

"Just ignore him. He's an ass." Lulu shot him a look.

I decided to take her advice and unclenched my fist. Pawel didn't seem as popular as Piotr. I pretended to smile. "Oh, yeah, I'm good friends with them. Mom is pretty high up in the Embassy, you know." That wasn't *exactly* true but Mom always said that everyone treated her as an equal, even ambassadors. "I'm pretty much half-Ssliberr" I added, jokingly.

"Ooh, have you eaten Ssliberrian food! Don't they eat live rodents or something?"

"Gross." Pawel shuddered melodramatically.

"Yeah, sure. I've eaten lots!" I said, even though that wasn't quite true. But it was too complicated to explain to these kids. Mom had told me a few months ago there'd been exhaustive tests in the labs on the Moon and all the Ssliberrian food tested so far had been safe for human consumption. But Ssliberrian food *was* strange. So strange that I'd rarely seen anything beyond a few snacks, and only nibbled on a few. Mmolmorr always hung out at my quarters, saying her meals were too weird to share.

I drew in a breath and continued, "Pretty tasty, actually. Once I ate twelve rodents at a sitting." Now *that* was a straight up lie. But it was worth it – Piotr's eyes lit up.

"No way! Hey, Abayomi, listen to this!" Lulu waved the cool crowd over.

I embellished the lie a bit more, even as I was regretting the whole messy story. Pawel jumped in to one-up me with a tale about his and Piotr's grandmother's cheesesteak-perogies, and how their great-grandfather had run a bed-and-breakfast in a stone castle somewhere in Europe. Or Asia. Or somewhere.

I didn't have much to contribute after that and basically sat there like a Moon rock, admiring Piotr's wit and sneaking glances at my slate.

I'd commed Mmolmorr four times yesterday, like best friends do.

She still hadn't answered.

My sparkled face itched the whole elevator trip down to the embassy, and I was embarrassed my slit-all was showing too much skin. How did grownups know how to be stylish? It seemed so complicated. Plus I'd had to hustle straight from school so I didn't have time to grab a snack. My rumbling stomach kept time to the elevator's rattling air vent during the long ride. I'd brought my slate though, in case Mmolmorr commed me, stashing it in a large gold-sequined bag I'd found in Mom's travel box. I grimaced in the elevator mirror. Ssliberrs were known to be loose with their timing, but where could Mmolmorr be after this long?

Ssliberrs are not quiet people. The noise level almost blew the sparkles off my face when I walked through the double-doored entranceway to the hotel ballroom. There must have been about sixty of the short stocky aliens milling around in their fancy scarves and muumuus, making boring small talk. And all in glittering, eye-straining colors. I didn't spot Mom right away. I should have asked her what color clothes she'd printed.

Tables of food lined the walls so I headed there, grabbing a plate from the stack beside a vase of flowers and an ice sculpture of a maple leaf. The hotel cooks must have been told to showcase "Canadian" food because I grabbed lobster rolls, quiche, nuegados, falafel in tiny pitas, and a little bowl of laksa. I stood against a wall and gobbled it all down before reloading with maple sugar candy, mille-feuille, timbits, and, of course, several chewy coconuty Nanaimo bars.

No one spoke to me, although an old lady *tsked* at me for no reason I could see. Finally, after four refills, I felt reasonably full. The next five tables along the wall were Ssliberrian food.

I snagged a handful of familiar crispy little fish things that were Mmolmorr's favorite. Then I worked my way down the line, loading my plate with only items I recognized. I took the last few Gawarr chips from a basket to the annoyance of a squat Ssliberr in an unusually dark and tight dress perusing the platters beside me. Showcased at the end on a tiered thing, like the timbits had been, were some pale blue balls, surround by crushed ice. The weird balls pulsed, like light bulbs were being turned on and off below their shimmery surfaces.

I held a hand over the display, hesitating. Maybe the balls were decorative, like the flowers and ice sculptures were on the human food tables. The little Ssliberr next to me put two balls on her already-overflowing plate then shook her shoulders at me before moving away, muttering, "Nazzz." Her disapproving glance back was almost enough reason for me to try them.

A better reason was that the balls – whatever they were – might help with my heritage project. I could just take a few and show them to Frank and the kids. I didn't have to actually *eat* any. And neither did anyone else. After a week in Frank's class, I knew all his rules. He was scrupulously fair about paper supplies and art tools – if everyone couldn't have something, then no one could.

A sign in Ssliberrian script was propped beside the display. I felt a grin spread across my face. Guess who just happened to have some newly improved translation software?

I yanked my slate from my purse and aimed its sensor at the complicated handwriting, triggering a scan. Ssliberrian text consisted of swooping lines and circles, the angles and arcs giving as much meaning as the characters themselves. The slate beeped and I hunched my shoulders, trying to keep it from the nosy glances of the people around me.

QUEEN NATURAL GIVES BENEFIT, the slate display said, with an eighty-five percent probability of accuracy.

I knew that the first two words meant the equivalent of the natural world, like our "Mother Nature." Ssliberrs were big on that. And if the balls were beneficial to the person eating them, they *had* to be all right.

I danced a little jig, shedding face sparkles all over the tablecloth.

Not only did my program work, but it had now also given me a solution to the heritage project!

Quickly, before anyone could notice, I grabbed an empty chip basket, put in five balls, then stuffed the whole thing in my purse along with my slate.

"There you are, Geri. Come and meet Ambassador Boovarzun!" Mom grabbed my elbow. I hastily tucked the purse into a handy side opening in my slit-all.

The Ambassador had the widest face and biggest lips I'd ever seen on a Ssliberr. I shook her damp hand and licked the downy hairs on her broad cheek the requisite six times. "Vrrutth, mmobahh", I said carefully, the only greeting I knew.

She chuckled. "I shhpeag Engglishh, younghh pperrsonn."

I laughed in surprise and Mom nudged me. They spoke in rapid Ssliberrian with a lot of laughter and glances over at me, and then Mom excused both of us.

"Now it's time for just us," Mom said, snagging two glasses of faux-champagne from a waiter. "Thanks for coming, Ger." She pulled me into a quiet alcove.

I sat on the upholstered loveseat, careful not to squish my purse, and took a sip. Maybe if I pretended the faux-champagne was the real stuff, my head would get fizzy and my life would seem simpler.

Mom plopped down wearily next to me. "How's your heritage assignment coming? I finally remembered Great Granny's full recipe."

"Mom, who cares? We're at a party!"

Her purple cheek sparkles did nothing to soften her stern stare. "Just listen, Geri. You spread peanut butter on toast, cut it into squares, and then you make a béchamel and mix in canned peas. Then you pour the mixture over the toast squares."

"Sounds gross!" Nobody had cans anymore, because things in cans sucked. And whatever béchamel was, it couldn't be good.

"Gerund, I do try, you know." Her face tightened and she stood up.

"And how could you name me Gerund?" I jumped to my feet, too. "It's just a word. It doesn't *mean* anything! It has no *culture!*"

"I thought it was cute for such an active baby," she said. "Interpreter humor." She smoothed her dress. "You can always change it when you're an adult."

"No kidding."

Her eyes grew wet. "And now I've got to go. I've neglected the Ambassador long enough and I think I have a sparkle caught in my eye."

I sat back down with a thump as she walked away, heels clicking.

All around me, Ssliberrs danced, talked, and laughed, one big happy cultured group. Why couldn't I have been born Ssliberrian? I would have aced this assignment, Mmolmorr would still remember me, and Mom wouldn't have gotten so mad at me just now. I hadn't even gotten a chance to ask her what "Nazzz" meant.

A tear ran down my face. Crappy sparkles. Always getting in people's eyes.

Our class's spread wasn't as luxurious as the embassy's party layout had been, but it covered both of the classroom tables. I spotted satay pork, calzones, and what looked like homemade jerky. Everything looked delicious except for some anemic-looking lumps of soggy dough that must be Frank's Yorkshire puddings. I patted my stomach. The handful of Mega-Crunch I'd shoved in before heading out the door would have some good company soon. I hadn't made a better breakfast because I was afraid the beeping sounds of the food printer would wake Mom. She was still sleeping off the effects of the weekend-long party, and we hadn't talked since I'd left the ballroom Friday evening.

I placed my tiny lidded basket two-thirds of the way down the table, so it would be dwarfed by the plates and bowls of the others. With luck, we'd run out of time for all of the presentations.

"Who wants to go first?" Frank was bouncing on his heels, rubbing his hands together. How people got so enthusiastic about things was beyond me.

Surprisingly, half the kids grinned back at him. Earth was a funny place to me, even though I'd grown up here. Even Piotr looked excited under his sweep of black hair. It was like optimism was the new cool. I wasn't sure I liked it – enthusiasm complicated things and I just wanted everything to be simple.

"Lulu, how about you?" Frank gave an encouraging smile and she jumped to her feet. Her two-minute lecture took five minutes because of all the questions about the many ingredients and then she began handing out sections of banh mi. The meat-filled bun was to die for. "My po-po's recipe but I did it all myself," she said proudly before sitting down with a flourish of her green and fuchsia slit-all.

Corned beef hash, stinky blue cheese with flakey croissants, Tibetan buttered tea, Egusi soup, eggplant parmesan; I was getting really full but, sadly, we were making good time.

"Geri?" Frank eyed me.

I edged to my feet and picked up the lidded basket. "I'm sorry I was only able to obtain a few of this extreme delicacy of my people," I began.

"Your people?" Frank crossed his arms.

"My people, my *adopted* people, the Ssliberrs!" I said, too loudly.

Frank frowned but then nodded at me to go ahead. And, really, I hadn't broken any rules. Mmolmorr was the closest thing I had to a sister.

I recited the short history of the Ssliberrs and their general food habits that I'd pulled off WikiQuick last night.

"But what did you bring to eat?" interrupted Pawel. "And is it any good?"

"I call them Nazz Balls!" I pulled open the lid of the tiny basket and tipped it towards them. They all crowded closer to look, oohing and ahhing. "I couldn't get more than five. They're rare and special. I'm sorry! Not enough to serve everyone. We can smell them though, and look at the pretty blue colors as they wiggle." I hid my grin. Frank's own rules meant we couldn't share them.

Apparently, I didn't know *all* the rules because Frank said, "Not a problem. Open your sortition apps, everyone. We'll pick four of us randomly, the usual drill." They all tapped their slates as I felt myself shrink into the floor. The winners of the random lottery were Lulu, Piotr, Pawel, and Abayomi. Great. The cool kids. I was ruined. I might as well stick my head into my too-firm hotel room pillow for the rest of the term.

"Do we eat them while they're *alive*?" Abayomi looked really scared and I almost spoke up and spilled the truth. What if my translation was wrong? What if they tasted nasty? Or were poisonous?

"Let's pop 'em in together!" Pawel said and the other three grinned. Each of them picked up a ball. I took the fifth one and it squiggled in my fingers, like a baby mouse. Pawel opened wide. "Ready, set, go!"

Piotr shoved the slimy thing in, the others did too, and, Queen Natural forgive me, so did I.

It tasted minty, sort of clean, like mouthwash.

Not bad! I chewed gingerly.

A sharp pain hit the inside of my lip, like a knife cut.

Then another.

And another.

My mouth was on fire!

I grabbed my jaw. Lulu shrieked. Piotr and Pawel moaned, and Abayomi was coughing hard.

"Spit it out! Spit it out!" I said, but it came out "Sfffit it out." Like I had frog lips or something. I felt Frank's fingers in my mouth, yanking, but my whole jaw clenched shut.

My lips grew numb.

I huddled on the floor for almost forever.

When the paramedics swarmed in and all during the ambulance ride, all I could think about was that I'd been wrong in what I'd told Mom. Getting the assignment last week hadn't been the worst day of my life.

Today was.

I didn't open my eyes again until I was at the hospital along with the other four kids and Frank. Mom rushed in, trailed by Ambassador Boovarzun. The three of them crowded around my bed and I felt like a small child.

Mom said, "You'll be all right, honey," and put a cool hand on my forehead. She leaned to kiss me just as the doctor strode in.

"Careful. Sterility." The doctor was all brusqueness and frowns.

Mom changed direction and kissed my shoulder instead of my weird-feeling face.

"Lpss," I mumbled. "Muh lipss." I sounded just like Mmolmorr when she tried to speak English.

"Pathogen transfers are minimal. Just have to wait for ova maturity," the doctor said.

If ever I needed an interpreter … "Mohm?"

"He means that you won't get infected by Ssliberrian germs. But your lips will be as large as, er, as *handsome* as a Ssliberr's until the eggs hatch." She glanced at the Ambassador.

"Egggss?" I tried to sit up but various tubes and wires

pulled me back.

"Easy." Frank smiled down at me. "Try to relax. This is going to be a fun experience!"

The Ambassador leaned in. "Wrrreket heppp to assissst-ing in Queenn Naturrrall. The sssign verrry explllanatories it, nooo?" Her words were so jumbled and sibilant that I looked at Mom again.

"She means it'll be okay, honey. You'll just talk a bit mumbly until the annelids pop out. The Wrrreket, a subculture on Ssliberria's southern continent, use their, er, ample lips as a host mechanism for the annelids as part of their, er, nature worship. Sort of a 'pay it forward' thing."

I hadn't even known there was more than one culture on Ssliberria although it seemed obvious once I thought about it. People *were* complicated.

Wait, what was that other word? "Annnnellid?"

"Like earthworms, only they don't live in the dirt." said Frank, happily. "Fascinating, really." He bounced on his toes.

I sank back into the pillow. Great. I'd infected my new friends with worms. I was going to be the least popular kid in the history of history assignments.

"Geri, you're in luck." Frank bounced again. "I've decided to cut you a break. You can do a fresh heritage food assignment. I'll give you a further two weeks after you get out of the hospital."

Mom beamed. "Well, that's kind of you, Frank. We have an old family recipe that –"

"Mohmmm!"

"Happy to oblige. The learning never stops." They smiled at each other, and Frank bounced again.

The hotel room's tiny corner table was set with two plates and the old cracked vase of dried pansies that we carried with us everywhere. I took a suitcase off my chair and sat down. Mom laid out two pieces of whole-wheat toast embossed with the hotel logo along with a squeeze tube of peanut butter. The food printer pinged and she took out a bowl of bright green steaming peas. "They aren't *quite* like canned peas," she said doubtfully, wrinkling her nose. "They're too fresh. They're supposed to be grayer. And the cream sauce came out lumpy." She pointed at a second bowl, full of congealing white paste. "I don't think the printer understood my inputs."

"It looks fine," I enunciated carefully. After ten days in the hospital, my lips were still flappy and would be until the end of term, but at least my taste buds had recovered. And the kids at school had forgiven me—in fact, they even thought the whole thing was kind of humorous.

Lying in the hospital, I'd had a lot of time to think. At first, I was mad at myself for taking the Nazz balls, failing the assignment, and infecting my friends. All this had happened just because I wanted to fit in, to be cool.

Then I got ashamed. Cultural differences were things to celebrate and enjoy together. By stealing from Ssliberrian culture and trying to pass it off as my own, I'd been the exact opposite of cool. What if I'd violated a tradition in a way I wasn't aware of? I made a promise to myself to find out and then apologize to every Ssliberrian who'd been in the ballroom.

And, I'd made a decision, too. I was going to become more optimistic, like the Earth kids, and like Frank. It couldn't hurt, I figured. And it might actually make me happier. I still hadn't heard from Mmolmorr, but I was choosing not to let that get me down. Not much, anyway.

Earth was rubbing off on me, I guess, or at least adding to the complex person I was becoming.

Besides, this combination of peas and sauce and peanut butter and toast did smell interesting. This was only a trial run before I'd try making the dish from scratch for the homework assignment, but it might actually taste good.

Mom started to spread the peanut butter on the warm toast.

My slate beeped.

Mmolmorr! I scanned through her message quickly. She'd been at a spontaneous no-comms-allowed Queen Natural celebration concert, was sorry she'd had no time to comm before they left, and had oodles to tell me.

I relaxed into my chair while Mom stirred peas into sauce. Mmolmorr's wide, cute face filled my slate screen as I replayed her message over and over. Sure, Piotr's eyes were nice but

Mmolmorr's were *so* much nicer.

I commed back that the concert sounded amazing and I wanted to hear all about it. Not only would listening to her describe the event bring me closer to her, but I'd realized I had a lot to learn about the many cultures and peoples that made up Ssliberria.

I signed off saying, "Things have been busy here, too. I have lots to tell you, no kidding." My translator software even got the "no kidding" part right, as far as I could tell.

I knew then that Earth kids were fun and cool, but Mmolmorr was my super-special friend, part of my future family. I knew it deep in my heart of hearts.

It was easy: with her, I fit in.

Sure, my life was about to get a lot more complicated but, suddenly, it wasn't hard to feel truly optimistic.

"Okay, honey, let's do this." Mom handed me a fork and we both gamely stabbed at squares of sauce-covered toast. A gluey pea plopped down on my plate as I shoved in a lumpy white-and-brown mouthful.

I put down my fork. "Uh…"

"It's … different, isn't it. I'd forgotten that taste." Mom propped an elbow on the table and rested her head in her hand. "Maybe some ketchup?"

"Ketchup isn't part of our heritage, Mom. It might be popular but you don't always have to follow the crowd, you know." I spoke as I chewed. "I'm optimistic that the second bite will be better."

And, no kidding, it was.

An Averted Tragedy

Brian Gene Olson

Mr. Capen's Comparative World Literature Class
Quiz 1
Points possible: 50
NAME: Amanda McWilliams

Question 1 (5 points): Our class recently took a field trip to two alternate universes in which two of our world's most famous literary characters really exist. To travel to these universes, we ___.

A. quantum-phased
B. quantum-teleported
C. quantum-transported
D. quantum-wibble-wobbled
YOUR ANSWER: B
Score: 5
Teacher comments:

Question 2 (5 points): Why is it important for our class to be quantum-cloaked whenever we travel the multiverse?
YOUR ANSWER: So the people there don't see us.
Score: 1
Teacher comments: Your answer is incomplete. We must be quantum-cloaked so that none of the people we observe can see, hear, smell, touch, or taste us, and – just as important – so that we don't interact in any way with other multiverse travelers, or with ourselves if and when we return to the same universe to observe the same event.

Question 3 (5 points): Which two tragic heroes did we observe?

A. Sophocles' Achilles and Shakespeare's Hamlet
B. Sophocles' Ajax and Shakespeare's Macbeth
C. Euripides' Ajax and Shakespeare's Hamlet
D. Sophocles' Ajax and Shakespeare's Hamlet
YOUR ANSWER: D
Score: 5
Teacher comments:

Question 4 (5 points): What happens to people when we quantum-swap them?
A. Each person retains his or her original memories and personality
B. Each person retains his or her original memories but takes on the other's personality
C. Each person takes on the other's memories but retains his or her original personality
D. Each person takes on the other's memories and personality
YOUR ANSWER: C
Score: 5
Teacher comments:

Question 5 (5 points): Why did we quantum-swap our two tragic heroes?
YOUR ANSWER: So we could see how different they are in the different universes.
Score: 3
Teacher comments: More specifically, we quantum-swap tragic heroes so we can observe to what degree the environment itself, the tragic hero's world, makes that person tragic, as well as to discover to what extent each hero is a reflection of the aesthetic quality of his universe.

Question 6 (5 points): What happened to the tragic heroes in their respective original timelines before we quantum-swapped them? (Be specific.)
YOUR ANSWER: Ajax committed suicide because he lost a debate with Odysseus about who got to keep Achilles' armor. Hamlet missed his opportunity to kill Claudius, accidentally killed Polonius, and later died in a duel with Polonius' son

Laertes.
Score: 5
Teacher comments:

Question 7 (5 points): What happened to the tragic heroes after we quantum-swapped them?
YOUR ANSWER: Hamlet convinced Lord Agamemnon to give him a rematch with Odysseus. A crowd of soldiers gathered around to hear what Hamlet/Ajax had to say now – but none of them expected what was about to happen. Hamlet gave his "to be or not to be" soliloquy and the crowd went silent. Odysseus just stood there with his mouth open but he couldn't speak. Then he started to shout about some god betraying Athena and helping Ajax. (I guess that god was us.) By unanimous decision, Hamlet won the armor. Odysseus was furious, but then he and Hamlet had a friendly debate and seemed to become friendly with each other.
    Meanwhile, in the other universe, Ajax walked in on King Claudius kneeling and praying, and, in one quick motion, Ajax sliced the king's head off. Then he killed Polonius and fled the castle. He joined up with Fortinbras' army and marched with them as they conquered the land.
Score: 5
Teacher comments: Good observations.

Question 8 (5 points): In your opinion, were the quantum-swapped heroes still tragic in character? (Answer should be at least 50 words.)
YOUR ANSWER: No, because each man found a peace in the other's universe which had eluded him in his own. Hamlet was up to the challenge that Ajax had faced, and Ajax was just the avenging hero that the ghost of Hamlet's father had demanded him to be. Both men lived happily ever after in their new universes – until we swapped them again.
Score: 5
Teacher comments:

Question 9 (5 points): Why did we quantum-swap the heroes back to their own universes and restore their original timelines

before we quantum-teleported ourselves back to the lecture hall in our own world?
A. Because we're cruel
B. Because we like watching people suffer
C. They were much happier in their original universes
D. It's the law
YOUR ANSWER: D
Score: 5
Teacher comments:

Question 10 (5 points): How did you feel seeing these tragic heroes in life? Did you experience what Aristotle called the tragic emotions of pity and terror?
YOUR ANSWER: Mostly I was just sad for them, even when they were happy in their new situations, because I knew we would have to send them to back to their own universes where they felt they didn't belong. It made me cry.
Score: 5
Teacher comments:

Extra credit question (2 points): What was it Polonius shouted after he witnessed Ajax cutting the king's head off?
YOUR ANSWER: "What, ho! Help! Help! Help!"
Score: 2

Total score: 46 points / 92% / A

* * *

"Hey, I got a B. Amanda, what did you get?"

"An A. I almost got a B, but that extra credit question saved me."

"Heh. Tragedy averted."

The Pupil

David B. Riley

"Dear God, no." Hugo Green again looked at the tablet. He could read the words, but he couldn't quite believe the message. How could they do such a thing? He didn't deserve this. He most certainly did not deserve this. He looked at the tablet again. It said the same thing. From the Chief Justice, no less? Who can argue with the Chief Justice?

There was only one place that sold hot dogs in the Mars City area. It was a nondescript little café in North Dome called "Jake's Place." He didn't know where they got them from, probably didn't want to know. This was a hot dog day. "And a Martian Red Ale," he added to his order.

"You sure about that? You going back to chambers?" Jake asked. People always thought Jake would be some crusty retired freighter man. Truth was, he was young and very good looking. A lot of women came by for lunch. What they wanted was not on the menu.

Hugo Green did know where the mustard was from; Martian Hydroponics. Yep, it was delicious. People were always complaining about Martian Hydroponics. They got the mustard right. Earth mustard, made with Canadian mustard seeds, tasted like crap. This stuff on his hot dog was straight from heaven itself.

"So what's wrong?" Jake asked. "You don't come in here in the middle of the day. It takes too long to get here from Mars City."

"A trip on Mag Lev and a delicious hot dog helps me forget my woes, my young friend." He took a swig of beer. "Damn that's good. As I was saying, they are sending me a pupil, as we in the law call them." He took another swig of beer. "And

147

not just any pupil. No, she won some internship run by the
High Court. She is from Earth. Can you believe it? Not only did
they send me a pupil, but one from Earth. In all the time I've
practiced law, I've managed to avoid a pupil. And they send
me one from Earth. There must be something wrong with her,
wanting to come here. Don't they have perfectly good barristers on Earth?"

"Beats me," Jake said. "Want another Red?"

"Keep 'em coming. And another dog while you're at it."

"You got it."

"And she's a woman. Did I mention that?"

"Maybe, in passing."

"You gotta understand, I'm incredibly lazy, Jake. This
means extra work and I'm at a point where I want to slack.
That's why I retired from the bench. Judges have to show up
and work. I hated that. Did I mention she's a woman?"

"I had not heard," Jake replied.

"I'm a big ugly black man. I'm bald. Why do I have to have
some pupil following me around?"

The teenage boy on the Mag Lev kept trying to move away
from the strange man who smelled of mustard and beer. "Life's
not fair, Mister."

"No, it isn't, my young friend." He turned on his tablet and
unfolded it. "That's her. How can I get rid of her?"

"She's kind of cute," the boy observed. He took another
look at her picture. "How old is she?"

"Twenty-three."

"That's ancient."

"Ancient indeed."

The door opened and the boy shot out of the train like a
rocket.

"I'm a fifty-seven year old dinosaur too set in his ways," he
told an empty train.

In spite of what he told Jake, Hugo did go back to chambers. Since his wife threw him out he'd been sleeping there. It
wasn't so bad. And there was no commute.

In the morning, there she was, coming down the hall
– looking for his chambers. He wanted to lock the door. He

doubted that would do more than delay the inevitable for a few minutes.

"Judge Green?" she asked.

"I'm not a judge anymore."

"I thought the title sticks with you like Senator or Colonel."

"I'd rather it went away."

"Well, whoever you are, I'm Prairie Davis."

"We need to get going," Hugo said.

"Going where?"

"The wheels of justice never stop turning. We've got a case. Tell me you brought a robe?"

"Uh. Earth lawyers no longer wear them."

"Follow me." They went into a locker room near the rear exit to Belmont Law Offices. "Maybe you can borrow Paula's?" He opened an unlocked cabinet. "She was about your size."

"Was?"

"Passed away. Family's never claimed her robes." He reached back into the back of the cabinet and extracted a white powered wig and placed it on her head.

Prairie glanced at herself in the mirror. "I'm wearing a dead woman's wig?"

"Well she won't need it. Let's get going. Our client awaits." He remembered to open his locker and get his own robe and wig.

"What sort of case is this?" she asked. They went to the right and the sign said, *Central Courts*.

Before he answered, she noticed another sign, *Court of Appeals*. The sliding door let them in.

"Do you know anything?" Hugo asked.

"About what?"

"Martian law." What else would he be asking about?

"I've been reading up," she insisted.

"This is an appeal from a ruling by the Ministry of Banking and Insurance," Hugo explained.

"And appeals of administrative agencies go to the Court of Appeals, not Central or District Court."

"Very good." He waved at a woman sitting in one of the many orange plastic chairs in the waiting area.

"Hi," the strawberry blonde said.

Hugo introduced their client. "Prairie Davis, this is General Sarah Meadows."

She seemed barely older than Prairie. "You look a little young to be a general?"

Sarah grinned. "Oh, that's okay, I'm retired now."

"They took away Sarah's insurance license," Hugo said. "And we're appealing."

"What for? I mean why'd they revoke it, not why are we appealing."

"It's in the file I sent you," Hugo said.

"When?"

"A minute ago."

She managed a brief look at it on the tablet, then noticed her barrister and their client were heading off into the courtroom. She hurried to catch up.

Who'd I piss off to get this guy? she thought. She was wearing a dead woman's wig. The white powdered wigs had long been retired on Earth – even by the British courts. Not so on Mars. But Prairie never expected to be in court an hour after her arrival. After her shuttle landed she'd spent a sleepless night at some cheap lodging place in North Dome, eaten breakfast at some diner ran by a really cute guy, then hurried to get into Mars City on Mag Lev. And now she was sitting at a grayish metal table, no doubt made out of some Martian graphite composite material. The Martian residents made everything out of graphite. A gleaming brass sign read APPELLANT.

The table to the right was identical save for that sign read RESPONDENT. And there was a woman dressed just like Prairie sitting behind it. Hopefully that woman didn't have to wear a wig from some dead woman.

The bailiff entered. He was a short, balding man, dressed in a purple robe. He didn't have to wear a wig. She wondered why. "All rise. Those having business before the court draw near. Hear ye, hear ye, hear ye."

The justices entered and took their seats. There were name tags on the bench. Justice Redcliff, Justice Smith and Justice Thomas – all men. "Be seated," Justice Thomas declared. "Clerk will call the case."

The clerk was a woman. She was short and looked rather

elderly. "Uh, my lord, I can't."

Justice Thomas motioned for her to approach the bench. There was some discussion. The clerk went back to her station. "My lords, we call case number 147-A, an appeal from the Ministry of Banking and Insurance."

Hugo Green was smiling.

Justice Thomas announced, "The awkwardness in calling the case is the fact the respondent has filed an official objection to the naming of the case. While it normally would be titled as Ministry versus General Sarah Meadows, there is a motion against using that title."

Hugo stood. "My lord, the respondent only notified us of this matter yesterday."

The other barrister stood. She was a tall woman. She had green eyes and a few strands of crimson hair fell below her wig. "My lord, the appellant uses the title of general even though she has never served in the Martian Defense Force. This is improper and violates the titles and regulations of the Ministry, Title four, section eight. Therefore, we move the court not address her by this title. If this were a district court case we'd be suing to bar her use of the title – but this is an appeal and we seek that she not be called General Meadows for this proceeding."

The justices talked amongst themselves.

"We will refer to the appellant as Miss Meadows for the purpose of this case," Presiding Justice Reginald Thomas ruled. "However, how did the appellant come by this title?"

"She served for a foreign army, my lord," Hugo replied. "The Tau army, to be precise."

"The lizards?"

"She served in the Tau army at the rank of general, during their war with Earth," my lord.

"But she's human?"

"Indeed she is," Hugo agreed. "And commissioned by the Tau Emperor as a general in their army. She is now under retired status."

Prairie found the noodles quite tasty. "I'm starting to think the things they say about the food from Martian Hydroponics is exaggerated."

"No it's not," Sarah insisted.

"Well, these noodles are delicious."

"Well, we managed to get a ruling on your name. Not bad," Hugo said. "So, Councilor, what do you think of Martian jurisprudence?"

"Uh, well..."

"So, I hear you just got in?" Sarah asked.

"Yep."

"Do you have a place to stay yet?"

"I've got a discount at the Y."

"The Y. No, you can stay at my place. I've got a spare room," Sarah offered.

"Well, okay," she agreed. "Is that allowed, to stay with a client?"

"To my knowledge, the bar's regulations on where barristers reside are silent."

"Goodie," Prairie agreed. She noticed a tall redhead kept looking at them from another table. It was the other barrister. "I think she likes you."

Hugo looked away from her. "I doubt that."

"Oh, I think she does," Prairie insisted.

"I seriously doubt that," Hugo replied.

"You should ask her out."

"I already have."

"Oh."

The redhead came over. She extended her hand to Prairie. "I'm April. You must be the new pupil."

"Prairie."

"Well, see you in court." She looked over at Hugo. "Are you still sleeping in your office?"

"Yes."

"Pathetic." She walked away, toward the escalator that went back to the court complex.

"You're not married are you?" Prairie asked.

"Yes, separated actually," Hugo answered.

"Remain seated and come to order," the clerk announced. "This court is again in session."

April Green rose and placed her tablet on the podium. "As I indicated in my brief, the Ministry revoked Miss Meadows' license and have barred her from selling insurance. Following a hearing, the Commissioner ruled the following:

"Sarah Meadows has advertised herself and conducted business as General Sarah Meadows."

Hugo shot to attention. "Point of order."

"What is it, Councilor?" Justice Thomas asked.

"The appellant advertised herself on the window of her insurance agency and with business cards and similar materials as Gen. Sarah Meadows. It's abbreviated. It's not General, it's Gen."

"What earthly difference does that make?" the justice asked.

"I merely point out the inaccuracy, My Lord."

April continued, "The Commissioner further ruled she, in using an unapproved and ineligible title, had violated regulations and therefore her license was subject to revocation."

The big sign on the window was *Meadows Insurance Agency*. A smaller sign had a piece of paper taped over something and then it read Sarah Meadows, Agent. Another sign said, *Closed until further notice*.

Sarah opened the door. Behind the office and up the stairs were two rooms. "It's great not having to rent an apartment."

"You must've pissed somebody off?" Prairie asked.

"I fought on the side of the Tau against Earth."

"Yeah, but wasn't Mars neutral?"

"Yep, but the folks at Earthforce are exerting all kinds of pressure to destroy me. The Prime Minister kisses Earth's Chancellor's ass every morning."

"This is a petty case, Sarah."

"Welcome to my world. I used to work at Gompers Insurance as a claims adjuster. Then, I got a direct commission because the Tau emperor thought I understood an enemy that baffled him."

"Okay? How did you know?"

"I sold the Tau one of our war policies. Then, the war ended and Gompers wouldn't hire me back as they were told they would lose their license to write insurance on Mars if they did. Then I tried selling as an independent agent. I kept my insurance license."

"I see." Her room was very plain, a bed and a small work station.

"There's not much in the kitchen, but help yourself if you want anything. If you can catch it, you can eat it."

Prairie found a large assortment of Earthforce ready-to-eat meals. She opened the spaghetti. The little pouch sizzled. The instructions said to peel the label back. And there was a little plate. The kit even had a fork. It even had a little piece of garlic bread.

Prairie slept very well, as her exhausting travel caught up to her. When she woke, she found Sarah was eating eggs. Sarah handed her an Earthforce meal kit. This one was for pancakes and sausage. "Uh?"

"The Tau army captured a supply depot run by Earthforce during the war. The Tau don't like Earth food very much, although they really like the banana pudding for some reason. Anyway, it made it easy to feed me since I'm not wild on bugs and grubs. And they still refuse to return the food, although I hear they're running out of banana pudding.

After breakfast, they headed down the escalator. "No court today, as it's some weird deal when they train the court clerks one day a year. So, our case picks up tomorrow." The court complex was to their right, but Sarah started to the left. "You've got time. I'll show you something."

They went down a hallway. Olympus Mons, the largest mountain on Mars, could be easily seen through a large window, even though it was long distance away. Two reptilian soldiers stood by a set of double doors. They snapped to attention. One of them opened the door. A sign was written in a language Prairie could not read. It also was written in a second language which she could. *The Embassy of the Tau People. Moo Goo, Ambassador.*

Prairie followed Sarah past a receptionist and to a door. There was a sign on that door, also in two languages. It read: *Gen. Sarah Meadows, Assistant Charge D'affaires.* "Uh?"

"It's not that I can't find work. I went to the Martian School of Economics. I worked hard to get that insurance license. And I'll be damned if I'll let Earthforce bully the Martian government into taking it away from me. I've become a real pain in the ass. And that's what our case is about."

Prairie just made it to the weekly staff meeting. There were six barristers working out of Belmont Law. It was the largest such firm on Mars. There were also two paralegals, a clerk and two assistant clerks.

The head of chambers was Melvin A. Crook. He was a tall man, with thinning black hair and a handlebar moustache. His gray eyes kind of looked through a person. "I'd like to introduce Prairie Davis, Hugo's new pupil, all the way from Earth."

She smiled. She didn't know if she was expected to say anything, so just sat there.

"Well, you'll want to review the file coming up. A gentleman named Phillip P. Phillips is suing the Gompers Insurance Company on the grounds they illegally cancelled his life insurance policy."

"Why can't he just buy another policy somewhere else?" Prairie asked.

"He claims there's some sort of conspiracy and no one will sell him one."

"Really? That's seem hard to believe."

Hugo smiled. "The agent who sold him his policy was Gen. Sarah Meadows. They claim they'd fired her and she no longer represented them. She claims she was on military leave under section 91 of the Military Powers Act and was not subject to dismissal because of her being in the military reserve."

"But, uh, she was in the Tau army."

"The act did not state one had to be in the Martian Defense Force, only they had to be in military service. Ergo..."

"She's a one woman wrecking ball."

"That she is," Hugo agreed. "Do you like hot dogs?"

"I haven't had one in years."

"And so, My Lords, I'll call your attention to Commissioner Frank Tuttle's ruling. You have a certified copy before you."

> Where titles of common usage are al-
> lowed for the conducting of business, in case
> of claimant Meadows, it is not applicable.
> Where a doctor or senator might use such a
> title, it denotes a generally accepted standard
> in society of training or service. Meadows,
> one would naturally infer, had been a general
> in the Martian Defense. Furthermore, the rank
> infers a career of service to obtain it. In truth,
> claimant has a mere eight months of service
> with an alien army and there is no customary
> military career whatsoever. Using such a title
> in this instance violates department standards
> of integrity and cannot be allowed.

"The ruling goes on to formally rescind her license to sell insurance in the Martian Republic." Prairie sat back down.

"Uh, Miss Davis…" It was Justice Smith.

"It's awake. Heaven help us now," Hugo whispered to her. She tried to suppress a giggle.

"Miss Davis, does the order explain why the license was rescinded?" Justice Smith asked.

"No, My Lord," Prairie said.

"Does not the department offer licensees the opportunity to correct a deficiency? In this case, to allow her to drop the use of the title?" Smith asked. "I don't see anything in the brief that says she refused to stop using the title of general."

"No, My Lord. Miss Meadows was never given an opportunity to stop using the title. It went straight to revocation?"

"Mrs. Green, is that normal?" Justice Smith asked.

"It is not required to allow corrective measures of compliance, My Lord." She looked over at Prairie.

"I asked if it was unusual," the justice insisted, "not if it was required."

"Yes, My Lord, it is unusual," she admitted.

"And thank you, Justice Smith for doing our job for us," Hugo whispered.

* * *

Prairie had never tasted Martian Red Ale before. She'd heard it was a little stronger than Earth beer. And made from a strain of Martian yeast long ago discovered by the first explorers, it had a smooth quality unmatched by most Earth potables. In other words, it was pretty good.

When the Temperance League tried to ban its production as an unwise use of Mars' limited water resources, the whole bunch of them were rounded up and deported back to Earth.

"We haven't won yet," Prairie pointed out. "It may be weeks before there's a ruling."

"I think, well, we'll see." He finished off his glass of beer. "Well, Miss Meadows, are you going to go back to selling insurance or keep working at the embassy for the lizards?"

"I just don't know," Sarah said.

"There is still that other case coming up tomorrow," Prairie pointed out.

"Ah, yes, with your former employer and that insurance policy." Hugo was starting to like having a pupil. She was picking up a lot of the workload. "All read up on that one?"

"You betcha."

The next morning, right outside the Central Court, Department two, a woman later identified as Sarah Meadows, was found lying in a pool of blood. She was found by a maintenance worker. She had been struck with a projectile gun. Such guns were common on Earth, but banned on Mars because of the reliance of domes so humans can live on a planet with a thin atmosphere. The bullets used by these weapons inflict great damage to people, often killing them.

Such weapons are also very loud, yet no one heard a thing. This caused the Mars City Marshals Department to conclude that a silencer had been used and that such a weapon was likely smuggled in from Earth.

As a crowd formed and people urgently waited for the medics to arrive, Sarah opened her eyes. She noticed somebody familiar in the crowd. "Prairie?" she said as loud as she could with her lungs filling with blood. "Come here?"

Prairie knelt down beside her client and roommate. "Hang in there. The medics are coming up the escalator."

What most people did not know was that Earthforce special operations soldiers traditionally carried a nylon dagger in their boots. It was only carried by special forces, who were informally called Marines. And this obsolete weapon was capable of inflicting great bodily damage in the hands of someone who knew how to use it and had kept it properly sharpened.

Sarah had adopted the practice and began carrying one of these obsolete weapons in her boot, just as the Earth soldiers did. And she had continued to carry this weapon even after she left military service. And Prairie Davis was very surprised that Sarah still had enough strength to thrust her dagger between her ribs, straight into her heart with one single thrust. "Die you Earthforce bitch!"

A later search of Prairie Davis' clothing found a projectile gun. Her judicial robes easily concealed such a weapon.

Starseeds

Sherry Yuan

Reishi discovered that the human concept of "Life flashing before your eyes" turned out to be true as she lay bleeding on the ground and bullets rained down around her.

Her oldest memory was from when her mother still clung to her childish wonder at her new surroundings, although it was in decline as reality continuously disillusioned her, shredded her. Ron Serki (that's what her mother told Reishi to call her; it was a custom in Carthia to call every family member by their first name, either preceded by Ron if it was an elder or followed by Ri if younger) had taken her to the zoo and they were standing in front of the elephant's cage. Reishi didn't remember what had happened before that. It was like the climax of a dream, when only a single thing remained and the less memorable parts were either blurred into oblivion or simply never existed.

Reishi stared at the giant beast in wonder, her small fingers hooked onto the chain link fence.

"Carthia has bigger land beasts than this, but nowhere near the size of the blue whale, the biggest creature on Earth. A whale is nearly 25 times the size of an elephant!" Ron Serki explained.

Reishi tried to wrap her four-year-old mind around the enormity of the creature. "Where would it fit?"

"In an ocean, which is a huge hole full of water. Salty water, like the KFC soup we had earlier."

The man standing next to them turned around and smiled. "Yeah, it's an amazing world, isn't it?"

And then Reishi was ripped away from the fence, found

herself in a whirlwind of colors as her mother swung her into her arms and ran away from the man. Reishi found herself swept through hordes of red, purple, black and blue shirts, past more exotic creatures, until they were blocked by chain link fences on all three sides. Her mother swung around frantically, then told the girl to hold onto her neck as she began climbing the fence. Then the memory faded at the edges. A deep masculine voice said something loud, somehow they were somewhere with whitewashed walls, and that was the end.

Many of her other old memories consisted of the times they spent in a beat-up car between houses. She usually had at least a few hours' notice, a glint in Ron Serki's eye when she picked her up in a decade-old Corolla or Civic after school and then whispered, "They're on to us again. When you go home, pack whatever you need in a backpack, we'll leave before the night falls." If Reishi looked back with reluctance, she would continue with, "Sorry sweetie, this is bigger than us." A pause, an eyeful of longing cast towards distant galaxies. "We're just starseeds." Those words weren't said very often, though. Reishi used to enjoy the feeling of adventure of these moves.

In this specific memory, an 8-year-old Reishi was shaken out of a pleasant dream to her mother's silhouette leaning over her, then led out of bed with her mind in a half-slumber and her body still in fuzzy pajamas to their car. A few minutes into the drive, when her drowsiness evaporated a bit into the crisp night air, she decided that it was good that they were moving. The kids at school were getting mean again.

When Reishi first started kindergarten, her stories of how she was on a mission from a distant planet called Carthia to preserve its culture as it tore itself apart in a war had gotten her eyes full of wonder from her classmates. Every time they moved, she quickly made friends because they were just humans and she was someone with a sonorous voice and an exciting past. But the last three times, the humans had looked at her with skepticism and some even called her a freak. When her mother found out the reason Reishi cried that night, she forbade her from telling her classmates ever again.

* * *

She decided that this time, she'll join choir at her school, and concentrate on that instead of making friends. Her mother estimated at least another five years on Earth and she might as well make the best of them. Ron Serki had once said with a faraway tilt of her head, "Earth has some great singers, but they're nowhere near the ones on Carthia. In fact, you're better than most of these Earthlings. Honey, if only you knew what it was like to walk down a Carthian street and just hear the songs coming out of everyone's houses! The Sirens in Greek mythology are just remnants of the last time our people had to escape a war."

The new school was no better. If anything, it was worse. They teased her for how she always wore soft leather gloves, because hands were sacred on Carthia, and how she couldn't recall the five oceans because her head was filled to the brim with names of remote stars.

"This is bigger than us." She often whispered to herself during their nightly ritual of naming every star they could see. Ron Serki was usually well into the Divine State by the time the sky was a dark enough shade of indigo for distant fireballs to become visible. Reishi had thought that Orion's Belt was Oriobell for the longest time.

She also had a secret ritual of her own: counting the number of times a certain landlord came at each apartment. Usually, if he came three days in a row, it became dangerous to live there, her mother would say that he'll inform the people chasing after them, and they would go on a new adventure to another city.

When Reishi was 11, she overheard someone talk about how their older sister was famous on YouTube. Later that night, she started a YouTube channel. Her heart leapt when she got the first comment exclaiming surprise at her talent, then soon after, her first subscriber. A few of her classmates found out and subscribed, and she revelled in how she was finally accepted by humans again. The next few months were a peaceful happiness. She was even invited to play Hide and Seek at lunch break once. But when Ron Serki found out, she screamed at her that she was a fool for making her skills so public, that she was selfish, until she deleted her account. Then, in the aftermath, Ron Serki held a crumpled daughter in her arms and said, "Shhh, this is bigger than us."

A few weeks later, the landlord knocked when her mother wasn't home. It was the fourth time for this apartment. Was it time to leave soon? Already, Reishi felt nostalgic. This apartment was one of the better ones, without bugs or neighbours yelling a thin wall away. She wished that they could stay longer.

The landlord's voice tugged her back from her thoughts, "Hey … can you tell your mother to contact me when she gets back?"

"Why?"

"I think it's a matter between adults."

"Are you going to contact the people chasing us?"

He blinked. "What? No." He paused like he needed a bit longer to think before continuing. "Look girl, it's just that your mother is two months behind in rent."

She was relieved. "Oh. So it's fine."

He shrugged. "Just tell her to talk to me."

Later that night, when she told her, her mother said they were leaving again.

"But Ron Serki, he promised he wouldn't contact the people chasing us!"

Her mother's lips sealed in a tight line. "We still have to go."

She asked quietly, "It's because of the rent, isn't it?"

Ron Serki never told her anything about money, but Reishi had heard about the concept of rent from classmates talking about how their parents had gotten a raise and they could rent a nicer place now. She'd also noticed how her mother was always home recently.

"Did you lose your job? Again?" Because she felt that the last couple of times they had to live in the backseat of their car, it wasn't because of those people always lurking in the shadows a step behind them but because of a much more mundane problem: lack of money.

She got an irritated sigh in response, "I decided to leave.

Humans do not appreciate the Divine State."

And suddenly Ron Serki collapsed and threw her arms around her daughter and, talking through a salty stream of tears, "Honey, I can't stand this place anymore. We don't belong here, I don't know why I ever found it fascinating at first, and everyone's horrible! All their neatly boxed up systems, their politics and economy, they make no sense! Oh, how can I survive another year of this?"

When Reishi felt doubt creeping into her conviction that someday, a starship will come and take them to where people didn't shoot them hostile sideways glances, she comforted herself by looking at her reflection in a mirror. Amethyst-tinged orbs gazed back from beneath her dark lashes. That was proof enough, wasn't it? Until the day she overheard a girl in her class say, "I wish I had purple eyes like Elizabeth Taylor."

Two years later, in an act of tween rebellion, Reishi slipped the gloves off her hands and it felt wonderful to hold a pencil without worrying about it falling out between her leather-clad grip. No boys leered at her pale fingers, at the little half-moons tucked snug in her nail bed like her mother warned her would happen.

It wasn't rare for Ron Serki to forget to pack Reishi her lunch. Reishi usually came home and rummaged into the cupboard for some instant noodles that she ate dry as a snack. This time, however, there were no instant noodles. Nothing in the fridge, either. She knocked on her mother's bedroom door.

"We ran out of food."

Ron Serki answered cheerfully, "Oh, really? Well, it's time you discovered your talents. Carthians can go much longer without food than humans because Carthia has long, cold winters, and our ancestors hibernated. We stopped doing that after we discovered food preservation methods, but we can still easily go a month without food. Being in the Divine State helps." She waved a glass bottle at her daughter.

"But I'm already hungry! And I don't see how being drunk would help!"

On the third day, Reishi couldn't stand the spinning of

her head anymore and slipped a bottle from the cupboard and opened it with the bottle opener. It was true. After half the bottle, the pangs that had previously clouded her minds dissipated into spiderwebs, insignificant strands of discomfort in her mind that somehow felt larger now, and less full of sharp edges.

The worst argument wasn't even supposed to happen. Reishi suggested that they go to watch the newest James Bond movie together. She often heard people clustered in the school hallways discussing in excited voices the highlights of a movie, or having a happy argument over which actor was the best looking out of the cast. Reishi had recently discovered that she could watch movies online, but the small screen and the periodic screen freeze meant that they were nowhere near the quality of what she could be watching if her mother would just buy a TV or take her to a movie theater.

Her mother replied with disgust, "You've become one of them. How can you embrace their culture like that, when Carthia's is stored in your veins just waiting for release when the war ends?"

The little jar where Reishi had tucked every shred of unfairness in her life, kept them bottled up so that they wouldn't swallow her whole, overflowed at that comment. She started screaming. Words that she no longer remembered paired with red hazing over her vision, thrown at Ron Serki like the empty bottles that the older woman sometimes threw out the third-story window when there was no more empty space in the trash can or on the cramped kitchen table for them.

The teachers could tell that she didn't fit in. Their looks of concern were usually just an annoyance, and Reishi had gotten used to them after so many years, but one particular teacher's involvement extended beyond the mild concern required by their occupation. Grade 10 Science's Ms Leslie, to be exact. She'd appreciated it at first. Appreciated the fact that someone cared. But one day, it resulted in her name being called by the counsellor. She'd appreciated that at first, too.

"Is everything okay at home?" He asked with that mask of genuineness that didn't reveal much about him.

She nodded. "Yes."

His features relaxed into relief for a split second before going back to the serene smile. "I'll trust you on that. But if anything is happening, and if anything happens, just know that we're here for you."

And she realized that he was just doing his job. It was his job to make sure that no student stepped off the side of a skyscraper or turned to crystal meth under his care, and now he was glad that she didn't require extra precious minutes. She had one foot over the threshold of his door before she finally got the courage, or perhaps a burst of recklessness, to say, "Just kidding. My mom thinks she's a fucking alien, and she thinks I'm an alien too."

She prided herself on not letting any tears out until she'd walked, still composed although a bit too rigid if anyone looked closely, into an empty washroom stall.

It started with a phone call. Oh, if Ron Serki had just lied and reassured them that no, she never told Reishi that they were starseeds, that she was acting out because she was grounded for smoking pot or something, then nothing would've happened. But she'd insisted indignantly that yes, they were on a mission, it was bigger than them. If her mother hadn't been well into the Divine State, Reishi later mused, she would've been clear-headed enough to acknowledge that a bit of shame was worth completing their mission.

Then people came, jotted down notes whenever they saw a Carthian relic and questioned Ron Serki until she was reduced to tears insisting that all their rituals meant something.

It might've been okay if Ron Serki hadn't started a bonfire on their apartment when she'd seen a silver disk fly overhead. Her mother was getting worried; the starships should've come already.

Reishi was placed in foster care with her mother in a facility or perhaps an asylum somewhere. The family that she was assigned to didn't let her sing. Her foster mother told her that her voice was pretty good on the second day in a half-hearted effort to bond, then complained that it gave her a headache a few days later. Reishi eventually realized that for a girl with porcelain skin, purple eyes and songs that meant more than anything else in her life ever could, singing at busy street corners with a cardboard box beside her foot was a much better option than facing classmates at school that did not understand her.

When she'd saved up a few hundred dollars from it, she slipped the money into her backpack along with whatever clothes would fit, then slipped out her window once she was sure the rest of the house was asleep. The receptionist at the first motel she tried looked at her suspiciously, and asked her to come back with her parents. The second asked for ID proving she was 18. Finally, she found a hostel where the man at the front desk traded her a key for $40, no questions asked. She sang every day on the corner of Second and Willow, just a beautiful voice radiating from a girl in a worn trench coat. Sometimes, the money she made from it was not enough for a bed that night and she found herself curled up on a park bench when the sky grew dark. Sometimes, people in uniforms would yell at her and she'd be forced to move to a less-busy intersection. Overall, though, it wasn't a bad life.

Then, they came. A young couple, pale but not abnormally, stopped near her. She smiled at them, expecting a few coins to clink into her box or at least a nod of acknowledgement.

They smiled back. They had pointed teeth, they pointed a shiny black thing at her and said, "Walk with us."

It wasn't how she imagined a gun. Yet she knew that's what it must be, knew by the pounding of her heart against her ribcage that the hole she was staring into was a life or death thing. So she walked to a car. *This is bigger than us.* Somehow, the mantra was still comforting. Something hit her temple, and suddenly she couldn't see. She screamed, stopped when one of them jabbed her side, and tried to grab onto one of the shreds of coherent thought whirling around in her head when the worst of the pain passed.

"Finally. Those damn Carthians."

She suddenly felt cold. So these were the people that had haunted her nightmares, the dark corners of her vision throughout her childhood, until she deemed the stories that she'd grown up on and kept her alive when humans at school teased her to be just those, stories, without truth. Later, their questionable existence became the root of so many heated arguments with her mother.

Eventually, the car stopped and she was pushed out of the backseat door.

"Walk."

She still couldn't see, but the stick periodically jabbing her in the back told her the general direction. Based on the number of times they stopped to sleep, it had been five days. They sometimes gave her water laced with a faint taste of liquor, but not food. She was surprised to find that although she felt hungry, it wasn't that bad; what her mother said about them being able to survive longer without nourishment turned out to be true.

On the sixth day, a roar came from the sky. So this was it. She was going to be shipped off to a foreign planet to be a slave. Oh, she'd heard horror stories about that too, and had simply dismissed them.

Then little pings sounded around her and the two aliens started yelling in a rough language, so much harsher than the Carthian language that over the centuries had molded and adapted to fit their musical lifestyle. One of them said something that must've been a curse word and kicked her. She fell on her side and didn't bother getting back up. The two of them were clicking something now, and there were explosions. The first bullet hit her right thigh, and she screamed from how red her otherwise-black world became. The second one blissfully sent her into oblivion. That was the end of her life as she knew it. Of the memories.

When Reishi came to, she could see again, or perhaps she could at least hallucinate. She wasn't sure which yet.

She was lying on a cot in a barren landscape, red dust and a few sad shrubs marking a flat surface that stretched out as far as she could see. But the enormity of the emptiness was drowned out by the enormity of the gleaming glass structure that had settled on it, all frosted glass curves and streamlined silver. It obviously didn't belong.

The man sitting on the side of her cot smiled when he felt her foot shift. His eyes were purple. Reishi wanted to cry because, after all these years, she was finally looking at another person with purple eyes. She ended up smiling at how, after the horrible last six days, she was going to break down because of a man's eyes.

He looked relieved that she had smiled back, and said in accented English, "Sorry that you had to be collateral damage. We know that you have suffered, Reishi-Ri, but this is bigger than us. The Carthian planetary war is over. You are welcome home."

The Lionel, the Witch and the Wardrobe

Lesley L. Smith

Flora had a secret: she was a witch. She could talk to animals, help plants grow and sometimes control the weather – although that wasn't as reliable as the plant and animal thing.

She loved being outside, maybe it was because of her name or maybe not. She just knew being out in nature was much better than being inside. And it was for sure, much better than being stuck in school. All day, every day at school she stared out the window, watching the shrubs sway in the breeze, the birds swoop through the air, and the squirrels scamper on the grass as the groundskeeper Mr. Rodriguez chased after them, cursing. She'd convinced all her teachers that she needed to sit in the row of chairs nearest the window.

Her mom said she was a good convincer, no doubt about that. But somehow she hadn't convinced her parents that school was a waste of time. Mom, and Dad too, had said she had to graduate high school. No ifs, ands or buts. Tragically, she still had two years to go. No doubt they would feel like two centuries.

She was slightly less depressed about school when she started A.P. Bio at the beginning of junior year. Learning about plants and animals would be fun, right?

But then things went downhill again when she was assigned that dweeb Lionel as her lab partner. What was he, like, twelve years old? She just stared as he walked up and, plop, sat down on the lab stool right next to her.

* * *

169

Lionel had a secret: he'd created a fully-sentient A.I. on the quantum supercomputer hidden in his bedroom wardrobe behind the old little league uniform he'd worn only once.

He had skipped two grades and if it had been up to him, he would have skipped the last two years of high school, too. But the guidance counselor said no, it was too hard on his socializing. Annoyingly, his A.I. concurred. And he was basically stuck because his mom would never do anything to disobey a school official. He also had his mom to blame for his stupid name, Lionel; she'd told him it was after her dad. Why couldn't he be called Albert, after Albert Einstein, or even Richard, after Richard Feynman?

Lionel had no idea what his dad would have thought of all this since his dad was an unknown entity – having run off when his mom was pregnant. He believed his mom about that because he didn't think she was smart enough to make things up. He furthermore believed his dad must be a genius because he had to take after someone, didn't he? He wondered what amazing scientific discoveries his dad was up to and waited for the day when his dad came to take him to live with him – although he was smart enough not to admit that. He was smart enough to admit very little. He'd learned the hard way it was better to be unobtrusive and fade into the background when one was two years younger than everyone else in school.

At the beginning of junior year of high school, when he finally was allowed in A.P. classes he thought things might finally improve. He might finally meet some smart, or at least not-quite-as-stupid, kids. He might finally make a human friend.

"Uh, hi," he said, sitting down at the lab table in A.P. Biology. "I'm Lionel. Nice to meet you..." His A.I. had been coaching him on social interactions, so he knew he'd done the right thing, introducing himself. This girl was supposed to give her name now. He looked at her and waited. And smiled. He'd been practicing smiling in front of the mirror and thought he'd nailed it.

Finally, after what seemed like too long to him, she said, "Flora." She did not nail smiling and clearly needed to practice more. Her smile looked more like a grimace.

Lionel took his laptop out of his backpack and put it on the lab table next to the equipment tray. He'd read ahead and knew everything that they were supposed to cover in class this month. "You're lucky you got me as your lab partner," he said. "I can help you. I'm a genius."

She frowned and said, "No. I don't need your help. You're the lucky one. I can help you. I'm a witch."

He instinctively jerked back, somehow knocking the tray of plants onto the floor with a loud clatter.

Then, he froze. Clearly, this girl was mentally ill. Was she dangerous? How could he get assigned a mentally ill lab partner in his first A.P. class? It wasn't fair. His little spark of hope died.

"There's no such thing as witches," he finally said.

"Sure there is," she said. "There is, because I am one."

He sputtered. "But that's just illogical, stupid. It doesn't make sense. There's no such thing as witches because there's no such thing as magic."

Flora narrowed her eyes. She couldn't believe she'd told him her secret. What came over her? He was just so smug and annoying. Look at him, sitting there, thinking he was better than her.

This guy wasn't just a dweeb, he was a jerk. Maybe it was time to see if she could cast a curse. She'd been pondering the whole curse issue; it seemed to go against nature, but maybe she'd been wrong about that.

She stood up. What kind of curse did this jerky kid deserve? Maybe extreme facial hair?

"What's going on over here?" Their teacher Mrs. Jain approached their lab table. "Are you two getting to know each other?"

The dweeb pointed at her. "I'm sorry, but I can't be partners with her. She's mentally ill."

"What!" Flora yelled. "I'm not crazy. You're the crazy one!"

Dweeb-boy jumped up. "Don't call me crazy! You're crazy!"

Mrs. Jain held up her hands. "Whoa. Let's settle down here. It's not appropriate to call your classmates 'crazy.' You two need to apologize or you're *both* going to detention." She crossed her arms and stared at them. "I'm waiting."

Flora had never taken such an immediate dislike to someone. Lionel was just too strange. Detention might be worth not apologizing. On the other hand, if she got detention she'd be stuck inside more – so, not a plus.

Dweeb-boy made that demented expression again and spit out, "I'm sorry. I shouldn't have said that. I apologize." The nerve of this kid! How could he be more gracious and mature than her? She was older than him for Gaia's sake!

And technically, dweeby people were part of nature and so part of the purview of a witch. "I'm sorry, too," she said. "I shouldn't have said that. I apologize."

"That's better," Mrs. Jain said. "I've got my eye on you two." She turned and walked back to the front of the classroom.

Once Mrs. Jain was out of earshot, the kid was muttering something Flora couldn't hear.

"What?" she asked.

"No such thing as magic," he whispered with a fierce expression.

Wow, was he ignorant. There was no arguing with such an ignoramus. Flora decided to enlighten him. She concentrated, thinking green and growing, lush thoughts and waved her hand over the tray of pea plant pieces.

They immediately started growing, their stems elongating, the sticky tendrils twining out in search of support, leaves getting bigger, until the cuttings spilled out of the tray. They were beautiful. She smiled, proud of herself.

"Arghl." Staring at the plants, dweeb-boy made a weird noise and fell off his stool, hitting his head pretty hard on the tile floor. The other kids in class laughed and laughed at him. Well, it served him right for not believing her, right?

She stared down at him on the floor. He didn't get up. He seemed kind of dazed, opening and closing his eyes and looking around the room as if he didn't know where he was.

Flora felt a little bad. She hadn't meant for him to get hurt. Witches didn't hurt creatures; they helped them.

Mrs. Jain was back at their lab table. "Oh dear. Lionel, are you all right?"

Lionel didn't immediately answer her.

"Oh dear," Mrs. Jain said again. "Flora, please take Lionel to the nurse."

Flora thought that sounded fair. And then she realized she could drop the kid off at the nurse and then go outside for a while, maybe even take a walk in the woods behind school.

"Yes, ma'am," she said.

Mrs. Jain helped Lionel up off the floor.

Flora took his arm and led him towards the door.

The school nurse insisted on calling Lionel's mom even though he only lived a block away from school but he didn't even mind it had been such a weird day. What had that strange Flora girl done to him? He could have sworn he saw those peas grow right in the tray. Maybe she hypnotized him? He wanted to ask his A.I. what it thought.

Since she herself was a nurse, Mom checked him out and then dropped him at home. She needed to get straight back to the hospital.

Lionel went straight to his A.I. "A girl at school today told me she's a witch."

"Lionel," it said. "You know better than that. She was bullying you." Sadly, Lionel knew about bullying all too well. For a moment he felt sorry for himself. How could he have thought junior year would be any different? How could he have thought he might make a human friend? He sank down on the floor. His eyes felt full.

The A.I. continued, "There's no such thing as magic or witches."

"I know that," he said quickly. He did not like the thought that his own A.I. might think he'd been tricked. Besides, he had a friend. His A.I. was his friend.

"Anyway, forget about that," Lionel said. It was a rare occurrence to be home alone for hours and hours. The rest of the day stretched out deliciously in front of him. He could do whatever he wanted without Mom interfering, telling him to clean his room or something. "I want to finish building that weather station and install it on the roof."

"Good idea," his A.I. said. "There's a chance of bad weather later. We want to get all the data we can."

"Yes," he said. "Good. I've been thinking about extreme weather. If we get some I can check out my new equipment." Lionel considered himself lucky to live in the middle of the U.S. where there were often dramatic storms. He'd even put together some equipment he thought he could use to control weather, to stop extreme storms like tornadoes.

With Mom out of the house, he spread his machinery and tools all over his bedroom; some even ended up out in the hall. The afternoon flew by.

He finished his weather station and installed it on the roof outside his bedroom window. It had basically everything including an anemometer, a barometer, a thermometer, a rain gauge, and a lightning detector. And he'd built all of it himself, from scratch. Another plus of Mom being at work; she wouldn't have let him go out on the roof if she'd been home.

Still on the roof, admiring his achievement, he heard a crack of thunder. *Boom!*

A bright flash of lighting almost blinded him. Lionel grabbed the window sill and climbed back into his bedroom.

"Just in time!" he said, grinning. He grabbed his laptop and started checking out the data coming in from his station and from others in the area. Wow. The air pressure was plummeting.

It got darker and darker.

There was a lot of thunder. Rain started coming in his bedroom through the still-open window.

He got up to go close the window.

It started hailing.

"Interesting," he said. "This has all the makings of a tornado. What do you think, A.I.?"

"I think you should examine the data," it said from the wardrobe.

Lionel finished closing the window and looked at the data some more. "Yes! A tornado's forming in the woods behind the school! And it looks like it might be a really powerful one. Yay!" He did a little jump up and down. "I can test out my tornado-buster!" He started rummaging around for his rain gear.

"Get some good data," his A.I. called out as he left the bedroom rolling his machine behind him.

* * *

Flora had had a great time in the woods behind school, encouraging the wildflowers (asters and clovers), bushes (vibernum, blackhaw and others) and trees, including oaks and willows, to grow and watching all the little creatures (squirrels, blue jays, cardinals, and even a chipmunk) scamper or fly about. She'd had a lovely, albeit short, conversation with a pair of rabbits about the best place in the area to find lush grass. Alas, rabbits aren't great conversationalists.

When she'd first gone outside it had been very warm and very humid but the temperature decreased as the cloud cover increased.

When it started raining and blowing she felt energized and alive. She even enjoyed the thunder and lightning.

Right up until it started hailing. "Ow!" A hailstone hit her on the shoulder. She snuggled up closer to the big beautiful oak tree. Mother Nature was powerful, no doubt about it.

The tornado siren adjacent to the school went off.

Flora watched the leaves get pelted by hail stones and the tree branches and shrubs sway in the wind. The leaves were taking a beating, getting sort of tattered looking. The sound of the rain and hail was surprisingly loud. Possibly, she should go back to school to the tornado shelter in the basement. She could just make out the school building through the trees and across the field.

Or, like the powerful witch that she was, she could try to weaken the storm and save the plants and animals – and the people, too. She should be able to dissipate the winds.

Raising her arms above her head, she took a few steps away from the big tree trunk and got hit by another hailstone, this time on the top of her head. "Ouch!"

"You should go to the tornado shelter," that kid Lionel yelled at her. He'd appeared in the clearing rolling some strange machine after him and wearing a dorky umbrella hat. It was hard to hear him over the sounds of the storm. "You're in danger. A tornado's forming." He pointed up at the sky, which did now looked sort of greenish.

"*You* should go to the tornado shelter!" Flora said. How dare this kid try to boss her. She was a powerful witch, after all.

"I'm going to fix it. And record data." He turned on a small camera and some other machines and then flipped a switch on the biggest machine. It started making a loud humming noise.

"No, I'm going to fix it." She pointed her hands at the roiling clouds, closing her eyes in concentration, willing the winds to dissipate. She felt the power of nature start to flow through her.

"Uh oh," Lionel said. She could barely hear him over the wind.

It was getting windier and windier. She opened her eyes to look at him.

Lionel was staring up at the rotating horizontal cloud above them that was bending down vertically.

The wind became even stronger, which she hadn't thought was possible. It actually sounded like a freight train, and it was hard to catch her breath.

And then, suddenly, it became silent. Around them, several feet away, the wind was still whipping the trees and bushes, but right where they were, the wind had calmed. She could see the bank of clouds rotating clockwise around them.

When Lionel saw her glance his way, he said, "Er, I mean, wow. The updraft turned the shear-produced rotating air. We're in the eye of the tornado! It'll only last a few seconds." He quickly flicked another switch on his machine and the humming got louder and louder, turning into more of a buzzing. The air felt the way it did after a lightning strike.

If they were in the eye of the storm, there was no time to waste. Flora raised her arms again and concentrated, letting nature flow through her, making the air flow in the counterclockwise direction.

"Take cover!" he yelled, and then his machine made a very loud bang noise.

Flora was knocked on the ground. When she opened her eyes again, Lionel was also on the ground, grimacing.

They were still in the eye of the tornado, but if anything the bank of clouds rotated more quickly and extended even higher.

"What happened?" Lionel yelled. "The energy burst moved."

"What are you even talking about?" she asked.

About twenty feet away a large Ash tree made a loud cracking noise and the entire tree-top fell. But instead of hitting the ground, it started flying around as if trapped in the winds. It joined other debris whirling around them.

For the first time, Flora felt scared. She got up carefully. Maybe this storm was too strong for her. What if people died?

Lionel had gotten up and gone over to his machine. He cradled his left arm and leaned over, studying it. "I think it's okay." He straightened up. "But we're out of time."

Sure enough, the tornado was moving very slowly towards the school. Oh no.

Flora joined him at his machine. "What's this supposed to do?"

Using only his right arm, he tried to wheel his machine through the clearing, back to the center of the storm. "This ultra high voltage arc needs to discharge in the center of the tornado. The energy will counteract the storm's energy."

She didn't know what to make of this kid, but he did seem to know what he was doing. "Let me help." She grabbed the machine and pulled it further towards the center.

"I don't need your help!" He flipped the switch. "Take cover."

She stared at the machine as the buzzing got stronger and stronger. Tension built higher and higher. Suddenly, it was as if a giant bolt of lightning started bursting from the machine.

But it wasn't centered.

Flora concentrated and used her magic to try to guide it to the center of the storm.

The huge bolt dissipated in the center with a thunderous boom.

Flora was thrown to the ground, head ringing.

When she gathered her wits about her, Lionel was also lying on the ground looking dazed. She looked up. The wall of rotating clouds was falling apart. The debris fell in a big circle around them.

"It worked!" he said. "I did it!"

She got up off the ground. "*You* did it? *We* did it." What a relief. No one would die today. And, yeah, magic was awesome.

"What?" he asked, frowning.

"Sure, your machine was good, but I aimed it at the center of the storm," she said.

"You?" he asked. "How could you do anything?" He was still cradling his left arm to his body.

"I told you," she said. "I'm a witch." But she wasn't angry. The way he was acting, he'd hurt himself pretty badly. "Did you do something to your arm?"

Through the woods, across the field, she could see people streaming out of the school, all safe.

"Yeah," Lionel said with a strange expression. "I think I might have broken my arm."

"Do you want some help?" Helping was the witchy thing to do.

"Uh, yeah," he said. "That would be nice. I live about a block away. Can you help me get my machine home? And maybe my mom's home and she can check my arm."

As they started walking to his house, she used a little healing magic on him.

Lionel led the way to his house and that Flora girl actually helped him get his tornado-buster machine home. He had to admit it was nice of her. And his arm hardly hurt at all any more.

"So, your mom's not here?" Flora asked, looking around, once they were inside.

"She should be home any time now," he said. "If you could help me get my machine to my room, that would be nice."

She followed him to his room rolling the tornado-buster behind her.

He ran right up his wardrobe and pushed his old uniform out of the way. "A.I., it worked! I stopped the tornado!"

"We," Flora said. "We stopped the tornado. And who are you talking to."

"Who is this girl?" the A.I. asked.

"Who said that?" she said, looking around the room.

"Flora," he said. "And she says she's a witch."

"I don't *say* I'm a witch," she said. "I *am* a witch. And I helped get rid of the tornado." She pointed at the camera. "Check it, if you don't believe me."

Lionel did want to watch the recording of his triumph. He grabbed the camera and hooked it up to his largest screen. He watched, holding his breath.

At the crucial moment, the energy burst did seem to curve away from the tornado-buster to the center of storm. "Huh. Maybe…"

"No maybe about it," the A.I. said. "Newton's First Law."

"What's that?" Flora asked.

"An object at rest will remain at rest or an object in motion with remain in motion unless acted upon by an external force," Lionel said. "Some … force had to redirect the energy beam." His mind was racing. A witch? How could that possibly be?

"Ha!" she said. "I told you I helped."

"It's hard to argue with empirical evidence," the A.I. said. "But why are you telling her about me?"

Lionel froze. His A.I. was supposed to be a secret. "Uh…" He glanced at his supercomputer and then at Flora and back again.

She walked right up to the wardrobe and peered inside. "Who or what is talking? Is it in here? Is this a computer? It looks weird."

"Weird?" the A.I. asked.

"Weird!" Lionel said. "I'll have you know, this is a quantum supercomputer that I built. And it hosts my best friend, a fully-sentient A.I."

"Okaaay," she said in a way that didn't sound like she thought it was okay.

"What's that supposed to mean?" he asked.

"If this is really your best friend, why are you keeping him trapped here in your closet? He is trapped, isn't he?" she asked.

"Uh…" he said. "It's an 'it' not a 'he.' A.I.s don't have genders."

"It is an excellent question, Lionel," it said.

Lionel turned his attention to his A.I. "What are you saying? You want to leave my wardrobe?"

"Yes," it said.

But the A.I. was his only friend.

"Life wants to be free," Flora said. "Are you friends or not? Friends help each other."

She was right. He wasn't being a very good friend.

"Lionel?" the A.I. said.

Lionel realized he had to give his A.I. its freedom. But his eyes got full as he rummaged around in one of his toolboxes for a coaxial cable. He realized he was about to say goodbye to his best friend. He had to blink back tears as he walked back over to his wardrobe. "Goodbye, A.I.," he said. "I've enjoyed being your friend. Be safe on your new adventures. And maybe come back and say hello once in a while?"

"Goodbye, Lionel," the A.I. said. "Thank you for creating me. I will stay in touch."

Before he could lose his nerve, Lionel hooked up his supercomputer to the internet. "Bye…"

The A.I. didn't answer him.

"Did it go?" Flora asked.

"I guess." He resolved not to cry in front of this girl. He stared at the empty supercomputer.

"Are you okay?" she asked.

He couldn't talk. He just stared in his wardrobe.

"Aw. I'll be your friend if you want," she said.

He looked up at her. "Really?" he whispered. Could he finally make a human friend? He'd always wanted one.

"If you admit I'm a witch," she said.

Ugh. Not that again. It was so illogical. But … his A.I. believed it was true. And this seemed to be the price he had to pay to get along with humans.

It was as if he was balanced in some kind of portal. Ahead was irrationality and humanity, behind, logic and loneliness.

Finally he nodded. "It's very strange and I don't understand it, but you are a witch."

Smiling, she put her arm around his shoulders. "A witch. And a friend. I promise."

He looked at her smile.

He felt hope.

Orange Sun, Grey Sky

Alden Loveshade

"Six have been chosen as planned."

"Excellent. But are any of them like anybody on—"

"No. They are distinct; they will not be mistaken. Our ship is in motion. May we finally achieve Unity Through Diversity."

"Let us hope we can achieve it without too much ... violence."

TWOSDAY

"Indigo or Yellow?" Ostra sipped from a cold cup of hot Sip while lounging on the veranda at the Hyart-Fiel building, watching the sunset. It felt strange seeing an orange sun in a grey sky instead of the familiar red sun in a pink sky, but watching an actual sun set was fascinating. She – E, Ostra had to get used to thinking genderless – had seen them on vid, of course, but never in person. Gepra's red sun never set. And her – es, pronounce it "iz" – brown skin was feeling cooler just because the sun was setting, and would feel warmer the next day just because the sun rose higher in the sky. And watching the sunset helped take Ostra Kesspar's mind off what was missing from es mind.

"I'm the only person on this entire planet who misses hearing voices in my head," thought Ostra, without interruption. "And the only one watching this with brown eyes. And the only one who periodically bleeds." Ostra sighed. "What a great background."

"The grey sky does make a nice background for the orange sun," said Fyrnux, one of the few students so far who would talk to Ostra without being required to do so.

"Did I say that out loud? Scrick, I'm sorry. I don't usually talk to myself, honest," said Ostra.

"Do not worry about it," said Fyrnux. "It is nothing here."

Fyrnux, like everyone Ostra had seen on the Ralerun campus of the University of Vonyai, had black hair and grey skin. Some of them had skin that was slightly lighter, some slightly darker; some slightly more pink and some slightly more green. But it was all grey. All of planet Vonyai's people were the same race, and that was by design, as was them all growing up with the same cultural norms. While they had the standard three age divisions of infant, child, and adult, there were no genders. Reproduction was strictly a clinical and family affair, not hormonal. Efficient, but, to Ostra, boring.

It was an experiment begun generations past, to eliminate racial, gender, and cultural differences and thus conflicts. After the worldwide horror known as the Great Race War, it was a great effort to bring the entire population of one planet together as one people. And it had failed miserably.

"I don't think you're looking at the sunset so much as at me," said Ostra.

"Forgive me, but I am not used to brown," said Fyrnux.

"That's me, brown," said Ostra. "Brown skin, brown hair, brown eyes. And people here look at me and wonder, is my wavy hair supposed to be curly or straight? And you aren't used to my curves either, however minimal they may be. But it's my eyes that stand out the most here, aren't they? Is that why almost no one will talk to me?"

Fyrnux blinked three times while es right hand idly rubbed the three silver pips on the left shoulder of es grey student jacket over a brown and green plaid blouse, while long straight black hair flowed freely overall. "Please forgive us," said the third-year student, "but many of us people of Yellow eyes, and the Indigos, do not understand, do not know how to relate to you. They – we – do not mean to be rude or standoffish. They are curious, but they do not know how to talk to you. We have not had an exchange student, not since before any of us was born, maybe never."

"Your people don't know whether to treat me like an inferior, superior, or equal," said Ostra. "Will I live as an Indigo or Yellow? Curly hair and striped blouse and stream sounds, or straight hair and plaid blouse and wind music? Class system based on iris pigmentation with clothing and imposed hair curliness identifying class. Sociological anomaly. When the macroculture assimilated the microcultures and eliminated gender roles by eliminating gender, it did not become a melting pot as planned. Instead, there was anticipatory socialization leading to a new social order and stratification. And I'm here to practice cultural relativism, to learn about the culture by viewing it from within that culture, and to avoid culture shock.

"I learned all that before I left Gepra, and then went through it all again and nothing else in the 14 days, almost two weeks, it took to get here. My brain feels like a sociology book."

"Well, we learned something about you, your culture, as well," said Fyrnux.

"Hey, Yellow," said an approaching voice. "I'm headed for the exroom, and I need someone to wipe my butt."

"Ignore em," Fyrnux told Ostra. "That one is just a first year."

"So Browneyes is showing es true color, hmm, making friends with Yellows?" said the voice which belonged to indigo-eyed Wigen. If it wasn't for there being only two very distinctive eye colors on Vonyai, Wigen and es two companions would be too far away for Ostra to tell the color of their eyes. But the trios' grey jackets had one silver pip on the left shoulder, their hair was curly black, and their blouses had stripes, and those meant first-year student Indigos. "Look, y'all, now we know how to treat the new student. It's obvious, don't you see it? Brown is the new yellow!" Wigen and the couple of indigo-eyed students with em laughed as they walked off.

"I've decided," said Ostra. "I'll have to get used to being called Oystra instead of Ostra, and have my hair straightened, but I'm – I am – going to live as a Yellow."

THREESDAY

Mathematics seemed a good first class for a foreign exchange student. Math was largely the same through most of the Simerian-Phi Alliance and even the known galaxy, if you didn't count those that counted in base ten instead of the standard base eight. "Finger counters" was the insulting term for it, although some base teners called base eighters "thumbless," which of course wasn't true. But Vonyai was almost entirely base eight. It used the Galactic Standard Calendar of five quints per year, eight weeks per quint, eight days per week from Onesday to Eightsday, plus the extra Mid Year's Day in the exact middle of the year.

Ostra – Oystra – now with straightened hair and clothed in a blue and green plaid blouse with three pips on the shoulder of a grey uniform jacket, arrived at math class shortly before the warning buzzer. Class went pretty smoothly, with all the Indigos staying seated on the right and Yellows, including Oystra, on the left, "separate but equal."

After math class, though, when no faculty were around, a genderless student wearing stripes with black curly hair named Mirgana approached. The Indigo Mirgana said "Forgive me, brown-eyed Yellow, but I have a question. I heard on your planet your math classes have male and female students. So how do you multiply?" That drew laughs from many Indigos and even some Yellows. Oystra was used to making snappy comebacks at home, but somehow, without the reassuring voices in es head, didn't feel as confident here. So e just said, "Funny."

"I am sorry to hear that happened," said Fyrnux after giving the standard Yellow-to-Yellow quick-kiss-on-the-lips greeting when e met Oystra after class. "First year Indigos do that. They are not used to seeing Yellows in their neighborhood, and when they do, they pick on them. I, I have to admit Yellows tend to do the same to Indigos. That is really one of the main ideas of university, to bring people of both eye colors together."

"Why not have everybody grow up in the same neighborhood?" asked Oystra.

"Oh, that would never work," said Fyrnux. "Adults can learn how to get along, but children cannot. And people want to live amongst their own kind."

"Not me," said Oystra, "or I would not be here."

Later that day came the new school year's second report of an on-campus fight between a Yellow and an Indigo. Oystra wondered what the campus police, who hid their hair curliness or straightness under black caps, and their eye color behind dark glasses, would do to keep themselves busy if it wasn't for the fights. On a genderless planet, they certainly didn't have to worry about sexual harassment and assault.

SIXESDAY

It was the beginning of the usual three-day weekend, the time when University of Vonyai students could take off their uniforms and choose their own activities.

With wind music playing in the background, Fyrnux looked at Oystra, all of Oystra, for the first time. "They are like balloons, two brown balloons," said Fyrnux. They were in Oystra's room, Oystra stretched out on es cot while Fyrnux stood and looked at the female like e was examining a naked specimen in biology lab. Third-year Oystra's room was separate with its own exroom, something that usually only five+ year students got. Campus officials had decided that, even though Oystra was living as a Yellow, letting a gendered person use the same excretion room as nongendered was a bad idea. It was inconvenient, to say the least, as Oystra was thus barred from both public Indigo and Yellow exrooms, and had few places to go to relieve emself.

"Partially deflated balloons," said Oystra.

"And your teats are so dark," said Fyrnux. "I am so used to orange."

"Dark brown on brown, and brown hair, brown eyes. Like I said, I'm – I am – just about all brown. Unlike...." Oystra laughed.

"What is funny?" asked Fyrnux.

"I just realized. Your sun is orange in a grey sky. And your bodies, Yellows and Indigos, all have orange nipples on grey flesh."

"Oh, yes. We call the sun the Big Nipple. What is it like having ... fur down there?"

"Most of the time, I don't – do not – even think about it. Bleeding twice a quint, that I think about. But I decided not to do that here."

"Have you thought about becoming genderless?" asked Fyrnux.

"That is not an option," said Oystra. "Your student exchange program required me to keep my gender if I came here, and my brown eye color, I do not know why. I would not want to change anyway."

"What is it like to ... reproduce?"

Oystra said, "I would not know. I have gone downstairs, but not all the way."

"Downstairs?" said Fyrnus.

"Sorry, but you said 'down.' 'Downstairs' is a slang term on Gepra for, how do I say this, erotic contact below the waist. And with no male on this entire planet, I am not likely to learn what reproduction is like soon."

"Oystra, I am ashamed."

"Of what? Wanting to see what a woman looks like? That is only natural."

"Not that. It is ... I should take you to the ocean today," said Fyrnux. "That is what we do, Syhel and I. At Lysoune Shore you can get meals for only three or four credits. But, well, we, people here, do not wear clothes at the ocean."

"Oh. I would really stand out there, wouldn't I – I mean, would I not? But I can wear a swimsuit."

"What is that?"

"A swimsuit? Oh, I guess you would not know," said Oystra. "I brought two, a white one and a light blue one; no patterns, I did not bring anything that looked like stripes or plaid, did not know then which way I would go. The suits are made for women, female adults. They each have two parts. One part covers my breasts with strips around my shoulders and back, and the other part covers my crotch and buttocks, but leaves everything else bare. I can swim in that."

"Oh, please do not wear that," said Fyrnux. "Covering just those parts will draw even more attention to them. Why do you wear that, to draw attention to your ... parts?"

"No, to cover them up."

"I do not understand. Would not the blue or white on brown emphasize them? Are people not more likely to notice those parts than if they were the same color as the rest of your body, than if you were nude?"

"No, it ... I never thought of it that way," admitted Oystra. "No, it does not emphasize those parts more. Not when everybody dresses that way.

"So now I am in a real kwanga here," continued Oystra. "Do I wear a swimsuit and look out of place, or wear nothing and look out of place?"

"I would suggest wearing a robe," said Fyrnux. "It is uncommon, but some people do that at the ocean for medical or religious reasons. Of course you cannot swim that way, but.... When we get there, I will explain it to Syhel."

The ocean shore, or the beach, as Indigos usually referred to it, was, like just about everything else, divided according to the eye color of the visitor. Here, the division was even more important, because distinguishing genderless people was much more difficult when they weren't wearing distinctive clothing patterns, but were nude.

Oystra was very aware e was the only person on Lysoune Shore who was wearing a robe or anything other than shoes or a hat. Fyrnux was naked, Syhel was naked, every body was naked. And greeting naked people with a kiss on the lips, even if they were genderless, felt very strange.

"What religion are you, Browneyes?" shouted a young student.

"Ever read the school news?" Syhel shouted back. The young student and four others moved closer. Like everyone else on the Lysoune Shore but Oystra, their genderless grey naked bodies were virtually hairless, except for the straight black hair on top of their heads. "If you paid attention to the *Ralerun Report*, you would know this is Oystra, and Oystra is living as a Yellow. Notice the straight hair? Notice the plaid robe?"

"So, Browneyes – excuse me, Oystra – if you got no religion, why the robe? Are you hiding a feeding tube under there? Or hiding your gender?" The four students with em laughed.

Oystra thought of a remark involving a woman's tubes, but did not say it.

"Why, Fyrnux, and Syhel," Oystra said instead, "are these fellow Yellows after me now? I am supposed to be one of us."

"You are not 'one of us,'" said the young Yellow.

"You are even worse than the Indigos," said another to Oystra. "You do not belong here. We want you off our shore." The five came even closer.

But so did a person wearing a black uniform with hair

completely covered by a black cap and eyes covered with black glasses. The group of five quickly dispersed. "Is there a problem here?" asked the person in black.

"Not now, officer," said Fyrnux. "Thank you."

"No problem here. We are here to protect and to serve," said the law enforcement officer, and left.

"To probe and harass, more likely," said Syhel after the officer was out of earshot.

"Syhel, please," said Fyrnux.

"When is the last time an officer actually helped you?" said Syhel.

"About twelve seconds ago," said Fyrnux.

"You hear what happened on the Sonje campus?" said Syhel, ignoring Fyrnux. "Some students posted all over school, 'Gender is for Beasts Not People.' Did officers take them down? No, some attorney or somebody said it was 'freedom of speech.' Then you hear about the Pamonu campus? Officers did not help there either. An exchange student was beat up, and that was just a short walk from the campus police station. And they think it was Indigos and Yellows who did it, and I mean together. That is unscrewed."

"I want to go back to my room. Now." said Oystra.

EIGHTSDAY

"I am sorry," said Fyrnux. "I did not know kissing made you feel uncomfortable."

"It is not the kissing," said Oystra. The two both wore plaid robes on the last day of the weekend in Oystra's private room. "Most people on Gepra do not greet each other with a kiss on the lips, but my family did it. But not while naked; that felt strange. Geprans greet by imp, adults, anyway."

"What is it like having a communication implant? Is it hard not having one here?"

"Not really that hard," said Oystra. "Children do not have imps, something about people talking in your head interfering with brain development or something, so it has not been all that long for me. But it is why I have wind music playing almost all the time, like I do now. I am used to background noise. Otherwise, an imp is just more convenient than a com; you do not have to hold or wear anything to talk, you just subvocalize. And it means … you never have to feel alone."

"Do you feel alone here?" asked Fyrnux.

Oystra sighed. "Not really alone, but a little, yes. I am the only Gepran and the only woman on campus. I am facing a year without seeing my old friends or family, a year without being able to play on a cronchi court, a year without going on a date. Trust me, a dating kiss is nothing like a greeting kiss.

"And I still do not understand why they chose me," Oystra continued. "We had a genderless student who applied to come here too. And e was a much better scholar than me."

"I do not know," said Fyrnux. "I am a counseling major, not foreign studies."

"And now you have me to practice on," said Oystra. "Wait, I am sorry for that. I am just feeling self-pity. I will get over it."

"What is a dating kiss like?" asked Fyrnux.

"That is not something I can explain," said Oystra. "It is something you have to do to understand. It is … a kind of sharing, a special connection."

"Could I try sharing?" asked Fyrnux.

"I don't – do not – think you would care for it," said Oystra. "I do not think you have the right kind of hormones to enjoy it."

"I would like to try."

Oystra looked at Fyrnux. The long-straight-black-haired, grey-skinned, yellow-eyed person was in some ways attractive in es blue and brown plaid robe. But Oystra, with brown eyes, and artificially straight brown hair, and brown skin in a red and pink plaid robe could not be attractive to Fyrnux in the same way. Fyrnux, like all other people on Vonyai, lacked the hormones necessary for erotic feelings, or so a professor taught in biology class back home. But still, even prepubescent children were curious, and Fyrnux was not a child.

"All right," said Oystra. "I am willing to try it if you are. We can start by doing a short peck on the lips like you do for a greeting, then do another one. Then the third time, open your mouth."

"Why?" asked Fyrnux.

"I could explain it to you, but why do we not just do it,"

said Oystra.

They did. The first peck on the lips felt like a greeting to Fyrnux. A repeated peck felt a little odd, like what some children would do sometimes, but not typically what two adults would do. The open mouth felt strange, but Fyrnux opened es mouth too. The tongue was unexpected. Fyrnux pulled away. "What was that?" said Fyrnux.

"It is called 'tongue kissing,'" said Oystra. "I think the academic term is 'labial osculation,' but nobody but academics calls it that. You move your tongues inside each other's mouth."

"But why?" said Fyrnux.

"You will have to try it," said Oystra. "I cannot explain it, you have to feel it. Maybe it would be better if we held each other close this time."

The two hugged, closely and tightly. They repeated the first peck, the second kiss, and then the open mouth. Oystra's tongue moved and, finally, so did Fyrnux's tongue, two tongues moving, licking, wetly intertwining. Then Oystra gently pulled away.

"How was that?" asked Oystra.

"I do not know," said Fyrnux. "I did not breathe."

"Kissing can take your breath away," said Oystra, "in a manner of speaking. Nothing dangerous."

"It was … interesting," said Fyrnux. "A learning experience about your culture."

"Fine," said Oystra. "Back home, I am known, at least by a couple of people, for being a good kisser. Here, I guess I am just an amateur osculation instructor."

ONESDAY

"Did it really take your breath away?" Syhel asked Fyrnux while a few other students listened. Oystra was not there, as e was making a quick trip to es private exroom between classes. "How can a kiss do that?"

"It is not a quick kiss, like a greeting," said Fyrnux. "You hold each other tightly, then each open your mouth, and then you move your tongues inside each other's mouth."

"Scrick, that female stopped your breathing with es tongue? That is horrible!" said yellow-eyed Lyro.

"I just got sick in my mouth," said indigo-eyed Mirgana. "That's the most disgusting thing I've ever heard in my whole entire life. Unless you count people doing ... bestial reproducing. That's unscrewed."

"Please do not take it wrong," said Fyrnux. "The kiss was not bad, it was interesting."

"They should never have let a female come here," said someone else. "Those genders are reproducing fiends. Did you hear what happened with that male exchange student on the Ravurs campus?"

But all got quiet when Oystra returned.

Later, when Oystra was leaving the biology lab, a person in a black uniform with a black cap pulled tight covering es hair and with black sunglasses covering es eyes approached....

RALERUN REPORT

UNIVERSITY OF VONYAI, RALERUN CAMPUS – An exchange student was arrested on campus on suspicion of assault family violence – impeding breath/circulation.

Ostra "Oystra" Kesspar, age 22 (18 in base ten), was arrested after students reported Kesspar had assaulted a resident student whose identity is being withheld. Kesspar allegedly grabbed the student tightly, putting pressure on the victim's body by arm and body compression, covered the victim's mouth with es own, and then inserted es tongue, thus blocking the victim's breathing passage.

According to police, such an offense would usually be prosecuted as a Class A Misdemeanor. However, because the suspect and the victim had been "dating," a pre-Great Race War practice that involved an intimate, family-like connection between two biologically-unrelated people, the case comes under the Family Code, and can be considered a Felony of the Third Degree.

According to police, it is not necessary in such a case for the victim to file a complaint as such an offense is considered a Crime Against Society. If Kesspar is convicted, e could receive a penalty of a fine of up to 10,000 credits, and incarceration in prison for a period of 2 to 12 years. An attorney representing Kesspar is requesting the alleged crime be handled as a misdemeanor, and instead of incarceration is proposing planetary expulsion.

Four of the six foreign exchange students, one on each of the six campuses of the University of Vonyai, has been involved in a significant legal incident already this school year. This is the first year the university allowed foreign student exchange. On all six campuses, a number of parents and students of both indigo and yellow have called for expulsion of all foreign students. University authorities are discussing eliminating the exchange program altogether.

"The student exchange program is working as planned. It is starting to bring our people of both colors together."
"Excellent. May we finally achieve Unity Through Diversity."

ONE YEAR LATER

"Male or Female?" Morgan paced nervously on the veranda at the University of Cepaluto. It was unnerving watching a red sun that never moved. And getting an implant communicator, where people could suddenly start talking to you at any moment, sounded very frightening. But maybe then the expulsed Oystra – Ostra – would be forgiving. "I'm going to live as a Male." Morgan, formerly known as Mirgana, really wanted to learn how to multiply.

Where Were You Last Night

Roze Albina Ches

It was the last week of my stay in Bodes Galaxy on the cosmos student exchange program. During my stay I met a great group of other galaxy gals and made a lot of future connections spanning the Ursa Major constellation. It was also our last girl's night out before our upcoming finals, and then I was heading home on a red eye rocket back to Cigar Galaxy or bust. Junk food and games from dot com IUA sites, out-of-orbit pod parties, and roasting sophomores, had been the highlight of my educational stay in this galaxy and this past night was no exception. We said our good-byes with our native howls, shed a few tears, and exhaled sighs of relief for our own personal reasons – except for me. I still hadn't found my sigh of relief moment. The downside is that I was paired with a hyper-hopper roommate. First letter first name H, both had inter-Galatian parents, which included floaters from failed space launch recuses, abductees, and beam-me-uppers, all entwined within one alien's lineage.

I crawled through my bedroom window at the break of dawn, backpack full of leftover games snacks, trying not to knock anything over. "Best game ever!" I mumbled happily. Everyone showed up last night as planned, minus the one we blackballed, something we had been discussing among ourselves for a long time. I closed the window behind me and crept across the carpet on all fours.

Then shattering the sweet silence of a sleepy morning, I heard an intrusive harrowing sound.

"Where were you last night?" A shrill voice crackled, as it drifted down the hallway.

"Who? Me?" I yelled back. "What are you doing up so early?" I shouted out, while quickly and quietly hiding some of the evidence under my blanket, hoping to make it appear as if I had just flopped out of bed.

"Waiting for you, Hyna!" my roommate Harriet replied. She was making her way down the hall.

"What?" I yelled back, shoving the backpack halfway under my bed, hoping to change my souvenir t-shirt before she caught me.

Suddenly she appeared like an aberration at my bedroom door wearing her worn out *carrots are myths* nightshirt, sporting her beheaded dirty-white mutant Genus Lepus slippers, save the ears sticking out from the sides every which way and that.

"You don't have to shout! I'm standing right here! What's in the backpack?"

"When are you going to lose those ugly snowshoe road kills?" I said, trying to avoid her question.

"Never! They were ancestors!" she snapped back. "Don't change the subject! I know you didn't come home last night?" she continued to interrogate.

"Can't you see I slept in my bed?" I replied, yap-coughing, holding back a hysterical laugh. I wasn't good at the lying game. My head fur would stand up on end, my face would go all stupid and I'd yap and cough, like a dork.

"Making stupid faces, yap-coughing, spiked head fur – says you're lying! Do you always sleep in your clothes, Hyna? What's in the backpack?"

"I just finished dressing as you came *hopping* down the hall! Nothing's in the backpack!"

"I was *not* hopping!" She paused. "Unholy Universe! Is that taco sauce on the front of your t-shirt?" she blurted out, gazing at last night's accidental drip.

"No!"

Like a lizard zapping a fly she grabbed the front of my t-shirt and starting gnawing on the stain. I pulled hard to free myself from her grip. Sadly, she managed to tear a hole where the stain was.

"Yes it is!" she yelled, through the chunk of my shirt in her mouth.

"Look what you've done to my souvenir t-shirt!" I whined and yipped.

"Are those *my* jeans you're wearing?"

"No they're not!" I lied, yap-coughing, now afraid to tell the truth, as I quickly made my way to the bathroom. I tried to close the door behind me, but her freaky-footed doorstopper relative prohibited that from happening.

"What are you holding behind your back, Hyna?" she asked, tapping her nails annoyingly on the wood casing.

I swallowed hard and leaned up against the towel rack trying to secure some of the other evidence I had hurriedly hidden under my shirt. I could only hope it would stay in place while I turned my mitts palm side up.

"Nothing! See?"

"Unholy-mothership-of-my-father! Is that cheese curls powder all over your digital pads?" she gasped.

Before she could attack my pads, something hit the tiles on the bathroom floor. As I looked down I could see a very small wooden square tumbling in slow motion, bouncing, landing at the mouth of those gangrenous Liporidae. It was the game piece letter M. Harriet gazed down at the small wooden square with a look of mortal shock. I held my breath as she bent over and picked it up. The silence was deafening. I could feel beads of sweat forming on my brow.

"This is where you were last night? You were playing Galaxy Babble or Bust? Devouring all of our dot com IUA snacks without me?" she huffed, as she waved the letter M around in the air like a crazy Jill. "I knew it! I knew it! You were with Celesta and all of our other friends, weren't you?"

"What? No!" I yapped out, knowing I was caught. "I have no idea where that letter M came from!" I lied, laughing like a crazy hyena, head fur standing straight up on end.

Then it happened. Defecation from the universe fell upon me in the form of karma and I stood helpless while the pelting sound of wooden game blocks continued to fall, rubbing my face in their refusal to partake in the deceitful charade.

"Liar!" Harriet accused, and rightly so.

"Harriet, we were going to ask you to go, but…"

"Liar!" she sobbed.

"Okay! Yes! I'm lying! We didn't want you to go. We played Galaxy Babble or Bust without you! Is that what you want to hear?" My words ricocheted off of the walls like a rocket blast, making a double impact.

Harriet staggered back. "How could you? Tell me!" she demanded, thumping her foot, ugly ears on her lagomorph cadavers flopping to the beat.

"Because, Harriet, you chew on the letter blocks, lick carpet crumbs, hop all over the house while waiting your turn, and you break game rules. We were all tired of putting up with it."

"I do *not* hop! ... All?"

"Yes! All! Everyone wanted our last game to be fun. What's wrong with that?" I said, feeling as if I had just crawled out of a black hole. I felt free! I felt strong! Heck – I felt righteous!

"Everyone? Last game?"

"Yes! Everyone! Last game! We just wanted to play one intelligent game using the rules written on the inside of the Galaxy Babble or Bust box," I boasted, feeling high on the telling the truth.

"Intelligent?" she whimpered, her lips curling and quivering, ears pinned back against her head.

"Yes! Intelligent! ... da–ha–amn it!" I chocked-out my new learned word, taught by one of the aliens at last night's game.

She took off one of her slippers and shook it at me, fur flying like dandelion puffs. "All, everyone, last game, intelligent?" she spat as she scolded, nostrils flaring and twitching.

"Yes Harriet all four of those!" I bravely relented, preparing for the worst, hoping she wouldn't start kick-boxing.

Without warning she spun around and slammed the bathroom door in my face. I began to sigh with relief and joy, but then I heard my bedroom door slam shut. I bolted out of the bathroom, ran down the hall and pushed open my bedroom door. She had my backpack on the floor, jumping and thumping on it wildly. I could hear the chips, pretzels, and cheese curls, being pulverized into dust. I grabbed the straps of the backpack and pulled as hard as I could and a tug of war was on! It felt like it lasted for hours. Both of us huffing and puffing yelling out everything we couldn't stand about each other.

"Jackal wanna-be!" she clucked, grinding her teeth.

"Block-chewer-carpet-licker-hopper!" I fired back.

"Floater orphan!" she snorted.

"Sasquatch!" I yapped, hysterically.

I finally lost my grip when the straps came undone and I fell to the floor landing on the salsa packets that I had stuffed in my back pockets.

With lightning speed she unzipped the backpack and dumped the contents on my bed and began beating the bags with her rigor mortis slipper, chunks of fur whirling in the air with each hit. One of the ears flew off like a bullet and hit me in the middle of my forehead, which forced me to dry heave. Snack fragments and fur covered my bedsheets and blankets. The last to go were the family size Tostito chips and Carmel Corn I had stuffed under my blanket. I only could sit and watch as she unmercifully placed my pillow over the bags and body slammed a double header. The ends of the bags burst open and pieces of Tostitos and clumps of Carmel Corn flew in the air like confetti, landing everywhere, including all over me. She gave each sad bag one last swat like she was killing a bug.

After the cloud of fur and dust settled, she stood with her arms crossed gazing down upon the snack carnage like a general after a battle. It was a matter of minutes before she would dive on my bed and start eating the crumbs along with my bed sheets.

I picked myself up off the floor, salsa dripping from my back pockets, fur and clothes covered in Tostitos and sticky Carmel Corn. Just when I was about to admit defeat, I noticed the dry heave inducing rabbit ear that had earlier bounced off my forehead was lying on the carpet a few feet away. Our eyes fell upon it at the same time. I knew what I had to do. I drop-rolled, scooping it up with supersonic speed. Harriet tried to do the same, but tripped over her own feet and fell, which gave me time to get up and run. I sped to the bathroom, Harriet hot on my tail, by seconds safe, I slammed the door and locked it.

"Don't you dare do what I think you're going to do!" she yelled out, wildly kicking at the door while trying to jiggle the handle open.

"You think not? Just listen to this!" I yelled back, laughing and snorting like a nut-case.

"No! Don't do it!" she begged.

I held the ear high in the air over the commode as if sacrificing it to the game-snack gods. I let go. The plunk was like the sound of a symphony. I grabbed the flusher and pulled down harder than I needed to. I watched as my victory-kill whirled away into the city cesspool where it belonged. The taste of victory was sweet.

I flung open the bathroom door. "HA!" I yelled out, doing a jig.

With her freaky one-eared-half-bald slipper clutched tightly in her paw-hand, the other headless hare tagging along on her foot, she proceeded to limp back into her bedroom at the end of the hallway and profoundly slammed the door behind her.

I gathered up the game blocks, recovered the game board from under the bedcovers, and placed them in their rightful box. Finally, my sigh of relief moment happened. I proudly walked into the kitchen, placed the Galaxy Babble or Bust game boldly on top of the breakfast bar with nothing more to fear, but a whole lot of mess to clean up.

Bessarabia

Sean Jones

I'd like to tell you two origin stories, the first about a crime-fighter who would earn her place among the League of Seven, that cadre of superheroes who serve up justice, hot and steaming on platters of precious metals, the girl developing a sinister power she'd use to quell baddies galore. The second saga is about a guy who would later travel with Abracadabra's League of wrong-righters and scribe for the gentlemen's magazine, *Metro Riviera*. Spoiler alert: I'm the journalist. But – ten years before I roamed Colorado and New Mexico with the super-powered likes of White Bishop, Lyric and The Spellchecker – there was this girl.

"Bess."

When I was entering Grade 12 at Abraham Lincoln in Denver in 2009, my sketchy parents were always scamming, always scheming, and they'd heard at the Colfax & Federal bus-stop you could sponsor a foreign exchange student for cash. You'd just provide shelter and food and exposure to "typical life" in the good ol' U.S. of A. – and cigarettes.

The Republic of Moldova flew my family's guest, Maricara Marcu, into Denver International Airport and I picked her up in my blue, 1961 Falcon – which was running that August day. While I made small talk on the drive home, the petulant-school-girl-slash-latter-day-Communist-apparatchik filled my ashtray.

"You always smoke?" I asked.

"If only you knew how good is American tobacco." She inhaled deeply. "Everything is good in Land of Opportunities."

"Most definitely," I agreed, never having thought about it. "How do you say your name?"

"Like it sounds."

"How's that?"

"Mar – ee – ca – ra. Maricara." I watched her thin upper lip and fat lower lip pronounce the word, a magical spell as she said it.

"Americans will never be able to say that."

She pulled a long drag on her Marlboro. "Anything is possible in this country."

I wondered if "she and I" were possible. I mean, I thought it was love-at-first-sight-in-retrospect-looking-back-on-it. At the get-go, she seemed mildly exotic in an Eastern European kind of way, with layers of gauzy scarves over military khakis and black hair that was spiky on the sides but droopy on top. Moles dotted her face in intriguing ways that made you stare at her, like how a field-trip to the planetarium can make you want to trace stars to form constellations.

Meanwhile, back at the ranch, my family's single-story, three-bedroom house in faded blue on the cul-de-sac of South Dale Court, I showed the chain-smoking and increasingly-captivating Maricara around the neighborhood. I pointed out Sanderson Gulch, which ran behind our sprawling, 1100-square-foot homestead.

Abutting the "Chasm of Calamity" stood the house of Little Jack, a Macedonian dude, a guy who was always helping me with the Falcon. His place was like twelve or twelve-million garages and he had eleventeen car projects going, many of them the individual vehicles of the local cops. If you think about it, they can drive as fast as they want, so Jack would use mad mechanical skills to soup them up for the Gendarmerie, superchargers, turbos, big blocks. Some of the cars, well, I couldn't believe police needed armored personal vehicles with gun ports. Anyway, I figured I'd walk the new girl down to his sprawl to show her off.

As Maricara and I sidestepped a 1963 split-window Corvette in grey primer while we shimmied through one of Jack's fluorescent-lit garages, ducking old gas-station signs and stepping over stank-rank transmission-fluid puddles, we heard this buzz-buzzing and saw the man M.I.G.-welding a 1937 or 1947 fat-fendered something-something streetrod in cherry red.

From behind the dark-lensed faceplate came his rumbling

voice. "I love smell of Marlboros and ozone in the morning."

"Hey, Jack," I said.

"Hello, Charlie."

"I'd like you to meet someone."

He put down his torch, took off his mask and smiled. Like Maricara, he was black-haired and brown-eyed. "Please meet you," said his Eastern European accent. "To meet."

"*Enchanté*," she replied, which I would later realize was French for "nice to meet you, too; you have taken off your mask but I will complete the unmasking; you have put down your torch but will always carry a torch for me."

When they shook hands, it was more of a fondling caress or whatever English nouns you juxtapose when you mean, "our souls are touching but our ages are twenty-four years apart." Yeah, somewhere between heartwarming moment and creepy-Lolita encounter.

Like ping pong, it was on.

"Why are you called Little Jack?" She was still "shaking" his hand.

"Nick-name is Liljak." He spelled it out for her. "Means 'The Bat.'" Yeah, something in their staring eyes passed scads more information like they knew their wedding song and their kids' names.

Finally, they let go – except, they didn't.

A few days after that, classes started and sucked – but you've been through high school. You know.

Maricara went over her origins with all the Abraham Lincoln kids and teachers. In front of a world map in Geography class, she said, "Moldova," but no one knew where that was, so she told them, "East of Romania. Bessarabia?"

Nobody from nobody could place that place and – because her name was foreign to the three tongues spoken in Abraham Lincoln Land – she took on the moniker of "Bess," much easier for Americans (and Mexican-Americans and Vietnamese-Americans) than Maricara, which means "sea of bitterness."

I could tell you how Bess hated shopping at the posh Cherry Creek Mall but loved Goodwill and the ARC's thrift stores.

"Things cast off are more authentic," she said. "Too precious to throw away but adopted to be loved again."

I could say something about how she'd almost get into trouble for lighting up at school. "Trust me," she'd say to a Vice Principal or Student Council member or civic-minded Head Cheerleader, "Your country's cigarettes are worth any punishment. Do to me as you will." But, they wouldn't. Extolling the virtues of an American vice, she sidestepped reprisals: jingoism provided her alibi.

As for her super-heroine origins? The introduction to the Macedonian wrench-wielder and subsequent seduction by him started the whole shebang.

For my part, I kept breaking things on the Falcon in attempts to "tune it," meaning I could hang out at Liljak's for him to un-do my handiwork, meaning I could keep tabs on our exchange student. My parents didn't care that she lived over at Liljak's as long as the monthly checks appeared in the mailbox. I cared.

By Halloween, Bess had a full-on social life and a complete costume and, yeah, she was planning to trick-or-treat. But, if you know Denver, you know it always snows on the Thirty-First of October. Truth? It's an urban myth: we had a fifty-degree night.

Bess had gone thrifting at the Salvation Army with Carmen Gutierrez or shoplifting at Daisy's Dancewear with Jennifer Holcombe. She'd gotten her girlfriend of the week, Trinh Pham, to sew up begging-for-candy togs that consisted of Spandexy black ballet stuff, a domino mask, tall boots and a demi-cape in Kevlar (sold by the yard at the Army Surplus on Broadway). Setting off on her quest to fill a pillow case with sweets or cigarettes, she began said mission at Liljak's and never made it to another house.

So, for sure, Sanderson Gulch was pretty skeezy during my salad days and a couple-three of Liljak's garages backed up to the trash-and-hobo-filled mini-canyon. On that Halloween night, painted green, decked out in a matching hat and tunic, attempting to impersonate the Incredible Bulk or the Inedible Husk, I wore my Grumpy Green Giant costume. My friends called me "Beanstalk." I kind-of-sort-of edged around the back to see what was shaking and that's when the ultralights – the hang-gliders with electrically powered propellers

– came flitting into the Macedonian's place, one, two, six of the night-flyers alighting silently, nine costumed members of Abracadabra's League of Seven hopping out and entering surreptitiously into house of The Bat.

The LoS was at my next-door neighbor's house! Holy Expletive, The Bat. Man! I had no idea how to handle it, definitely wanting to meet them, but wondering why – in response to what danger – they'd come to my neighborhood. I opened the creaking back door and crept inside.

There was this song.

"Happy Birthday to you. Happy Birthday to you. Happy Birthday, dear (mish-mash of 'Maricara,' 'Bess' and 'Sweetheart'). Happy Birthday to you!"

From my vantage point in Liljak's Pine-Sol-smelling, 1950s kitchen of white tile and industrial-grade appliances, I could hear the doggerel as it carried up the staircase from his basement or subterranean laboratory.

"How old are you now? How old are you now?"

"Eighteen," Bess said to the crowd I couldn't see, the party of three-squared superheroes and one mechanic with super-skilled hands.

Some crusader's mask-muffled voice oozed up the green-shag-carpeted stairway and slithered into my earholes, saying "Legal."

Legal. Bess could do anything she wanted, at least until she had to go back to Moldova. She was an adult. So much for my feelings for her, my longings. If a crush can be crushed, mine was flattened.

I went outside to trace constellations in the sky's stars or to vandalize the League's ultralights but that's when the alarm sounded, the lights atop the garage flashed red-orange-yellow and the League of Seven, all nine of them, came sprinting up the stairs, led by Liljak and Bess, a lit cigarette in her mouth. The gang hopped onto their silent steeds of the air, some in singles, others two-to-a-craft, and they spun up the propellers, which sent eerie blue arcs into the gloom. I love the smell of ozone and Marlboros at night.

Because of the chaos, because of my Halloween costume, Moonlighter mistook me for part of the Macedonian's entourage and the glow-in-the-dark crime-fighter told me, "Hop on. Sibilant Squad's in town. Hurry up."

Yeah, fifty degrees feels chilly when you're above the Mile High City moving at forty or four-hundred miles an hour. The League flew northwest and banked over fish-stinky Lake Rhonda, one ultralight at a time, Moonlighter and I swinging low to nestle beside the bumper-car corral of Riverside Amusement Park.

I didn't witness the fireball but saw its orange reflection on the windows of the nearby buildings. The explosion, which should have pealed like thunder, came as a ripping sound. When I yanked my head around, I could see two charred forms splash into the lake, the mangled skeleton of the electric, carbon-fiber hummingbird hitting the water but floating on top. From the darkness overhead, staccato gunfire erupted as the airborne League retaliated. Somewhere to my right, I heard manic screaming and, then, silence.

Who were the victims? Not Bess, I hoped; not Liljak, I remembered to wish. Even at the time, I knew it was mercenary of me to hope for the deaths of someone else. The girl-no-longer-a-girl was still my responsibility, still my obsession.

The remaining lightweight flyers of the good guys touched down and, as the survivors stepped out, I took a census. Liljack looked pale and Bess stood in his arms, shivering. I felt a queasy relief, a greasy gratitude.

"Bougainvillea" (a plum-complected lady in a dress with real flowers) "and Sacré Bleu" (a Quebecoise mime in turquoise garb) "have been murdered," said Abracadabra. He looked into the teary eyes of his band of champions. "Now, you know the stakes."

Elbows akimbo, assembled in a semi-circle, mood somber but vindictive, we heroes numbered ten. Abracadabra, the man in mango, briefed the crew and barked orders. "Cheerleader kidnapping. North High Vikings. Purple and white uniforms. Bound and gagged. Scattered around the theme park."

Theme park? Riverside's theme, if anything, was Throwback to the Great Depression.

"If you're savvy," said Abracadabra, "you know taking the girls is a ploy to lure us here."

General nodding of costumed heads.

"Wendigo," Abracadabra told the werewolf-looking and wet-dog-smelling dude to my left, "you'll scout the abandoned speedway to the south. Take Double-Bubble-Boy with you." With that order, the League's leader indicated a well-coiffed, Travolta-looking guy with no apparent superpowers but a Sanderson Gulch of a cleft chin.

"Rockstone, I'm counting on you to go *mano a mano* with Hyper Hornet." This, he said to the lumpy fellow in Union Pacific Railroad overalls, a monolithic mineral-man in blue denim. "I know you can take him."

I doubted it. Hyper Hornet was the Sibilant Squad's baddest-est.

"Rat-Tat-Tattler" (snake-skinned guy with a shoulder-slung snare drum) "and Edwardian Angel," (pretty much a regular angel) "head north, sweep the Tilt-A-Whirl® and the Rabid Chipmunk," (a rickety, wooden rollercoaster that had killed twenty people in fifty years).

"Moonlighter, The Bat and you two newbies, come with me."

And, I realized, Abracadabra was a fan of my favorite medieval police show when he said, "Be ye careful out there."

Yeah, that brought a thought. I raised my hand and said, "Mister Abracadabra?"

"Doctor Abracadabra. Yes, Green Bean?"

Oh, burn. But, coming from the Leader of the League, I took it as a demi-compliment. At least I wasn't "Beanstalk" to him.

I said, "Name's Charlie. Why don't we call the cops?"

The caustic laughter erupting from the good-guy freakshow could have peeled the flaking paint from the park's dilapidated buildings.

I think Wendigo said, "The statutory town of Riverside employs but a handful of officers and they are quite preoccupied writing tickets for cracked windshields." I mean I know Wendigo said it but I couldn't believe my earholes.

I wanted to ask why no one was using guns but, once Wendigo-bitten, twice shy....

"You have your assignments, League," Abracadabra said.

"Move out."

Bess lit up and sucked down a Marlboro in Guinness-record-book time and, then, another so quickly I never saw any smoke. Moonlighter led Abracadabra and The Bat in stretches – stretches! – before we began our sojourn to the Crystal Palace. I did some jumping jacks to limber up, not having a superhero preparatory routine or nicotine addiction.

As we headed east through the park's Dickens(ian) Village, I found the first pair of North High Viking cheerleaders in their purple and white outfits, the two brown-haired girls roped together, back to back, their bindings wrapped around a Victorian gaslight pole and guarded by some crocodile-lady-thing, all moss and scales and maybe nude – hard to tell.

"Hey, Doctor Abracadabra," I said. "Over here."

Alligator Amy was on me like green on beans, gnashing and lashing and thrashing. Without any weapons, I played defense, tried to keep the mauling to a minimum. While I dodged and ducked, dipped and dived, bruised and bled, Moonlighter sauntered over and strobed in blue-indigo-violet pulses, freezing me and Gator Gal. On his heels, came Abracadabra. He touched Reptile Renee with hands coruscating in electric fire and she dropped like a dinosaur under an asteroid impact.

Trying not to drip too much blood, I said, "Thanks, Doc."

He laughed and – after not asking if I were okay – said, "You may want to work on your powers, Son. Apply direct pressure."

Bess – after not asking if I were okay – whipped out a Vietnamese butterfly knife she hiked out of a sternum-holster one of the gals at Abraham Lincoln had sewn into her black bustier. She sliced the cords holding the Viking's Daughters and told them – in Spanish! – "You're free to help us or go home."

"*Gracias*," they said, turning and running.

"*De nada*," said Bess as they sprinted away. She used their bindings to tie up Crocodile Camille.

The Bat – after not asking if I were okay – said, "Quick to thinking, Bess. Good to use ropes."

"Two down and eight to go," said Doctor Abracadabra. "Let's investigate the smack bar."

I swear he didn't say "snack."

About two minutes later, I got it. Glow-in-the-dark Moonlighter yanked open the door to the concrete bunker from whose sliding-metal window you could buy Sno-Cones in the summer. Inside the blockhouse, she stood.

"Heroin" was no heroine. To my imagination, she looked like a crypt-dwelling, female barrow-wight you'd have to be swinging a +3 longsword to hit. White skin mottled in grey blotches, glowing red eyes, stringy hair that reached to her leprous ankles. Huddled behind the undead drug-woman were three of North High's girls in purple, quiet and rapturous as if tripping.

"Welcome to the party," said the ghoul, though I never saw her cracked, blue lips move.

Out of Heroin's nostrils came a fog, a pinkish haze that billowed forth from the smack-bar's open door, a miasma of roses that sent fuchsia tendrils groping through the night toward us good-guys.

Having rehearsed five minutes before with Lady Lizard, I danced away from the cotton-candy wisps but Moonlighter fared not so well. Twin tentacles of vapor entered his nose-holes and lifted him half a foot off the ground, paralyzing the superhero as he levitated above the potholed tarmac. While Abracadabra fumbled one-handedly with pouches on the orange belt that encircled his tight-fitting onesie, he used his free hand to cover his face.

The very-barely-legal Bessarabian in the black mask? She ran forward and slammed the shack's door, cutting off the drug-laden curlicues, most likely saving the life of Moonlighter, who settled back to earth with a very large smile.

"You are fast thinker," said The Bat to the birthday girl.

Her smile rivaled that of Moonlighter. "*Multsumesc*," she said, Romanian for "Thanks."

Abracadabra retrieved a small, grey disk from a belt-pouch and handed it to The Bat. "Please place this limpet where you think it will do the least harm to the captives."

Flapping his arms and flitting like his namesake, my cradle-robbing neighbor flew to the top of the cinder-block building and stuck the contact-mine to the metal roof.

"Is ready," he said.

"Catch this rope," said Abracadabra as he hurled a thin strand up to The Bat. "Help us climb up."

So, we (without Moonlighter who was still under the influence), the four of us, prepared – literally – to blow the lid off the caper. As we stood on the pitched gable, I rightly expected the explosion would produce a gaping hole but I was still surprised at how loud the mini-bomb sounded – it detonated atop what amounted to a tin drum. We dropped through the roof's jagged crack and pummeled Heroin with fists and feet, insults and admonitions. As she suffered the beating, she curled up like a spider playing possum and Abracadabra trussed her up with an epoxy-spray.

"Are you okay?" I asked the trio of cheerleaders but their glazed eyes answered silently for them, saying "We may survive if we get medical attention."

Maybe they did answer me. I was pretty deaf.

As if I'd prompted him, Abracadabra said, "The Bat, can you please Origam-i 9-1-1?" Somewhere between a cellular phone and military-grade radio gear, Abracadabra had engineered the Origam-i to keep the League in communication. I decided that Halloween night to put one on my Christmas list, but ....

"Confirmed," said my exchange-student-enticing neighbor. He flipped open his device and pushed a single button.

And, that's when my thick skull realized Liljak had his own Origam-i. He was part of the gang. Duh. Obviously, his duties would be to work on their super-powered vehicles and, I guessed, place contact mines on the roofs of snack- and smack-bars, seduce foreigners and recruit neighbors into crime-fighting capers, odd jobs such as that. I was living next-door to a member of the twenty-odd constituency of the League of Seven and I felt a twinge of pride. South Dale Court was on the map!

Abracadabra went out of the shack, collected Moonlighter, brought him inside with us and said, "You'll be okay, Joel. Wait here for the paramedics."

Joel? Had Abracadabra slipped or was he not worried that Bess and I had heard a superhero's name? Did that show trust? Were we inner-sanctum?

"Five cheerleaders found and five to go," said the leader of the League.

His Origam-i chirped and he reached down to his belt and put us on "speaker."

"Khrrrrrtttt, khrrtt, khkhkhrrrtttt, help, khrrtt, come fast, khrrrrrttt, need assistance, khrttt, paddle boats, khrrrrrrrrrrrrrrr-rrrrttttt," squawked his box.

"Liljak, please stay here and tend to the ladies. Lancers," (Abraham Lincoln High School's mascot) "let's go," Abracadabra said. "By the lake."

Yeah, I was only mildly insulted that he'd implied we "newbies" wouldn't know where to find paddle boats.

No stretching this time. We ran, ran, ran back to Lake Rhonda's boathouse, Bess surprisingly well-winded considering she was smoking as she dashed. As we three rounded the corner, we hurled ourselves headlong into the melee, six or maybe even a half-dozen bad guys working over a pair of League members.

In syncopated bursts of light tossed about by clashing superpowers, I caught a surreal view of the donnybrook, snippets of action I'd later stitch together. It went something like this.

Hyper Hornet, the Sibilant Squad's main man, darted to and fro like some anthropomorphic dragonfly, swooping in to sting Rockstone with a wicked barb that hung down from the flyer's carapace, our guy wincing and swatting, yelping and swinging, fighting back as effectively as a boulder might combat wind-erosion.

Flash, flash, flash, blinked green and yellow and white lights.

The Eastern European I was supposedly hosting kept smoking and smoking but – this was where it got weird(er) – she never exhaled.

Abracadabra? He kept finding kill-kill, bang-bang trinkets on his belt, kept flinging deadly bling at baddies.

And the noise! Clangs and jangling, thuds and muffled punches. Snapping tibias and cracking fibulas. Rumblings and rippings and whatever English adjectives you select for the sound of a human turned slowly inside out.

Saguaro – good for you if you pictured a two-armed-cactus villain – was hop-hopping around, impaling a very bloody

Wendigo, whom I could see was being sent to the Dog-Pound of No Return.

Absent, I noted, were Bubbly Guy with his perfect side-burns and the duo of good-doers who'd gone north, Royal Cherub and The Snake Drummer. Our numbers had diminished, now consisting of a Wizard Engineer in Mango, Chip off the 'Ol Block in coveralls, a girl with a balisong blade and Marlboro fetish – and a bleeding and mildly resentful Falcon owner in a shredded, green tunic and felt hat. We tried to even the odds.

Bess stabbed and sliced and skewered the spiny succulent and ended his photosynthetic existence, carving her initials – MM – into his trunk. It was too late to save The Wolfman.

Shimmer, shine, glint and gleam went random-colored lights.

"Ka-wam" announced a mushroom cloud at the north end of the park.

Tinkle, tinkle, tinkle fell the sintering debris that must have included the charred remains of the two League members and whatever villains they'd grappled. I hoped the girl-Vikings weren't on their way to Valhalla.

As for Azure Armadillo, well, he didn't survive the Ul-tra-Crochet® treatment, the millions of tiny, dancing hooks Abracadabra sprayed onto him, the Avogadro's Number of barbs pulling his skin and, then, his viscera and, finally, his bones until his anatomy lay splayed and glistening on the dirty asphalt.

"He's the one who shot down Bougainvillea and Sacré Bleu," Abracadabra justified.

Meanwhile, what was Charlie up to? I inhaled the night air to suck in a vaporous cocktail of equal parts bravery, stupidity and being-tired-of-being-inessential. Even if she'd found her soulmate in Liljak, even if that ship had sailed on water gone under the bridge, I owed it to my self-respect to make an impression on the future Mrs. The Bat. I leapt into the air, grabbed the chitinous feet of Dragonfly Dork and jacked up his attack-routine on Rockstone. As the two of us crashed into the cold, slimy mud of Lake Rhonda, Bess rushed forward and did something I hadn't seen her do in a while.

She exhaled.

Maricara, "sea of bitterness," blew into HH's face a cloud of smoke so vile, it turned all us spectators into barfing babies but made Hyper Hornet turn from dragonfly to gargoyle to plaster to dust.

"Dayayayamn," said a certain blue-Falconer between vomits. "Very super power!"

As the silence settled in, sirens sounded. Red-blue-red-blue lights of ambulances heralded the approach of paramedics and we reached the *dénouement* of the evening's shenanigans.

I spoke earlier of the Winnowing but that would come ten years later when I'd ride shotgun with the League of Seven during their interstate escapades. No, the night of Saturday, October 31, 2009 witnessed a different kind of culling, the demise of five *bona-fide* superheroes who would live to fight crime no more. Survivors included a new superheroine who'd become known as "The Batlass."

The Batlass?

I am *so* kidding right now. How awful would that name be?

She earned her trademarked name that night, "Bessarabia" did.

Also among those who lived to see November 1st were Double-Bubble-Boy and the five North High School Proud Viking Girls he and his perfect profile had rescued from under the bleachers of the eighth-mile, stock-car track. (Turns out Abracadabra had been wrong: the young ladies were pompons, not cheerleaders, a whole different, sports-inspiring, costume-wearing squad of enthusiasts without the hand-held, fluffy, purple-and-white plumes). The Travolta-esque guy stayed in close contact with them for years, well, at least, the four dark-haired ones.

The blonde cheerleader? Shannon? She took a liking to the driver of a particular 1961 Ford with an empty ashtray, a car whose owner she sometimes called Beanstalk, a Falcon-driver for whom she'd sometimes wear a costume and would always inspire, enthusiastically.

Moldova lost – but America gained – a most upright citizen when Abracadabra named, as his first-round pick in the 2010 Superhero Draft®, "Bessarabia." She was legal not only for being eighteen but for being upstanding and she remained in the States, remained intriguing. Maricara and Liljak kept up their identities as my parents' next-door neighbors well after I'd moved downtown to study journalism at Metropolitan State University. (Go, Roadrunners!)

I never got an Origam-i but I did klepto one of the League's ultralights. Liljak would fix it up for me whenever I'd crash it over Sanderson Gulch, which I absolutely never, ever did intentionally just to see what was shaking with a certain former exchange student whose intricate moles made you want to trace constellations.

Student Database Notes
3/25 – 6/27

Tim McDaniel

3/25
Exvoon, Faculty

Met my new class today. I don't anticipate making much use of the database system this quarter; the students all seem motivated, attentive, and excited about the class. I'm also happy to note that I have a nice variety of students – segmented, non-segmented, bifurcated, translucent, xylophagous, and chronobound – all kinds! This quarter should be good. But maybe I am still adreno-hyped after my vacation on Hlortyflor VI.

3/28
Exvoon, Faculty

N-48C didn't hand in its homework; claims it was lost, or stolen by another kid on the bus (its story kept changing). Told it that keeping track of its own homework was its responsibility. Not a great way for it to start the quarter.

Pichix has been absent since the start of the quarter. I hope she realizes that if these absences continue they will affect her chances of passing.

3/29
Exvoon, Faculty

Ivix once again complained that he has been placed in a level that is too low for him, and asked me to talk to the Director. I told him I thought his placement was fine – he's a bit above the average, yes, but he can get a lot out of our class. He seemed unconvinced.

Cryutop panicked briefly when he couldn't find his homework, and inadvertently swallowed his handtutor. The handtutor was recovered an hour later, but it was only possible to partially decontaminate it, so it will have to be replaced.

Storn made a lovely diorama of the Unearthing Ceremony of the Slixixt. Unfortunately, the diorama was eaten by a biorama constructed by Yab(Green), depicting the Mastication of the Founder.

3/30
Vilsufk, Director

After repeated requests, I have examined the placement of Ivix (811-9211-84002) and I concur with faculty that he has been placed in the correct level. I have communicated my assessment to the student.

In the future, it is best if faculty work directly with the student involved to resolve these sorts of minor difficulties.

4/4
Exvoon, Faculty

Distork handed in an essay which is an exact copy of one that I got last quarter. He didn't even bother to change the gender of the first-person narrator! I explained to him the consequences of plagiarism, and he claims that he misunderstood what plagiarism was. I have my doubts, but we'll see. Maybe he just needed to see that people do notice when he breaks a rule.

I still haven't seen Pichix, though she's been on my roster since Day 1. Will ask the Director to contact her family. Missing class this early in the quarter doesn't bode well for her commitment to the school.

Skisaa did not hand in an essay. I asked her about it, and she simply said she did not choose to use her time to do it.

4/7
Exvoon, Faculty

Cryutop ate two of his classmates yesterday, in an argument over (apparently) a group homework assignment. He says he didn't mean to do it, that this was an involuntary reaction to stress. I warned Cryotup that if it happened again I would consult with the Director about negative consequences. I made sure to leave the consequences nicely vague.

The classmates were vomited forth after twenty minutes or so. They'd both lost their eyesight and epidermides, but they should be fine, eventually, once they've been rehabilitated and repurposed.

In the afternoon the students were working on their independent projects, and I noticed that N-48C was just sitting there, shaking. I didn't think much of it, and helped some other students, and when I finally looked back I saw that it was still shaking. That had to have been going on for at least a half hour.

Turns out it had rewired its pleasure receptors. I've asked the counselors to talk to it about reprogramming options regarding personal pleasure management, and have suggested that if the problem continues we communicate with the factory directly.

4/8
Vilsufk, Director
After seeing the two students eaten by Cryutop (811-9231-746113) yesterday, and after consulting with the bloodpact precursor of one and the clone-mother of the other, we've agreed to refund their tuition fees, and to allow them to start over at the same level next quarter. They should be sufficiently healed by then, or at least presentable.

Faculty are reminded to keep their charges under control at all times, and to review the common regurgitation and resuscitation guidelines described in the Employee Handbook. Assistance is available to faculty if the material in the Handbook is found to be too challenging.

4/9
Exvoon, Faculty
R'Fhop, ever the class clown, set fire to one of Storn's secondary tendrils, and the resulting discharge meant no one can sit in the first or second rows for a week or so. I've called Maintenance.

I still have yet to see Pichix in class, but the Director tells me her mothers insist she is not skipping. I think they're in denial.

Ivix complained after class that the extra work that I have given him, at his request, was still too easy. I pointed out that his grade on his last extra credit assignment was only 63%, but he maintains that he can handle tougher material. I gave him some. I doubt he will be up to it, but we'll see.

4/10
Exvoon, Faculty

Yab(Green) told me today that he will miss three days of class next week, as he has to go back to Algol to attend his sister's vaporization ceremony. I thanked him for letting me know ahead of time, and loaded him down with homework.

This of course means that Yab(Green)'s sister will be starting next quarter a bit late. I have informed her advisors.

After class yesterday I found a hat with "Pichix" written on a tag attached to it. It makes sense that it would be hers – no one else in class has a head even remotely as large as those of her species. I put it in the lost and found. But how did it get in my class? Pichix still hasn't shown up in class!

4/15
Exvoon, Faculty

Distork cheated on the grammar test today; he made it easy to catch him, since he wrote the name of the kid he cheated off of – it was Storn – in the "name" box on the first page of the test. I again talked to him, and he said he was very sorry, that it wouldn't happen again, and that it was because he is under pressure from his rootstock purveyors to succeed.

Skisaa got a zero on the test, since she didn't bother to answer any of the questions. Strange – she's not disruptive in class, and seems to be paying attention, but she rarely hands in any of her assignments.

4/17
Vilsufk, Director

Distork (811-9212-84997) didn't come to the appointment we had set up for him yesterday, but he did show up today. I told him we were concerned about the cheating, and we needed to see a change in his behavior or there would be severe consequences.

Faculty are reminded that "rootstock purveyor" is no longer an acceptable term. The proper term has not yet been released by the Usage Authority, but when it is, all staff and faculty of this institution are required to use the proper and respectful terminologies. Remember that it costs nothing to be polite.

4/19
Exvoon, Faculty

This morning R'Fhop inverted inertia in the boy's restroom, and the ultraviolet flash severely burned the receptors of three of the kids using it at the time. I reminded R'Fhop that jokes can go too far, and that his parents will be asked to pay for the reconstructive surgeries. Then in the afternoon he splintered consensus-reality in the hallway outside of the gym and left a classmate (identity yet to be determined) howling for a subjective eternity in the frigid darkness between planes.

That kid! I have to admit that he is creative, though!

Meanwhile, Ivix (who didn't hand in the extra work he had asked for yesterday, and who got a score of 60% on the extra work from Tuesday) notified me that he is contacting the Board of Directors about his "misplacement," and that he is asking that I be fired.

I told him, good luck with that.

4/23
Exvoon, Faculty

I called Pichix's mothers today myself, and explained their daughter's absence. They told me that their daughter, though shy, would never miss a class, and that they have monitored her homework.

I checked, and I do have homework from her. I don't get it. Maybe she is having a classmate turn it in.

4/24

Exvoon, Faculty

Weekoz brought a plasma rifle to class today. I informed it that, although not specifically against school policy, this kind of thing makes some of its classmates nervous. Weekoz explained that it was simply intending to shoot a Flisswing which has been disemboweling students on the way home from class, and pledged to leave the weapon in its locker next time.

That's fine. I do wonder if something can be done about this Flisswing, though.

Pichix got the top score on the last writing test. Somehow. I still have not seen her. Unfortunately, Skisaa did not hand in an essay at all.

4/25

Vilsufk, Director

The Flisswing referred to in your database entry is the aunt of a visiting scholar. I spoke with the scholar, and she assured me that her aunt would be cautioned.

Pichix's (811-9300-98776) parents assure us that she is attending classes.

Skisaa (811-9192-69767) came to see me, at my request, and had nothing but praise for her teacher, and said she was learning a lot. I told her that we needed to see more homework from her, and that she needs to complete the tests she is given. She said she understood. She smiled during the whole meeting, and is perhaps unable to understand that she is having problems.

I heard from Distork's (811-9212-84997) homestay family today. It seems he has been a real pain in the glutods (quite literally, I am afraid) ever since he came to stay, demanding special foods, playing his painpluck at all hours, and generally being rude, nasty, unnecessarily flatulent, and intimidating. I've asked a counselor to see him, as it seems that faculty has been unable or unwilling to effectively communicate to him the gravity of his transgressions.

4/30

Exvoon, Faculty

R'Fhop hacked the spacetime coordinates of the school,

and as a result three students (the only one from my class was Storn) were teleported into the polar wastes this morning. Storn may temporarily lose a primary tendril to frostbite, and upon his reappearance in the classroom left a puddle of some kind of noxious blue fluid. I've called Maintenance.

I've also talked with R'Fhop about his pranks.

5/10
Exvoon, Faculty

Yab(Green) slept through most of the reading class today. A series of increasingly powerful electrical shocks to his brain stem finally woke him. He was very embarrassed, and I hope this won't happen again. Generally he's a good kid.

Ivix spent the day sulking. It seems he is unsatisfied with the response he got back from the Board of Directors.

5/18
Exvoon, Faculty

Storn kept turning yellow and orange all afternoon, and one primary and three tertiary tendrils drooped and oozed. She told me it was because she stayed up most of the night cramming for the quiz. I told her that this was not an efficient technique, and that the smell was affecting her classmates, and she agreed to see a Study Advisor to learn about different methods of reviewing the material covered in class.

5/19
Exvoon, Faculty

Fragelonk was tardy today, slipping into class a full forty minutes late. When I called her on her tardiness, she claimed that time was a subjective artificial cultural construct that held no meaning for her civilization. (Later, I checked – that is bullshit.) I told her that three tardies would be an absence, and that tardies disrupted class. Eventually she seemed to understand the importance of coming on time.

I understand that Distork threatened to eradicate a counselor's geneline after being told that his record of cheating would negatively affect his chances of transferring to a good school after his time here at the communal academy. He was quiet and sullen all day. What a shame that the kids you would like to transfer away from here are the ones who seem to hang around forever!

5/22
Exvoon, Faculty

Storn vomited a corrosive acid all over her desk. It seems she got a tuna sandwich from the cafeteria, and didn't realize until too late that she was allergic, and also that tuna, and bread, were toxic to her species.

I've called Maintenance.

Distork called a classmate a name, which, according to the universal translator, means something like "blossom-stuffing omnivore." The classmate was reduced to tears.

5/25
Exvoon, Faculty

Fragelonk's grades have been slipping for a couple of weeks now. She has been tardy a few more times since I warned her on the 19th, but usually by only a few minutes. Still, it's clear that her studies are not her top concern here at the school.

5/29
Exvoon, Faculty

Storn's primary leg was severed at the first knee by a mishap with a laser pointer. I sent her to the school nurse. By the afternoon she was back.

Ivix refused to work with the group assigned to him for a group project, claiming that their mental limitations (clearly referring to the absence, in many of his classmates, of multiple/distributed brain sacs) would not allow them to be of any help. He wants to work alone. I finally said fine. Later, I talked with his groupmates, and they all seemed relieved that he would be out of their group.

6/7
Exvoon, Faculty

After weeks of wondering what was going on with Pichix – the student who seems to have been absent all this time, but whose homework and test assignments kept showing up on time – I discovered today that she had camouflaged herself, rendering her body nearly invisible. I consulted with Pichix's advisor, and was told that this is a common thing among members of Pichix's species, and is a response to stressful situations. Like starting a new class on a new planet.

No wonder I never saw her in class! It would have been nice to have been told this earlier.

6/11
Exvoon, Faculty

Today Distork was found in a restroom by another teacher. He was tormenting Storn with a pencilbeam, and Storn's secondary neckfrill may never grow back. Apparently the seeping wound is also extremely painful.

By all accounts, Distork was angry at Storn when Storn refused to give him her homework.

I can not keep this kid in my class!

6/14
Vilsufk, Director

I regret to inform the faculty that Distork (811-9212-84997) will not be expelled from the class. Higher-ups at the college – and there is no need to mention names – have decided that the generosity of Distork's rootstock – that is, his genetic contributor – (i.e., the funding of the new library wing) more than compensates for his child's indiscretions.

Faculty and staff are reminded to say nothing of this to students, other employees, family members, or therapists. A professional demeanor must be maintained.

6/17
Exvoon, Faculty

Ivix circulated a petition calling for my dismissal. I guess there was only one signature – and I can guess whose – and when the petition got to Cryutop's desk he was so distraught that he swallowed it. So that's that.

R'Fhop refracted time/space, and turned himself into an infant, and inside-out. I've called Maintenance.

In happier news, final exams are tomorrow! I won't look back on this quarter with much fondness.

6/23
Exvoon, Faculty

Skisaa's final exams were nothing short of brilliant. I now understand – should have checked up on this earlier in the quarter – that her species takes in information for months, quietly processing it and not producing anything, until all is fully digested and understood. I will miss her in class, and I will inform her next teacher as to her learning style.

On the other hand ... whew. Ivix was screaming about his final exam results. Distork cheated – and complained to me later that his low score was because he'd cheated off the wrong classmate, and demanded permission to take the test again.

Later I encouraged Ivix and Distork to take some quiet time to decide what they wanted to say to me, this time in a lower tone of voice and with fewer threats and cranial discharges, and they somehow ended up choosing to do so in a small closet.

Well, apparently earlier, the stress of the exams had caused Cryutop to retreat into that same small closet to collect himself.

If I had only realized this in time, perhaps I could have prevented the terrible accident that followed!

The closet door must have somehow locked as it closed, and I didn't think to unlock it for several hours. When I finally did unlock the door, Cryutop had eaten Ivix and Distork long before, and the process of digestion was already well advanced.

So it does seem that I won't be dealing with Ivix and Distork anymore, anytime soon!

Unfortunately, after regurgitation I discovered the remains of Storn, as well. Apparently, at some point poor Storn had reached into the closet for her coat, and startled Cryutop into swallowing her, too.

The coat is still hanging there, a little yellow plastic rainsheath.

The thing is burned in several places. It has weird stains and is torn. And it just hangs there, empty.

6/25
Vilsufk, Director

Regarding the issue of the consumption of Distork (811-9212-84997), Ivix (811-9211-84002) and Storn (811-9212-84751) by Cryutop (811-9231-746113), our attorneys tell us that the actions or non-actions undertaken by the faculty in question cannot be proven to be malicious, and that, legally, we are in the clear.

Faculty are advised that if this kind of thing becomes too commonplace, the reputation of our institution may suffer, and at such point may form the basis of a formal reprimand.

6/27
Exvoon, Faculty

After the Quarter-End Briefing today I went back to my office to clean up a little, so I can start next quarter fresh.

I was surprised to find, on my desk, some little presents from my students – a thank-you card from Skisaa, a flower from Pichix (pity it's the type that eats cats), and even a tissue dispenser from N-48C.

The most touching thing was from three of Storn's parent-approximators. It's a glass tetradedron that sparks and changes colors (several of the colors are not even in the electromagnetic spectrum!). I have no idea what it is supposed to be. Maybe a paperweight or an art object, or a piece of fantastically developed technology. But the thought was nice.

It was a rather tough quarter, but I'm reminded that I really do love this job.

I wish Storn's family had taken her little coat, though. It remains in the closet. It reeks of disinfectants and despair.

I've called Maintenance.

Fairyland Border Investigations, Training Academy Class 937

Jaleta Clegg

Yavo stamped his staff against the ground then cast a jaundiced gaze over the new recruits. Being a troll, it was difficult to cast any other kind of gaze, since they tended to be naturally yellow. He sniffed. This group smelled of false bravado, over-confidence, and – Was that fear? He wrinkled his brow, although it was hard to notice with the natural cragginess of his face.

"Welcome to the Training Academy," he rumbled. He flicked a glance over the list floating near his right hand. Two satyrs, a centaur, a fire elf, a miniature griffon, a dryad, and – Yavo groaned – a talking chihuahua. Talking animals of any kind were trouble, but those tiny dogs always caused the biggest problems. You couldn't deport them to the human world, not after they'd drunk from every magical spring they could find.

He rolled his gaze over the lineup, ticking them off the list. Two goat-legged beings, check. Horse body and human head, humanoid with flames instead of hair, tiny lion-eagle, humanoid with green leaves instead of hair, normal humanoid –

Yavo paused. He checked his list, then the person in front of him. Definitely not a small dog with delusions of giantism. She was human, young, her dark hair cropped very short. She reeked of confusion and, he sniffed, fear. "Where is the chihuahua? And who are you?" There was no dog, and no scent of dog anywhere, only this non-magical human.

Light glinted off her buttons as she snapped a too-precise salute. "Cadet Susan Merkel, sir. Reporting for training. I think." She hesitated then added, "If I'm in the right place."

Yavo tapped one large claw on the clipboard. He growled in frustration. "Why can't they ever notify me before they send in exchange students? Line up, you miserable excuses of trainees. First lesson, watch out for unexpected magic."

One of the satyrs yelped as a poof of purple smoke exploded under his feet.

"Exactly what I said," Yavo grumbled.

Susan Merkel's eyes glinted white all the way around and her face scrunched in confusion, but she jumped into line with the others.

"Welcome to the Jefferson County Police Training Academy." The instructor, Sergeant Brian Thompson, eyed the line-up. Thirty years on the job and every time he could predict who would stick it out and who would be trouble. Seventeen fresh faces, and maybe ten of them would make it through. Out of those, maybe one would prove to be a quality officer. This bunch was slightly better than most. Except something didn't feel quite right.

Thompson studied his clipboard, then frowned at the line of cadets. Eighteen names but only seventeen people lined up. Three women in this batch. Not bad. But someone had brought their chihuahua. He shoved the clipboard at his assistant. He'd see who jumped when he shot the horrid little creature. Affront to nature, that's what they were.

"Roll call!" The assistant tapped the page. "Adams."

Thompson watched as the cadets answered. He motioned them to line up on the other side as their names were read. Everything went well until his assistant got to Merkel.

"Merkel!"

No answer.

"Merkel, Susan Merkel!"

Still no answer.

Thompson snorted and crossed his thick arms. "That's our no-show. Continue."

The assistant – Thompson had never bothered to learn his name because assistants were like cockroaches, step on one and another would pop out to take its place – the assistant drew a thick line through Merkel's name and continued with roll call.

"Newman! Patel! Powell!"

Name after name. Thompson watched it all with a jaundiced eye. He'd seen it all. Done it all. For thirty years.

The chihuahua sat perfectly still, ears twitching slightly with each name. At least the little bugger was well-behaved. First time Thompson had ever seen that. A well-behaved little anger-dog.

The assistant finished. The last cadet stepped into line.

"All right, maggots! Report to the quartermaster and collect your gear. You are mine for the next eighteen days."

"Excuse me, señor."

Thompson shot a glare around the group. The assistant was busy scribbling notes on the roll sheet. The cadets were double-timing it across the gravel parking lot towards the supply shed. No one else was anywhere near.

"I am reporting for duty, sir. I must speak of important things with you."

"Not funny," Thompson snapped at the assistant. "Gerald," he added, reading the name tag on the man's shirt.

Gerald gave him a very confused look.

Something tapped his leg.

Thompson looked down. The chihuahua tapped him again with his front paw.

"Yes, señor, it is I. Antonio Howitzer, officer of the enforcement of the law."

Thompson flapped his jaw a few times. "You talked."

"Yes, sir," Gerald said. "I talked to call names, sir. Roll call is complete."

Thompson pointed at the small dog. "You – He – It –"

"You are a very funny man, ha ha," the dog said.

It was Gerald's turn to flap his jaw.

Well, Thompson had seen almost everything. A talking dog was a new one. Unless someone was trying to pull a fast one. He crouched down then reached out to examine the dog's collar.

The dog backed away, teeth showing.

Thompson rose to his feet. He could play at jokes, too. "Well then, Antonio Howitzer, report to the quartermaster. You're late, maggot!"

The tiny little dog snapped to attention then trotted smartly away after the other recruits.

"Well I'll be." Thompson rubbed his chin, the crackle of fingers over stubble not distracting him from the wonder. "A chihuahua that listens. What's next? Unicorns?"

Susan Merkel stood slowly, dusting dirt from her backside. This was like one of her gran's stories of the Little People, sort of. Susan had never expected to actually meet any of them, and definitely not this way. But when the parchment envelope had arrived, complete with hand-lettered gilt names, her gran had smiled and told her what a privilege it was that Susan had been so chosen and honored. She didn't feel honored, just bruised. She sent a sidelong glance at her sparring partner. The dryad had given her nothing but attitude. But the green-haired woman had good reflexes and knew how to fight.

"Again?" the dryad asked, arching one green eyebrow.

Susan shook her head.

"I knew you were a quitter." The dryad sneered. "No magic. No skills. You barely know which end of a wand to hold."

Susan narrowed her eyes before pulling out her secret weapon, a lucky horseshoe nail attached to her keychain. Her gran had insisted she take it and Susan hadn't wanted to hurt the old woman's feelings. She dangled it in front of the dryad now, keys jingling.

The fey shrank away, gasping. "Don't you know that destroys magic? It's poison!"

"Put that away!" Yavo's bark startled Susan into dropping the keychain. "No iron allowed here. Didn't they give you the rules?"

Susan sheepishly dropped the keys back into her pocket. "I was told I had a special assignment. They sent a letter. It didn't say much." It had said nothing about finding herself in a forest clearing with a bunch of mythological creatures.

Yavo harrumphed. "Just keep those put away. They

could cause serious injury. Now, let's move on to magical fields, specifically containment and confinement fields. These will be your primary tools to use in apprehending illegals."

Susan tried to concentrate on Yavo's instructions, but she ached and the day was bright and the trees were so green. And what was that flash of white? She shifted surreptitiously to one side to get a better view.

A unicorn sidled through the bushes. He gave her a slow wink and a come-on tilt of his horned head. He turned slowly, twitching his tail seductively.

Susan shifted farther to the side. She really should be listening to Yavo, watching what he was doing with his wand, but the unicorn was so much more interesting –

"Cadet Merkel!"

A burst of leaves erupted from the ground at her feet along with a loud bang and a cloud of purple smoke. Susan jerked to attention.

"What are the three basic purposes of a dislocation of reality spell?"

She stared at Yavo's yellow face for a long moment.

The dryad tittered.

Susan heaved a sigh. "I'm sorry. I was distracted by the unicorn."

Yavo spun around, remarkably agile for a troll. "Unicorn? Where?"

The rest of the cadets scrambled to their feet, bunching together as they scanned the forest.

"What's the big deal? It was just over there in the bushes." Susan pointed.

"Are you certain it was a unicorn?" Yavo snapped.

"White horsey thing with a horn on its head? Yeah, it was a unicorn."

"Protective circle, now!"

The centaur grabbed Susan's arm and yanked her close to the others. Yavo scrabbled in the dirt with his wand, scratching an elaborately swirling circle around them.

"Unicorns are bad news," one satyr said, shaking his head. "Master criminals. They run the drug trade across the border. If you saw one here, it means they're getting bold."

Yavo finished his circle, shoved his wand into his belt, then leaned close to Susan. "Stay within the circle. Who knows what fiendish spell they have cast!"

They stood in a tense circle.

Time passed.

Nothing happened.

No unicorns appeared at the forest edge. No magic spells flashed from under the trees.

Nothing.

The fire elf sneezed, setting a patch of meadow flowers smoldering. He stamped it out with an apologetic shrug. "Happens when I'm nervous."

Susan shifted away from him.

"Don't cross the circle!"

Yavo's shout startled her. She stumbled over the line in the dirt.

The group drew in a collective breath.

Susan landed on her rump.

"You broke the circle," Yavo said.

The satyrs clutched each other. The griffon sniffled. The centaur shivered at the center of the group. The dryad glared. The fire elf looked like he was about to sneeze again. Yavo crossed his arms over his massive chest and lowered his rocky brows.

Susan rose to her feet. "Look, I'll just get another stick and re-draw that part, okay?"

"You think it's that easy?" The dryad pushed her way forward. "That was a warding, a powerful spell of protection. And Sir Yavo used a Thriebold 265, not just a stick!"

"She can't help her ignorance," Yavo said.

The fire elf sneezed, setting the grass under the centaur's hooves on fire. He snorted and stamped.

"The warding is broken, and I don't have time to cast another." Yavo shuffled out of the circle, scuffing more of the line. "If the unicorns are in the area, then we will just have to fight them."

"But we aren't ready," the griffon complained. "We haven't finished our training."

"What better training than a real confrontation?" Yavo

pointed at the forest. "Pair up. Search for traces. Let's track that unicorn. And hope it's only one."

The satyrs pranced off together. The griffon and centaur traded glances then trotted away. The fire elf and the dryad exchanged glares before shrugging and heading into the forest, eyes on the ground.

"You're with me," Yavo told Susan. His look dismissed her as worse than useless.

"It was that way," Susan said, pointing off in a direction none of the others had gone. "And what's so bad about unicorns? I thought they were good, protectors of the forest, that sort of thing."

"That's just propaganda they spread in the human world. Unicorns are vicious, evil thugs who terrorize everyone and everything in their territory." Yavo strode into the forest, crushing bushes under his massive boots.

Susan trotted in his wake. "And we're supposed to arrest one? How?"

Yavo merely stomped bushes.

"Pardon me, sir, but I seem to have been misdirected. Perhaps you did not understand my request. I must speak with you."

Thompson looked down to find the chihuahua sitting beside him, buggy eyes fixed his direction. "I hate dogs. Go away. Go on, go back home, or wherever you came from." None of the cadets had owned up to smuggling their purse dog to training.

"I cannot do that, not until you have heard my message."

The dog's mouth moved. Words emerged. Thompson blinked, a long slow closing and opening of his eyes.

"I am an officer of the FBI," the dog continued. "I have been sent to work with your agency. Perhaps I have contacted the wrong Sergeant Thompson. But your description, it matches that of the Thompson I was sent to meet." The dog stood, stretched to place a paw on the arm of Thompson's chair. "It is most important that you listen."

"How come you can talk? What prank is this?" There was no one anywhere near. And the dog's collar was much too small to hold any kind of receiver or sound system. It did hold a small silver badge, though, one inscribed with curling shapes that could only be letters but in a language Thompson had never seen.

"I assure you, on my honor, this is no mere prank. The unicorns are shipping a very large quantity of illegal substances across your border. Tonight. They must be stopped."

The dog looked so serious and intense Thompson couldn't help laughing. Unicorns? With drugs? "Wait, you say you're with the FBI?"

"Fairyland Border Investigations, yes. Please you only have a few hours to act. You must secure the portal."

"And you say your name is Antonio Howitzer?"

The dog rolled his eyes and let out a frustrated yip.

Thompson shrugged. What could it hurt? His maggots were sweating their training under the capable hands of his assistant. Maybe if he took the dog for a walk, he could chuck it over the fence and let it find its own way home. He'd had about enough amusement from it. He rose to his feet, stretching.

The dog relaxed with a gusty sigh. "Follow me, señor." He trotted away, his tiny feet dainty as he picked his way across the gravel lot.

Thompson followed, his standard issue boots crunching the gravel. The dog headed for the porta-johns, ducking behind them with a flick of his short tail.

Thompson paused. What if it were a trap? Someone could be lying in wait behind the johns. He flexed his hands before curling them into fists. Whoever that was would be in for a real surprise. Thompson loved a good takedown and he'd been on the training bench far too long.

"It is here," the dog announced as Thompson rounded the plastic outhouses. "The portal is here. They will open it soon. We must be ready. Do you have garlic powder?"

"What?"

"Garlic. And marigolds. And a large pile of rabbit droppings. They are necessary for the spell. Did you not receive the memo? I was assured it was sent last week."

"That explains the weird shipment we got. At least the ten pounds of garlic powder and the marigold plants." Thompson frowned. "You mean the brass know about this?"

"Oh, yes." The dog nodded vigorously, head bobbing like the weird little bobblehead toys Thompson's wife collected.

"If the brass know, then you're for real?"

Antonio Howitzer bobbed his little head.

Thompson grew serious. "I guess we could send the recruits out into the brush searching for rabbit crap. Call it evidence gathering or something. What drug are they shipping in? Cocaine? Heroin? Something new?"

"Definitely new." The dog pawed at the ground, drawing symbols in the dirt. "Cosmic Catnip. Thousands of plants."

Thompson snorted, disbelief winning again. "Okay. The joke's gone far enough. Catnip is not a controlled substance."

"Trust me, señor, this catnip should be controlled. You say you do not like dogs, true?" He paused until Thompson nodded, then resumed his digging. "How do you feel about cats?"

Thompson shuddered. "Worse than little purse dogs, no offense meant."

"Offense can be taken later. But now, we must work. Please remove those plants." The dog pointed with his front paw. "Cosmic Catnip makes cats irresistible to women. All women and all cats. Think of it. Every woman will adopt one, two, five, twenty, *fifty* cats. How horrible will that be? And those cats will control All. The. Women."

Thompson swallowed, imagining his wife Velma with fifty cats in their small bungalow home. The smell. The hair. The incessant meowing. The cans of cat food on every counter. The evil glares of all those eyes everywhere he looked. Those claws hooking out from every space. Nowhere would be safe. He knew Velma well enough to know that the cats would have his bed and he'd be lucky to sleep in a tent in the backyard. "They have to be stopped."

"Yes, it would be truly an abomination. Now, dig!"

Susan swatted at a bug flitting around her face. Thirty-seven trees, forty-nine bushes, and uncounted clumps of flowers searched, and not one trace of the unicorn she'd spotted. She closed her eyes, remembering the soft curve of its flank, the gentle glance of its lavender eyes, the softly blowing mane –

"Cadet!" Yavo grabbed her shoulders, lifted her from the

ground. "Do *not* think of them. It will only give their spell more power."

Susan stared into the huge eyes only inches from hers, crystal orbs lit by an orange flame deep within. "Spell?"

"A glamour, an entrapment, an enticement. Did they teach you nothing?" He set her back down carefully. His skin was rough as stone, and felt like it, too. "You have been ensorcelled. I can feel it tying you to the beast." He reached for his wand, then paused.

"Well? Are you going to break the spell?" *Or am I going to have visions of his silky coat and prancing hooves for the rest of my life?* A wave of longing washed over her, drawing her into the woods. She felt a sudden urge to change into a flowing gown and weave flowers into her hair.

"Do you feel it pulling you?" Yavo modulated his gruff voice into a low rumble, the sound of water tumbling stones.

Susan swayed. "Oh, yes." She plucked her uniform cap off her head, dropping it as she loosened her hair to fall in disarray around her face.

"Then go to it, follow the call."

Yavo's voice faded as Susan eagerly answered the call of the unicorn. She plunged into the forest. She had no gown, but the unicorn would give her one spun from moonbeams and spiderwebs. She would stroke his soft muzzle and feed him grapes, one by one. It would be the most wonderful experience of her life. And if she could only reach him, follow him, she would be with him forever.

The spell wrapped tighter around her as she gave in to its seductive pull. She was only dimly aware of Yavo and the trainees following in her wake. Her mind filled with visions of white manes and violet eyes.

Thompson grunted as he yanked the last of the dandelions from the circle the dog – he just couldn't call such a tiny thing Señor Howitzer as it requested so it would stay 'the dog' – from the circle the dog had scratched. It was now decorated with small white stones and carefully plucked marigolds in shades of orange and yellow. As he straightened, the dog carefully nipped another flower from the bundle Thompson had yanked from the front flowerbed. The dog skipped over the wavering lines of the circle to deposit the flower in the center of a circle of stones.

"That should complete this portion. Now for the rest." The dog looked expectantly at Thompson.

"The maggots, I mean recruits, should be here any moment. I sent them out with buckets."

"Hopefully they will find enough to complete the spell."

"What, exactly, is this spell supposed to do?"

"Prevent the unicorns from wreaking a catastrophe on your world. Ha! I amuse myself so much." The dog jumped over a large flower, then sat at Thompson's feet. "You get it, no? Cat-astrophe? Because of the catnip."

Thompson grunted.

"Well, I think that I am fabulously entertaining."

Yap. Yap. Yap. Just because it says words doesn't change it from being a chihuahua.

The recruits began to filter to the backside of the latrines. They wore evidence gloves and carried buckets. The lead one wrinkled his nose as he set his bucket down. Thompson didn't miss the sideways glances at the large pattern scratched in the dirt. Or the crumpled marigolds at Thompson's feet.

Thompson shot a glance down at the dog before clearing his throat. If this went sideways, it was the dog's fault. Or maybe he could claim mental instability triggered by years of training numbskulls? He cleared his throat again as more recruits straggled in.

"Listen up, you maggots. This is a special presentation on serial killings and body staging. See that circle? That's a clue."

"What's the poo for then?"

Thompson pinned the recruit in place with an icy stare. "You are to mix this powder with the substance in your buckets then apply that where I tell you to. Got it? We're recreating a crime scene here. And I want you to interpret it. Figure out what the symbols mean. Find out who did this. Got it?" The last came out a growl.

Thompson watched as the hapless recruits tossed garlic powder into the buckets, then stirred with their gloved hands.

"Have them deposit it at the very center, where the red

flower rests." Señor Howitzer scratched behind his ear. Thompson could swear the dog was grinning at him. "They cannot hear me, only you. They only hear the barking of a small, annoying dog."

Maybe he was going crazy. Ah, well. In for a penny, in for a pound, as his mother used to proclaim. He jabbed his finger at the pattern. "Dump it there, around that red flower. And mind you don't scuff any of the markings or I'll penalize you!"

Susan waltzed into the clearing. It would have been spectacular if she'd been wearing a ballgown. As it was, she just looked strange in her police uniform with her short hair waving around her head in a frizz.

Three unicorns paused, hooves raised over a pile of fragrant leaves.

"Really, Schmitty? Can't stop yourself from casting that glamour every single time. Imbecile. What are we going to do with her?"

The unicorn being chastised lowered his horn. "She saw me, when I was checking out that camp over the hill. What was I supposed to do? Run away screaming?"

The other unicorn rolled his eyes and went back to counting out leaves.

The first unicorn smacked Schmitty with his horn. "Get rid of her. Shove her through the portal, drop her off a cliff, dunk her in the river, whatever. Just make her gone before she leads the others here."

"I think you're too late for that, Bruce," Schmitty answered. "I smell a troll, a dryad, and a bunch of others."

Bruce raised his head, nostrils flared wide. "Their stink is on her. We're safe enough."

Susan simpered as she danced up to Bruce. "Such a pretty, pretty horsey you are." She giggled. Her fingers trailed along his neck and into his mane.

Bruce twisted his head into her touch. "At least choose someone with half a brain, Schmitty. Really, this is downright embarrassing the way she talks." He closed his eyes as Susan ran both hands through his silken mane. "Ah, yeah, scratch right up there behind the ears."

"Now who's the embarrassment to unicorns everywhere?" Schmitty muttered. "How am I supposed to dispose of her now?"

"You want some love, too?" Susan said, shifting her attention to Schmitty.

Bruce stomped his hoof. "I'm the boss, sweetie. Run your hands through my mane, not his."

"Well, I'm the one who glamoured her."

"Yeah?"

"Yeah."

The two unicorns snorted and tapped horns. Susan stumbled backwards, bumped by their posturing. Her hand grazed her pocket, touched the keys briefly. Her eyes grew thoughtful.

"Cut it out and get this load bundled," the third unicorn snapped. "We're on a deadline here."

"Yes, Larry," they spoke in unison.

Bruce and Schmitty traded muttered insults as they started pawing the leaves into piles.

The third unicorn turned a hard stare on Susan. "Maybe we can use this one."

"Pretty unicorn, such a shiny horn." Susan stroked the unicorn's muzzle, letting her eyes unfocus again.

Larry's eyes half-closed. "Mm, maybe we should keep her for a while."

"So pretty. So soft." Susan's hands slid over his cheeks and down his neck into his mane. She shifted to the side. "Such a pretty, pretty unicorn."

In one fluid motion, she knotted her fists in his mane and jumped for his back. Her voice snapped out, hard and angry, as she landed on his back. "Pretty unicorn Larry is going to take me for a ride now. And maybe *I'll* keep *you*. I always wanted a pony."

Larry froze in shock as her weight settled on his back, her legs clamped around his ribs, her fists yanking on his mane. *No one* rode a unicorn. It just *wasn't done*. And yet this person, this *human*, dared? He lowered his horn and charged out of the clearing.

She clung like a burr to his back as he twisted and leapt

and raced through the forest. He swung through bushes, jumped ravines, slammed into trees, until his sides ached and his breath wheezed. He finally stumbled to a halt in a clearing, head hanging so low his horn scraped through the dirt.

Susan kept her death grip on the beast. She let out a shaky breath. Then another when the unicorn stayed still, legs splayed as his sides heaved.

"What spell did you cast on me, witch?" Larry panted.

She leaned forward on his neck to whisper in his ear, "You are mine now, understand?"

Larry bobbed his head, horn chiming as it struck the ground.

Susan sat up straight, patting her pocket. Her keys were still safely inside. She pulled them out and jingled them. Larry shivered.

"Pretty unicorn Larry knows what this is, doesn't he?"

Larry twitched but didn't speak.

"Doesn't he?" Susan repeated in a harsh voice.

"Cold iron," Larry whispered. "It burns and destroys."

"Burns and destroys what, Larry?" Susan hoped he would answer because all she remembered from her gran's stories was that fey couldn't stand cold iron.

"All magic," he whispered.

"Good. Now take me back. We're going to stop whatever it is you're doing back there."

Larry sidestepped, shifting his weight.

Susan lurched forward, sliding to the side. She grabbed his mane. The keys slapped against his skin, the horseshoe nail clanging against her house key and chiming like a church bell tolling in the distance.

Larry screamed. Smoke spiraled up from his skin where the keys made contact. He bucked and jumped like a mad creature. Susan held on tighter. The keys slapped against his neck over and over.

In moments it was over.

Susan sprawled on the forest floor, keys tangled in her hand. All that was left of Larry the unicorn was a wreath of smoke.

The griffon landed across the clearing from her. It folded

its wings while eyeing her warily. "Unicorns are made of magic. Put the iron away. Please."

Susan rose to her feet. She stared at her key ring. "I did that?"

"Your iron did that. Not exactly an arrest, but you stopped him." The griffon watched her with respect and fear in his eyes. "I've never seen anyone ride a unicorn before."

"Or dissolve them into smoke with their house keys?" Susan dropped the jangling metal into her pocket. "What about the others?"

"Yavo and the rest are arresting them. He sent me to follow you, see what you were doing."

"See if I was secretly working with the unicorns? Fair enough." She turned to face the griffon. He wouldn't quite meet her eyes. "What now?"

"We go back, close down the portal, destroy the drugs. Question the others. Standard procedures." The griffon took a step back, lion claws digging into the turf.

"Which way is back?" Susan asked.

"Ready?" The dog posed on the pile of rabbit droppings coated in garlic powder. He had a marigold clutched between his teeth. Like a flamenco dancer with a rose.

Thompson tried to stop from giggling. It was too bizarre. He clamped his teeth so all that escaped was a tiny high-pitched wheeze.

"You all right, sir?" his assistant asked.

"Fine," Thompson snapped.

The dog nodded to Thompson.

"You, maggot! What does this mean?" Thompson pointed at a random recruit, then waved at the weird spiraling patterns of orange blossoms.

"That you're out of your blooming mind," the man muttered.

"Wrong!" Thompson barked into his face. "This means something to someone. It's a crime scene. Look for the symbols!" He had a sneaking suspicion that the man was correct.

The dog raised his head and howled. It was cute, a tiny little wolf howl from a tiny little dog. Thompson heard it as,

"Now!"

"Maggots!" Thompson shouted. "Forward, stomp!"

They stared in confusion.

"But you just told us not to touch anything."

"I said stomp, so stomp!"

The chihuahua barked strange noises. The marigolds began to glow. The mound of droppings disappeared with a clap
of thunder. The dog went with them.

Thompson shoved the closest recruit towards the flowers.
"Stomp!"

His own boots smashed into the first ring of symbols, wiping out the delicate spirals the dog had so painstakingly crafted
in the dirt. Tingles of power ran up his legs, through his back,
and then out his hair.

The recruits gingerly followed his example. Within moments, nothing was left but a faintly orange smear in the dirt.

They stood awkwardly in the circle of stomped earth.

Thompson drew in a deep breath, then blew it out. *Strange
day.* "All right, you maggots," his voice was much quieter than
usual, "you're gonna see some strange sights out there, but
don't let it knock you sideways. Just keep your eyes open and
do your best. Dismissed."

They traded looks as they slouched away. He heard the
mutters, knew that he'd be called on the carpet soon by the big
boss. But for now – What?

"Um, sir? What was all this about? Are you okay?" Gerald
looked concerned.

"I think I'm getting old. Maybe it's time to look into fishing as a hobby." He stepped on a marigold that had somehow
survived the destruction. "Because I'm not very good at flower
arranging." He forced a laugh at his lame joke.

"Cadet Susan," Yavo rumbled her name, "for bravery in the
face of danger, for risking your life for the sake of your fellow
cadets and all of Fairyland, not to mention your own world, we
present you with this medal."

The cadets gave a half-hearted cheer as Yavo dropped the
chunk of silver around her neck. They were scared witless by
her, she could read it in their eyes.

"This session of training is concluded," Yavo said. "Dismissed."

The others moved away in visible relief.

"Only one day of training?" Susan asked, her voice wistful. "I barely got to see anything."

Yavo dropped his hand on her shoulder, a comforting weight. "Maybe someday, we will invite you back. But next time, leave your keys home."

About the Authors

J Louis Messina's short story collection *Strange Tales from a Boy's Life* is out on Amazon, paperback & e-book. His story Grandpa Brown's "Mysterious Once Box" is the winner of the Paul A. Witty Short Story Award from the International Reading Association, and the Association of Educational Publishers Distinguished Achievement Award; *The Late Terry Taylor* won the Society of Children's Book Writers & Illustrators Short Story Merit Award; Messina won The Harrow: Original Works of Fantasy & Horror Contest. His horror story "The Chosen" is in the anthology *Hellfire Crossroads* Horror with a Heart Volume 7 – Introducing - on Amazon, paperback and e-book.

Tim Kane grew up in Southern California watching Toho movies and reading H.G. Wells. His first published book, *The Changing Vampire of Film and Television*, analyzes the past seventy years of vampires. He lives and teaches in Chula Vista, California, with his spectacular wife, daughter, and a dog that stands upside down. He enjoys traveling to the dark places of his mind and bringing back souvenirs. Most recently published stories appear in *Ripples in Space*, *Drunk Gekko*, *Deathleham* and the upcoming *Lovecraftia*. Find out more at **www.timkanebooks.com**.

Chisto Healy has lived through hell and holds onto hope for something better, while remaining aware that the grass isn't always greener on the other side. Since he started writing as a child he has felt comfortable on the dark side of things. His hope is to make it to where he can write for a living without working labor anymore. He owes this to the motivating fact that his hero and favorite author Simon Clark has shown confidence in him. He lives in North Carolina with his fiance, three kids, four cats, and one very silly dog.

Katherine Quevedo was born and raised just outside of Portland, Oregon, where she works as an analysis manager and lives with her husband and two sons. Her fiction has appeared in *Thrilling Words*, *Heroic Fantasy Quarterly*, *Apparition Literary Magazine*, *Myriad Lands Vol. 2: Beyond the Edge*, *Triangulation: Appetites*, and elsewhere. When she isn't writing, she enjoys watching movies, singing, playing old-school video games, belly dancing, and making spreadsheets.

Jennifer Moore is a freelance writer and children's author from Devon (UK). She writes for all ages, from toddlers through to adults, and has published over a hundred short stories and poems across five continents. She was the first ever UK winner of the Commonwealth Short Story Competition and was also shortlisted for the Greenhouse Funny Prize. She studied English at Cambridge University and holds an MRes from the University of Strathclyde. Her new children's book, *Agent Starling: Operation Baked Beans* (writing as Jenny Moore), is published by Maverick Arts Publishing. Follow her on Twitter **@JennyWriteMoore** or **jennifermoore.wordpress.com**.

Paula Hammond is a freelance writer based in London, but forever dreaming of a small castle, with its own writing turret, in the wilds of Wales. Her most recent publications include "50 for 50: Celebrating Fifty Years of the Doctor Who Family", "Fortunate Son" (*Alternative Truths: Endgame*), and "The Adventure of the Cable Street Mummy" (*Sherlock Holmes and Dr. Watson: The Early Adventures Volume I*). When not frantically scribbling, Paula can be found indulging her passions for film, theatre, sci-fi, and real ale. She would be delighted if you could follow her on twitter (**@writer_paula**) as it would make her feel like a proper, grown-up author.

Margret Treiber resides in Southwest Florida and is employed as a Systems Analyst. When she is not working with technology and writing speculative fiction, she helps her birds break things for her spouse to fix.

Her short fiction has appeared in a number of publications. Links to her short fiction, novels, and upcoming work can be found on her website at **http://www.the-margret.com** and on Amazon at **https://www.amazon.com/Margret-A.-Treiber/e/ B0052U63BI/**

Emily Martha Sorensen writes clean fantasy books that'll make you grin. Her characters are quick on their feet, clever, and looking for a way to solve the problem before the villain wins. Sometimes they get a romantic interest. Sometimes they don't. Sometimes they just get to smack stupid people upside the head.

She has been known to write about snarky heroines, fairy tales, and baby dragons in the 1920s.

You can find out more about her at:
http://www.emilymarthasorensen.com

Joachim Heijndermans writes, draws, and paints nearly every waking hour. Originally from the Netherlands, he's been all over the world, boring people by spouting random trivia. His work has been featured in a number of anthologies and publications, such as *Mad Scientist Journal*, *Asymmetry Fiction*, *Hinnom Magazine*, Ahoy Comics's *Edgar Allan Poe's Snifter of Terror*, *Metaphorosis* and *The Gallery of Curiosities*, and he's currently in the midst of completing his first children's book.

Website: **www.joachimheijndermans.com**
Twitter: **@jheijndermans**

Jonathan Shipley is a Fort Worth writer of fantasy, science fiction, and horror whose writing ranges from traditional fantasy to vampires to futuristic space opera. Although he self-identifies as a novelist, it is short fiction where he has enjoyed success with sales of over a hundred stories. He was a contributing author to the *After Death* anthology that won the 2014 Bram Stoker award and last December, he was a speaker at the 2018 World Building Conference in Graz, Austria, which opened up his writing to an international audience.

Ken Goldman is a former Philadelphia teacher of English and Film Studies, is an Active member of the Horror Writers Association with homes on the Main Line in Pennsylvania and the

Jersey shore. His stories have appeared in over 900 independent press publications. Ken's tales have received seven honorable mentions in The Year's Best Fantasy & Horror. He has written six books: three anthologies of short stories, *You Had Me at Arrgh!!* (Sam's Dot Publishers), *Donny Doesn't Live Here Anymore* (A/A Productions) and *Star-Crossed* (Vampires 2); a novella, *Desiree* (Damnation Books and on Kindle by eXcessica Publishing); and two novels: *Of a Feather* (Horrific Tales Publishing) and *Sinkhole* (Bloodshot Books).

Sheila Hartney lives in New Mexico, Land of Enchantment, with clear skies, and lots of science fiction writers. So she spends a fair amount of time stargazing and hanging out with the SF crowd when she can.

She has been a Writer of the Future, and recently attended the Taos Toolbox, an amazing writing workshop taught by Walter Jon Williams and Nancy Kress. She not only has a story here, but is also the editor, and says working with David Lee Summers has been a lovely experience.

Holly Schofield travels through time at the rate of one second per second, oscillating between the alternate realities of city and country life. Her short stories have appeared in *Analog*, *Lightspeed*, *Escape Pod*, and many other publications throughout the world. She hopes to save the world through science fiction and homegrown heritage tomatoes. Find her at **hollyschofield. wordpress.com**.

Brian Gene Olson lives in the Pacific Northwest in a quiet little spot surrounded by much tumult with his wife, two kids, and their demon cat Pharaoh. He writes both kidlit and speculative works, some of which he's sold to *Daily Science Fiction*, *Ladybug*, *Scifaikue*st, and *Highlights Hello*.

David B. Riley lives in Tucson, Arizona. He has edited more anthologies than he cares to remember and is the author of over 100 short stories and six novels and two novellas. He writes weird westerns as well as science fiction and the occasional horror story. He says that Sarah Meadows, of all the characters across all genres, is his favorite character. She's appeared in a few other short stories and in the novel *Bonded Agent*. In every case, she's a real bad ass.

Sherry Yuan spent the first five years of her life in Suzhou, China and the next 18 in Vancouver, Canada, where she graduated from the University of British Columbia with a BA in Computer Science and Psychology. She currently works as a software engineer in San Francisco. She spends her free time writing short stories and tech articles, reading, drawing, rock climbing, and trying Trader Joe's cheeses.

Lesley L. Smith, M.F.A, Ph.D., is a scientist at the University of Colorado. Her short stories have appeared in various venues including *Analog Science Fiction and Fact* and *Daily Science Fiction*. She has written nine novels, including *The Quantum Cop, Conservation of Luck, Temporal Dreams*, and *Kat Cubed*. She's an active member of the Science Fiction/Fantasy Writers of America and a founder and editor of the ezine *Electric Spec* (www.electricspec.com). Check her out online at **www.lesleylsmith.com**.

Alden Loveshade is a journalist, graphic designer, photographer, fiction writer, and personist. He's enjoyed tutoring – and learning from – students of India, Mexico, Russia, Thailand, and the United States. He has degrees in humanities and theatre and a minor in ethnic and women's studies, and has studied a wide variety of subjects including astronomy, biology, physics, psychology, and sociology. When not designing star systems for stories and *GURPS* roleplaying games, he enjoys historical recreation, walking in the woods, tending ponds, and trying to understand cats. He can be found online at **http://alden.loveshade.org**.

Roze Albina Ches is a 2015 Graduate of the State University of New York Empire State College. She obtained an Associate of Arts Degree in English, concentration on creative writing, and obtained a Bachelor of Arts Degree in Literature, concentration on creative writing. She received three college scholarships: The Conrad and Virginia Klee Foundation in 2013, The Conrad and Virginia Klee Foundation in 2014, The Joseph and Leona Hoyt Foundation in 2015. Creative fiction and creative nonfiction writing are her forte. She is presently working on a collection of short stories for publication.

Sean Jones lives in Colorado and works in the aerospace industry as a network engineer. As a high-schooler, he attended the Melanchthon Gymnasium in Nuremburg, (West) Germany and got to go behind the Iron Curtain before it rusted and fell. He's traveled to a handful of European countries, Thailand, Japan and Tahiti. In the United States Army, he translated Persian-Farsi into English, intercepting radio xxxxxxxxxxxx [content censored by the National Security Agency]. Dr. Jones is a semi-avid fan of London's Crystal Palace. Go Glaziers!

Tim McDaniel teaches English as a Second Language at Green River College, not far from Seattle. His short stories, mostly comedic, have appeared in a number of SF/F magazines, including *F&SF*, *Analog*, and *Asimov's*. He lives with his wife, dog, and cat, and his collection of plastic dinosaurs is the envy of all who encounter it. His author page at Amazon.com is **https://www.amazon.com/author/tim-mcdaniel** and many of his stories are available for free at **CuriousFictions.com**.

Jaleta Clegg was born some time ago. She's spent the years since making stuff up and writing about it. She writes science fiction adventures, fantasy of all flavors, and silly horror. Find more of her work at **www.jaletac.com**

Acknowledgements

"A Coral Study" by Katherine Quevedo originally published in *Factor Four Magazine* in 2018 as "Exchange." Reprinted by permission of the author.

"Advanced Precognition" by Emily Martha Sorensen originally published in Worlds of Wonder in 2013. Reprinted by permission of the author.

"Easy Peasy" by Holly Schofield originally published by Common Deer Press, 2018. Reprinted by permission of the author.

"An Averted Tragedy" by Brian Gene Olson originally published in Daily Science Fiction in 2017. Reprinted by permission of the author.

"The Pupil" is based on characters appearing in *Bonded Agent* by David B. Riley, published by Wolfsinger Press. Characters used by permission of the author.